MW01268854

TELL
THE
TRUTH

DALE DELILLO

Fulton Books, Inc.
Meadville, PA

Published by Fulton Books 2022

ISBN 978-1-63985-277-2 (paperback)
ISBN 978-1-63985-278-9 (digital)

Printed in the United States of America

To Louanne,
for the support and confidence in my
ability and for urging me to continue.

To Annette,
for enthusiastically prompting me on to completion.

My love and gratitude to you both.

1

John Corfinio, wearing an ill-fitting black suit, climbed the broad granite stairway leading into the courthouse holding a cardboard coffee cup in one hand and absently tugged on his tie with the other. He glanced over at the large man carrying a legal briefcase matching him step for step ascending the stairs. "This sucks," Corfinio mumbled to his companion.

Attorney Arthur Bari sighed in reply while chomping on a soggy cigar stub that smelled like it died two weeks ago. "To *which* do you refer," quizzed Bari wearily, "the coffee, the infernal climb, or the situation itself?"

Continuing their upward trek, they passed two teens in faded jeans and flannel shirts sitting on the stairway, totally engrossed in comparing forearm tattoos. Neither looked up as the two men passed them by, while the particulars of their animated conversation were lost to the blaring horns of street traffic.

"Ughh," Corfinio grunted and grimaced, swallowing a mouthful of coffee from the plastic-lidded cardboard container. "Is it asking too much to expect a *half-decent* cup of coffee instead of having to suffer through *this* crap?"

He put the cup to his mouth once again then decided against the torturous liquid and tossed it into the metal waste container standing alongside the entry doors to the courthouse. "I mean, *half* decent would be a *vast* improvement. Is that too much to ask?"

"Ahh!" Bari proclaimed, waving a meaty fist in the air with an exaggerated flourish. "*So* then, at *last* we come to the crux of your discomfort, the coffee...*that* bad?" asked the lawyer as he switched his attention to examine his dead cigar and reluctantly flicked it into the waste containers topside the ashtray.

"Uh-huh." Corfinio nodded. "Apparently, it's asking for too much to expect a cup of *real* coffee with *real* cream and *real* sugar. No wonder people are so miserable in the morning. Especially around here! It should be *mandatory* that courts throughout the land serve decent coffee so shitheads like me can get a fair judgment. No wonder the judges are always in such a rotten mood. The *coffee sucks!* How can you expect to get a fair judgment from a guy who's gagging on a cup of sucky coffee?"

"Now you see," said Bari with just a hint of a smirk, "*there's* your first mistake. What makes you think that the coffee served to judges is the same coffee that's served to the likes of you? No, no, my ignorant malcontented friend—judges are 'special people,' and they get preferential treatment. *They* get the *good* coffee. But you *were* right about one thing."

"What's that?"

"The crispy, day-old coffee *is* served to shitheads like you."

"Oh, so now I'm a shithead?"

"Hey, pal, *you* were the one who brought out that point of *insignificata*."

"Well, you didn't have to agree, did you?"

"My job is to defend you, not bolster your ego."

"Say! *There's* an interesting concept," Corfinio sarcastically quipped, "*de*-fend. Not *o*-ffend!"

"Perhaps I'd be less apt to *o*-ffend if you were less o-ffensive, *Stultus*."

"What does—"

"Fool. Dumbass. Stupid. Take your pick. All the same in Latin. Stultus."

Pursing his lips, with a slight roll of his eyes skyward, Corfinio sighed heavily and turned the conversation. "Okay, so let's get back to the secondary point here. If the judges are getting all the *good* coffee, then why are they always in such a *bad* mood?"

"Isn't it obvious? It's because their entire day is filled with dealing with shitheads like you."

"Again," Corfinio stated flatly, rolling his eyes, "we're back to the 'shithead' thing again. I'm sorry I ever brought this up."

"Yeah," said Bari motioning, toward the entry doors, "I bet you are."

2

Pulling the oversized double oak doors open, they entered the courthouse foyer. Two rows of three-foot-high metal poles with black plastic links lined the entry from the doorway, funneling all incoming traffic toward a walk-though metal detection station. Three armed policemen stood on the opposite side of a short conveyor belt that fed into a baggage detector while idly discussing the Red Sox loss from the previous evening.

"Oh, look," whispered Corfinio, "it's Moe, Larry, and Curly...or is it Huey, Dewey, and Louie? I can see my tax dollars hard at work here, paying for three cops making ninety bucks an hour to watch a TV screen and confiscate fingernail clippers and keychains."

Bari shot his client a killing stare, motioning for him to shut up.

One of the officers motioned for Bari to set his briefcase on the conveyor belt and directed him to walk thru the upright detector. As the briefcase crept into the detection housing, a monitor over the housing revealed the contents of the satchel. Almost immediately, the alarm started to wail with a high-pitched staccato beeping. Unable to immediately detect the reason for the sounding alarm, another of the officers manning the station retrieved the briefcase as it exited the housing.

"Do you have anything metal in the bag, sir?" he asked, not waiting for an answer as he proceeded to open the bag.

Before Bari could answer, Corfinio mumbled from behind, "Only fifty-three ballpoint pens, a butter knife, and a carburetor from a '67 Impala."

Bari's head sunk onto his chest and groaned in frustration. A thin smile spread across Corfinio's face as the three police officers suddenly directed their attention toward him.

Visibly agitated at the ruse, the overweight middle-aged police officer with bad skin standing nearest to Corfinio stabbed a finger in his direction. Taking a half-step toward him, he growled, "What are you, some kind of wise guy? You think that's *funny*? How'd you like to spend some time in a cell, huh, wise guy?"

Still smiling, Corfinio answered politely but with more than a hint of sarcasm. "Well, gee, no—I'm *not* a wise guy, yes—it *was* kind of funny, and no—I *don't* think I'd like to spend some time in a cell. Does that answer all your questions, Officer?"

Temporarily stunned at the response, the policeman stood speechless.

"*Officer*, Officer," Bari cut in, quickly begging, "*please* pay *no* attention to my client. He's a complete *idiot*, obviously without a *shred* of sense. As you can readily see, neither of us is carrying any type of paraphernalia that would prove to be lethal or otherwise threatening to another person."

The officer in charge of inspecting the briefcase, not in the slightest amused at the unfolding event, nodded gravely in agreement stating that a metal clipboard which he held aloft like a trophy pelt had set off the alarm.

"If you would prefer, Officer," added Bari hastily, "I can leave that item here at the desk."

"That won't be necessary, Counselor," said the overweight officer, slowly regaining a segment of his damaged composure. "Apparently, your *friend* here thinks this is a time for fun and games. You would be wise to instruct him that this is no joking matter. I—"

"Yes, yes, of course," Bari cut in quickly, "I'm really *very* sorry about this whole thing. I *promise* you, there won't be any further outbursts from my client, 'the Moron.' He's just not right in the head. He comes from a long line of unbroken idiocracy."

"Nope, I won't say—" Corfinio started to say, shaking his head back and forth vigorously.

"Would you *shut up!*" Bari scolded, gritting his teeth, spinning to face his client. "What is *wrong* with you? Just...*shut up!*"

Corfinio, juvenilely pleased with the commotion he had produced with his off-hand remark, dragged his forefinger and thumb across his lips in a 'zippering' fashion, rolled his eyes skyward, and bowed his head in false submission.

Turning back to the policemen, Bari continued offering apologies as he and Corfinio walked through the metal detection portal without further incident. Exiting the detector, Bari grasped Corfinio's arm firmly and led him away from the glaring stares of the trio of policemen.

3

They quickly walked toward the center of the crowded concourse where Bari glanced down each of the tentacle-like corridors in search of a semi-secluded area to chastise his client.

"Hey, Arthur?" Corfinio asked. "Could I have my arm back?"

Without answering, Bari tugged Corfinio toward the end of a long corridor terminating with a pair of locked egress doors. Dropping his briefcase to the floor, he lifted both hands in supplication. Still rankled by the predicament his client had caused, he asked, "*What* the *hell* was that? Was that *really* necessary? Do you *want* to go back to jail? Are you some kind of *retard*? Do you have severe brain damage?"

Corfinio pondered the last question for several seconds before answering. "If I did…would I know it?"

Bari, unamused and visibly seething, stood staring intently at his client, waiting for an explanation.

"Oh, come on!" Corfinio finally replied with a half-grin. "It was *funny*. You *know* it was funny."

"Funny," Bari stated flatly.

"Yeah. Just because a goon in a blue suit thinks 'funny' is boinking some poor slob off the noggin with a phallic symbol doesn't mean it *wasn't* funny. Now if I had said 'fuel pump' or 'electronic ignition'…well, that's not so funny. Besides, who would have thought that old Mister Stick-up-His-Ass would actually believe that you would have had a carburetor from a '67 Impala in your briefcase?"

"I don't think that's what got his attention, Mister Shithead—"

"It always comes back to the 'shithead' thing, doesn't it?"

"That's right, shit for brains, I'm thinking maybe he didn't like the part about the steak knife. *Knife* being the key word here."

"Uh, *'scuse* me…it was *fifty-three* ballpoint pens and a *butter* knife," Corfinio corrected.

"What*ever*…that's not the point. The point is, that's an arrestable offense," Bari said in frustration.

"*What*?" asked Corfinio, genuinely surprised. "You mean to tell me that you can be *arrested* for bringing a *carburetor* into a courthouse?"

Bari completely ignored his client's last statement and surged ahead with a definitive explanation. "By suggesting that you have in your possession a device that *may* do harm or *cause threat* to another individual, *especially* in a federal building or in an area governed by federal authorities, *is* cause for *immediate* arrest. An arrest which *could*, by the way, result in a term of twenty *years* of incarceration."

"No kidding," Corfinio said evenly.

"No kidding, *Sir Doofus*." Bari paused after his delivered derogatory and sighed, still somewhat annoyed at Corfinio's lack of gravity for the situation. "Did I ever tell you about the time a group of protesters requested permission to audience a trial? When they signed in at the desk, the leader added alongside his name 'with bomb.' He's now doing twenty to life."

"Well, maybe he shouldn't have been stupid enough to bring a bomb with him then."

"He didn't. He only *said* he had a bomb. Twenty to life."

"Seriously? Even though there *was* no bomb?" Corfinio asked skeptically.

"Doesn't matter. A perceived threat."

"Wow." Corfinio furrowed his brow and thought for a moment. "How much time do you think he would have gotten if he had written 'with carburetor'?"

"Five years," Bari answered instantly.

"*Five years?*" Corfinio repeated, incredulous at the response.

"Absolutely. Illegally transporting potentially dangerous material without holding a Hazardous Material

Transportation License—*or permit*—into a federally funded or operated building. *And* if the carburetor had even a residual amount of gasoline or oil residue, then it would be viewed as an explosive device whereupon the offender could assume a sentence for no less than twenty years or as long as 'life.' So," Bari completed with a dramatic swirl of his plate-like paw, "there you have it."

Corfinio, incredulous, stood with mouth agape, shaking his head. "You gotta be kidding me," he whispered.

Bari turned his back on his client, the hint of a smile forming on his lips.

"Yes," he said, "I am."

Bari approached an empty bench located along the perimeter of the main concourse. He sat down looking back at Corfinio and waved him over. Bari reached into his briefcase, removed a manila folder, and proceeded to scan his handwritten notes, running his finger down the page. Bari had filed a motion for reinstatement of visitation on behalf of Corfinio, which had been suspended at the time of his incarceration. Upon his release, his ex-wife, Marsha, had filed yet another restraining order against him with allegations of physical abuse, emotional abuse, neglect, and domestic violence. Seated beside his lawyer on the bench, Corfinio leaned back, tilting his head against the cool plaster wall and stretched his legs into the aisle. Bari was mumbling something, but Corfinio wasn't listening, his mind drifting back to when this all began.

4

Eighteen months earlier

John and Marsha Corfinio's relationship had been slowly deteriorating, and the birth of their only child did nothing to improve the quality of their association. Six months later, after several unheeded demands for divorce, John was served with divorce proceedings and a no contact order by the county sheriff. He was told to remove himself from the premises immediately or face arrest. Not having much of a choice, John gathered an armload of clothes, a Wilbur Smith novel, and his truck keys. He slept in a run-down motor lodge that night and spent the following day searching out a place of residence.

After investigating several residential rental prospects, he finally decided on the Huntington, formerly an elegant fourteen-room Victorian home complete with servants' entrance and carriage house, which had been converted into a boarding house that rented to men only. It was owned and operated by Mrs. Morrelli, an attractive widow of seventy-two who made it abundantly clear that she tolerated "no liquor, no drugs, and no women" in her household. He also discovered during his residency that Mrs. Morrelli knew just about everyone within a distance of four blocks, including what they did, where they did it, and how they did it. Corfinio found this mildly entertaining and often engaged her in conversation after returning from home from work. He found her enthusiasm amusing when relating the latest gossip and neighborhood news. He also discovered that Mrs. Morrelli had a key gripe with the man next door whom, she insisted, "seems determined to turn this neighborhood into a slum."

"He's a nice enough man," she said with some reservation in her voice. "He's a lawyer, you know. He always looks neat and never brings any strays home, if you catch my drift," she said with a wink. "I should know, I keep an eye open for these types of things. The last thing we need around here is a bordello! But good *Lord!* Just *look* at that house—it's a first-class disaster! No, no"—she tapped her lip with her forefinger and shook her head ever so slightly, "that man should *never* own property!

"You know, John," she added coyly, "you being a carpenter and all, you *really* should ask him if he wants you to *fix* something!"

"Mrs. Morrelli," John announced with a gracious sweep of his hand and bowing at the waist, "how could

I *possibly* deny a fair lady such a small task?" He waved his arms about with dramatic flourish. "Inform the brutish clod that I shall challenge his lax ownership on the morrow!"

"Oh, *you*!" she replied with a wave of her hand, a rosy hue coming to her cheeks. "Don't you get flip with me!"

"Why, Mrs. Morrelli," said Corfinio in feigned shock, placing both hands over his heart, "how can you *say* that? You *are* a fair lady. In fact, when I see you, it's like my eyes have opened to the glory of the sun. If I were ten years younger, why, I'd chase you down and make you mine!"

"And if I were ten years *older* and half out of my wits, I might be of a mind to let you. But right now, I'm going to get one of my skillets and introduce it to your head unless you stop all this foolish chatter!"

"No need for violence, Mrs. Morrelli," Corfinio said playfully, taking two stairs at a time and heading for his room. "Tell the lout I'll see him tomorrow!"

The next evening, Corfinio climbed the front stairs of the adjoining house to meet the owner as promised. Before he could ring the doorbell, the door opened with a *whoosh!*

"Come in! Come in! Mrs. Morrelli told me to expect you!" He seemed overly enthusiastic in his greeting as he shoved a mallet-sized hand outward. "I'm Arthur Bari."

Arthur Bari, fast approaching middle age, stood two inches over six feet and looked more like a pro wrestler than a lawyer. An unruly beard covered all of his face, and a pair of heavy black-rimmed glasses set high on the bridge of his nose. In contrast to the undisciplined growth of hair on his face, a neat, thick mat of coarse, chestnut-brown hair covered his head, ending precisely at the collar of his white shirt.

Taken back by the suddenness of the welcome and the unexpected monstrous size of the man, Corfinio was tongue-tied for a response.

"Oh! I uh…uhm, was wondering—"

"And *you are*?" Bari interrupted, pleased with the effect.

"Oh, jeez! I'm sorry, I'm John Corfinio," he said, jabbing a thumb in the direction of the boarding house. "I live next door, and I was informed by Mrs. Morrelli… well, Mrs. Morrelli thought that maybe you might be needing some work done on your house here? Look, I told her I'd come to see you because she asked, but y'know, if you have someone or you're not interested, then…"

"Well then!" Bari proclaimed, waving his arms in a grand gesture of welcome and animation. "We *certainly* wouldn't want Mrs. Morrelli to get her *ass* in an *uproar*, now would we? Please! Come in!"

Entering the house, Corfinio was led into a small study, where he was invited to seat himself. Bari chose the high-backed leatherette in back of the large mahogany desk located in the middle of the room. As Corfinio looked casually around the room, he noticed the herringbone-pattern white oak flooring and five-foot-high, oak-raised panel wainscoting on two of the four walls. The remaining walls were covered in floor-to-ceiling bookcases stuffed to overflowing with law books, leatherbound volumes, and dust-covered ancient statuary.

"Before we start discussing the 'ill repair' my home has fallen into," Bari said with playful sarcasm, "can I get you anything?"

"No. Nothing, thanks anyway," Corfinio declined, shaking his head slightly from side to side.

"Are you sure?" Bari pressed, tilting his head to the side. "Maybe a drink? A beer?"

"Nothing, really."

"Coke? Coffee…anything?"

Corfinio thought a minute then blurted, "How 'bout a plate of beans?"

A blank look filled Bari's face for several seconds before he suddenly let loose with a rumbling laugh that seemed to shake the entire house.

"Beans!" he shouted at the ceiling. "Oh, I *like* that! *That's* the problem with society today, the complete and total abandonment of the *simplest* pleasures of the palette…*beans!* I have to admit, *nothing* satisfies the cravings of intestinal flatulation like a good plate of *beans.*

But," he said, throwing both hands in the air, "we're fresh out. So why not try the coffee?"

Corfinio relaxed and sat back in the chair. "Sounds good. Thanks."

"How do you take it? Bari asked, moving swiftly from his home office toward the kitchen.

"Black," shouted Corfinio toward the disappearing voice then added, "with cream and sugar!"

"Coming up!" Bari shouted back and then suddenly reappeared in the doorway. "Wait a minute—you *did* say 'black,' right?

"Yes."

"But then you said 'with cream and sugar.'"

"Yeah, I do that sometimes," Corfinio offered in explanation. "Some people never get used to it."

"Hm, I see," Bari replied. He disappeared again, returning several minutes later carrying two mugs of steaming coffee and proffered one to Corfinio.

Corfinio accepted the cup, thanked him, and proceeded to raise the cup to his lips when he noticed that the coffee was without cream or sugar. "Hey, the coffee is black."

Bari smiled and said, "Yeah, I do that sometimes. Better get used to it!"

5

The two men spent the better part of the afternoon exploring the property, returning to the home office, where they prioritized items of immediate detriment as opposed to cosmetic repair. It was no coincidence that the two items taking priority were facing Mrs. Morrelli's house. After a brief discussion as to the approximate cost of repair, Corfinio decided that a description of his personal situation might also be in order in hopes of soliciting legal counsel.

Bari leaned back in his worn leather armchair and rolled a half-chewed cigar between his forefinger and thumb. "So it becomes apparent that your actual *earning* power may not be conducive to prompt legal payment should that situation arise. Is that correct?"

"Well," Corfinio said, squirming slightly in his chair, "that's true, *but* I *always* pay."

"I would never insinuate that you wouldn't, but timely payments *are* appreciated. I *too* have financial responsibilities that preclude a magnanimous amount of *pro bono* work."

"Yeah, no, I get it," Corfinio agreed, but he clearly didn't. "Uhhm, okay. I don't know what that means. What's 'pro bono'?"

"Free."

"Ah!" Corfinio said. "And let me guess… I don't qualify?"

"Not even a little. You are *gainfully* employed and *quite* capable of compensating legal counsel." Bari leaned back in his leather chair and relit his cigar, tossing the match toward the ashtray, which missed by several inches. He leaned his head back, staring at the ceiling for a few seconds, and blew a lazy smoke ring. "However…" he added, letting it hang in the air.

Corfinio waited, leaning forward, anticipating some kind of continuation to the initial thought. "However *what*?" he finally blurted.

"Perhaps, in the event of diminished available funds, we may employ a system of barter," Bari suggested. "How do you feel about that?"

"Depends. What are we bartering?" Corfinio asked warily.

"Your professional services for mine. As Mrs. Morelli so aptly pointed out, I'm in dire need of residential repair and quite unable to meet her high standards of property maintenance. So? Shall we consider barter, or as

I prefer to call it, your upcoming period of 'indentured servitude'?"

"I'm not in a very good position to set terms or deny any offers, am I?" Corfinio asked rhetorically. "But if that arrangement is agreeable to you, I guess it works for me too. So when does my 'indentured servitude' start?"

Bari snickered good-naturedly. "As *soon* as the money runs out, my friend!"

"And how long does my 'indentured servitude' last?"

"Well," Bari mumbled, relighting his cigar, chugging on it twice, "I have a *big* house…and"—he paused to exhale a roiling cloud of smoke that looked like a head of cauliflower—"it needs a *lot* of work. You could be here for *some* time!"

"Not for anything, Arthur, but this sounds like a twentieth-century version of slave labor!"

"Yeah!" Bari said enthusiastically, flourishing a wide grin as his eyebrows raised and his eyes gleamed. "Ain't it great!"

Corfinio and Bari shook on the deal, both satisfied that they had gained reasonable access to the expertise of the other.

Over the course of the following months, an easy friendship developed between the two men, each appreciating the caustic wit and humor of the other. Insults and deprecations were the standard mode of communication when not engaged in legalese and thoroughly enjoyed by both. Anyone within earshot would generally cringe hearing the verbal assaults they heaped upon one another, which made it all the more entertaining for them.

6

Immediately upon taking Corfinio's case, Bari petitioned the court for child visitation. The court complied with the request, and a visiting schedule was issued in spite of the rigorous protests by Corfinio's ex-wife. The order designated that the visiting time occur between 10:00 and 11:00 a.m. on Sundays at the home of his ex-wife. A monitor was to be present at the time of the meetings ensuring the minor child's safety from any perceived threat issued by Corfinio.

The paperwork handed him by the Clerk of Courts indicated time, place, and duration of visit, "and shall not occur without the presence of an impartial third party." Arthur Bari considered this a minor victory and one that at least led in a forward direction for his client. Corfinio, on the other hand, was visibly miffed at the outcome.

"This is a good thing, John," Bari explained as they left the courtroom. "You *wanted* visitation, you *got* visitation. So what are you so pissed off about?"

"*Really*, Arthur?" Corfinio asked, waving the court document in the air, his face flush, anxiety and frustration apparent. "You call an *hour* 'visitation'? At *her* house no less! With an *armed* guard! The only thing they didn't do was stick a sheet of Plexiglas between us!"

"Hey, *Momuss Retardus*," said Bari, using one of his many pseudo-Latin invectives to deride Corfinio, "first point, one hour *is* visitation. *You* may not consider it as such, but it gets visitation established, which will eventually increase to longer intervals, providing you don't fuck it up."

"If *I*—"

"Second point," Bari continued, ignoring Corfinio's interruption, "*her* house is also where *he* lives, and this ensures to some degree that his mother will feel that the child is on safe ground. Third point, the 'armed guard' is her sixty-three-year-old aunt!"

"Let me point something out here, *Counselor*," said Corfinio with both hands gesticulating wildly, his voice climbing in volume, "*her* sixty-three-year-old aunt who *hates* me! Her aunt! *Hardly* 'impartial' by *anyone's* account! And...AND... I'm on *enemy* territory! What about *my* safety? *My* safety hasn't been considered here *at all!* Doesn't *my* safety count?"

"No, John. Not even a little."

Corfinio, dumbfounded, stared at his lawyer stunned by the reality of the answer.

"John? Look...you're *well* over six feet—what are you, 230, 240? You are not the 'threatened'—you are the 'threat.' Whether you are or not in reality does *not* matter. It's the perception that counts. They look at you and think, 'Well, he could certainly do some serious damage.' It doesn't matter if you really *would*—it's that you *could*. Thereby, John, *you* are the threat that needs to be protected *against*."

7

Arthur Bari had coached him in "proper behavior" prior to the visiting arrangement. "Pay attention to me, John—this is *vitally* important," Bari instructed, circling his desk, waving a thick finger at his client, clenching a cigar stub between his teeth. "Remember, be civil and especially pleasant when you greet your ex-wife. If she feels threatened by your attitude, you can expect that the visitations will be suspended."

"That might be difficult to do," Corfinio offered. "How can I *possibly* be even *semi*-decent with a hell spawn satanic bitch that deserves to die a slow and agonizing death of unmitigated pain and suffering?"

Bari continued to pace the room slowly as he relit the end of his cigar and tossed the wooden match into the overflowing ashtray on his desk. He blew out a gust of blue smoke at the ceiling and proceeded with his directives as if Corfinio hadn't interrupted.

"Be that as it may, you have to play nice. You cannot—*cannot*—touch the boy in a rough, playful manner, *no matter how seemingly innocent*, or especially in anger or retaliation of any form."

"Arthur," Corfinio replied impatiently, "he's *three! And* I only get to see him for an *hour!* There's hardly enough time for us to actually *do* anything fun, never mind being angry with him. Besides, what the hell would I be *retaliating* against anyway? What's he gonna do, hit me with a Tinker Toy?"

"If he does, I'll be jealous," Bari replied with a smirk. "But, John, seriously, my advice to *you* is to not touch him at *all*. Even in an *affectionate* manner."

"I can't even hug or kiss my own boy?" Corfinio turned, following his lawyer's circuitous journey, mouth agape in disbelief, waiting for his lawyer to reply.

Bari stopped pacing and removed the ash-laden cigar from between his teeth, tapping the heavy powder gently onto the mounded heap in the overloaded ashtray. He cocked his head to one side, barely squinting one eye behind the heavy, black-rimmed glasses. "John, *you're* under the reasonable misconception that this is your 'son.' But it's not—it's her 'weapon.'"

"*Oh, come on!*" Corfinio scoffed with a wave of his hand, dismissing his lawyer's comment. "I don't think—"

"*Exactly!*" Bari interrupted triumphantly, raising both palms in supplication, staring blindly above as if seeking the presence of God. "You *don't* think!"

Dropping his hands, he turned to face his client. "Have you learned *nothing*? She only has *two* objectives, one of which is to remain in the system that provides for her. The second of which is using *your son* as leverage to get *you* to provide the rest. Do you understand that, John? Am I getting through that *rock* pile of a head of yours?" Bari was exasperated with his client. "John, look. I know the situation is far less than ideal, but you have to see that she's looking for the opportunity to squeeze you out of your son's life completely. If you do something— *anything*—that could even *remotely* be misinterpreted as wrong or compromising, you *will lose* visitation. The court would rather err on the part of caution, rather than subject your child to your 'abusive' personality."

"But I'm not an abusive guy," Corfinio protested weakly.

"Says who, John? *You*? It doesn't matter what *you* say! All that matters is what *she* says. If she goes to court and says that she feels threatened or unsafe or that she fears for the child's safety, then *you lose! End* of story! *No* more visits! So until we can arrange for the visitation to take place at an alternate location *without* her presence, you have to be careful. *Very* careful. Don't *touch* him, don't *grab* him, and don't even *sneeze* on him for crissake. She'll probably claim you're a mycoplasma pneumonia carrier."

Corfinio stared down at the floor sullenly and exhaled a long breath of downheartedness. "Fine, Arthur.

I'll make *sure* to be on my best behavior," Corfinio said, sarcasm dripping heavily. "I have to tell you, Arthur, I *never* thought it would be like *this*."

"This ain't Disneyland, John."

8

Corfinio dreaded the first visit with his son because he knew instinctively that Michael would reject him as a stranger after so much time had passed. *He probably won't even remember me*, he thought. *I'm nobody to him now.* Michael was three years old, and Corfinio felt that whatever bond he had with the boy would surely be gone. He hoped differently, but in his heart, he knew to expect the bitter disappointment that surely awaited him.

Corfinio sighed heavily before knocking on the front door of his former home. He was surprised to realize that his heart was pounding, and sweat dripped slowly down the nape of his neck in spite of the cool, steady morning breeze. The seconds seemed interminably long as he raised his clenched fist to knock again when the door opened. The old woman's stone-faced ghastly countenance greeted him and, without any verbal exchange or eye contact, waved him into the living room. He stepped inside amid a scattering of children's toys strewn freely across the floor. A stack of folded laundry threatening to cascade onto the floor sat on the arm of the floral-patterned couch. Across the room, no more than fifteen feet away, Corfinio saw his son, Michael, standing by his mother's side.

The handsome boy stood just over three feet tall, with thick, curly, blond hair framing his renaissance angel face. Soft brown eyes nestled above his slightly pinked cheeks, and a nervous little smile exposed straight white baby teeth.

A surge of emotion like a sweeping ripple gripped him upon seeing his boy. He felt lightheaded and conversely heavy hearted at the same time. *Michael! My son!* He wanted so bad to run over and lift him up and hold him, but his feet remained glued to the floor. He felt the tears welling in his eyes and refused to give in to the raw emotion, mustering his inner strength to keep his voice steady as he addressed his son. "Hey, pal," he said softly, "how you doin'?"

Michael walked over to him with his arms extended.

Against his lawyer's explicit advice and direction, Corfinio bent down to embrace his son. He never saw the burning rage on the face of his ex-wife, Marsha.

Over the course of several months, an easy routine had developed in spite of the acrimonious relationship shared between John and his ex-wife. The visits went surprisingly well considering Corfinio had to deal with two hovering forces of evil determined to pounce on even the slightest infraction. Adhering to Arthur Bari's words of warning, he ignored every baited comment and snide remark aimed his way. He kept reminding himself that the focus was to enjoy what little time he had with his son until a better arrangement could be bartered, begged, or bought.

Most of his discomfort at being in 'enemy territory' dissipated once he was engaged in the company of his son. They would sit together on the couch while Michael would "read" books to his father, creating a story to match the pictures on each page. Corfinio would point at the words and ask, "What does that say?" and his son would reply, "I dunno, Dad, I can only read pictures!"

Some days were dedicated to crashing miniature metal cars on the carpeted floor, while others were given to creating new species of animals with colorful wads of Play-Doh. No matter the form of entertainment, Corfinio was always impressed with his son's intelligence and enthusiasm, confident that he had the smartest child in creation. A prouder father there never was.

9

After each visitation, Corfinio would drive two miles across town to the same café he frequented each morning before work. He had been a regular customer for sixteen years and enjoyed the homey atmosphere and the odd assortment of characters that made it unique. Quality Coffee had been owned and operated for twenty-seven years by Tim Ferrante, who claimed that if he ever took a day off, he might like it and never come back. "That's it!" he'd announce every morning to the aging assortment of long-retired political and social analytical geniuses. "I'm taking tomorrow off!"

The seated legion of old men would laugh and yell back, "You can't! Your wife won't let you stay home!" But somewhere under the laughter, they were petrified that he actually *would* take a day off. And the truth of the matter was, their wives didn't want *them* to stay home.

Corfinio's initial visit to Quality Coffee was an eye opener. He discovered that the contingency of unfaltering daily regulars fiercely staked and guarded their territory like chain-mailed pikemen at the battlements. Seating himself rather than taking his coffee to go gained him immediate attention from the rheumy-eyed gargoyles that immediately ceased conversation to stare unkindly in his direction. One of the white-haired, hefty patrons sitting across from him at the horseshoe-shaped counter stabbed a stubby finger in his direction.

"Hey, sonny, you're sitting on Lenny's stool."

Corfinio glanced up at the old man and grinned, thinking it was a playful ruse. "Lenny doesn't appear to be here right now," Corfinio said kindly and was met with solemn aged faces staring back at him. "Or," he added, realizing with subdued levity their somber dispositions, "I could slide over here," and moved to the adjacent seat.

The old man huffed and growled, "Now you're in *McGee's* spot. Everyone *knows* McGee sits there!"

Corfinio stood up, somewhat entertained by the situation and pointed to the third seat in line. "Here?"

"That's Big Mike's seat!" said the bald man, jumping into the fray. "And the next one belongs to Crazy Charlie!"

"Okay," Corfinio sighed in amused resignation. "Which of these empty stools *isn't* reserved?"

"That one over there at the end, next to the pole," said the white-haired old man. "But if you *really* want, you can sit in Crazy Charlie's seat. He gets madder than a wet hen when someone sits in his spot. We love to piss him off!" The old man chuckled, and his cohorts followed suit, nodding in agreement.

The front door pushed open, and Sergeant Paul Young of the local PD walked in and nodded in the direction of the assembled seniors. "Morning, men! Or at least whatever's left of it anyway," he announced good-naturedly as he approached the takeout counter. Sturdy and barrel-chested, head and face completely shaven with the exception of a thick, brown walrus mustache, Paul Young looked more like a lumberjack than a policeman. His size intimidated most people immediately, but his light-brown eyes reflected a man with a gentle heart and soul. There were certain offenders who would vehemently argue that point, but among the law abiding, he was well-respected.

Corfinio turned when he heard the booming voice of the policeman. "Hey, Paul."

"Hey, John! How you doin'? How's everything going with you?"

"Great! Have a job, a place to live, and I saw my boy this morning. What more can a man want in life?" Corfinio said good-naturedly as he sat down.

"A million dollars would sure help!"

Tim Ferrante walked up to the counter and handed Paul Young a cardboard coffee cup. "*Two* dollars will suit *me* just fine. Here's your coffee!"

"Thanks, Tim," Young said, handing the dollar bills to the proprietor, dropping a third into the tip jar.

The front door opened again, and an older, short, thin man with glasses walked in, glaring at Corfinio. "Whaddya think, ya *own* the place?" he demanded loudly.

The seated white-haired old man piped up quickly, "We *told* him not to sit there, Charlie! But *he* said, 'Screw Charlie and his stool, I'll sit in any damned place I want!'"

"Oh, is that a fact!" Charlie said, the ire visibly building, totally entertaining the crowd of seated old men.

"Hey, wait a minute—" Corfinio objected.

"That's it!" Charlie exclaimed, throwing his hands in the air. "I've taken as much of this abuse as I'm gonna take! *Paul!* Lemme borrow your gun!" He turned to the policeman with right hand extended, palm upward.

"Well," Young drawled, "I can't do *that*, Charlie, but if you want, I can shoot him *for* you."

"Fine!" Charlie agreed. "Just as long as I get my seat back!"

"How 'bout if I just move?" Corfinio asked with mock trepidation.

Charlie looked at Paul Young then at the assembled mob of instigating old men then back at the policeman. He tipped his head, scrunched his nose, blinked twice, and threw both hands in the air. "Works for me!"

Corfinio moved away from the trouble-causing stool, sliding his hands into the pockets of his jeans, and casually sidled up to Paul Young. "Y'know, Paul, I should probably think about finding another coffee shop on Sunday mornings."

"Ohh, come on," Young scoffed, "don't let Crazy Charlie scare you away. He's loud and obnoxious, but he's harmless—he's just crazy."

"It wasn't him I was worried about," Corfinio said. "It's *you!* It might be in my best interest to avoid a cop who *offers* to shoot me!"

"Don't worry, John. I wouldn't shoot you unless you *really* needed it!"

10

Several months passed before Corfinio approached his ex-wife about the prospect of extending the visits. He knew she'd probably refuse but felt he had to make the attempt. As always, she announced when the hour was up with an almost malicious satisfaction, cuing him to leave.

"Looks like it's time for Dad to leave, Michael," Corfinio said sadly, adding with a half-smile, "but we had a pretty good day!"

"Yeah!" Michael agreed enthusiastically. "See ya, Dad!" The golden-haired boy grinned, waved, and wandered off to the television.

Corfinio walked slowly to the front door with Marsha shadowing him close behind. He stopped as he stepped down onto the front porch. "Marsha," he began carefully, "I was thinking…it might be nice if I could get some extra time with Michael. Maybe make it a two-hour visit so we could have a little more time together."

Marsha stood facing him at the doorway, arms folded across her chest, her eyes suddenly dark and foreboding as if a cloud had passed across her face.

"No," she said with absolute finality, leaving no doubt that negotiations were completely out of the question.

Still, Corfinio couldn't let it go. "But why not?" He fully expected her refusal, a sinking, deflated feeling overwhelming him nonetheless.

"Because, I don't want *you* here one second longer than I *have* to!" Her words were pure venom, but Corfinio was beyond feeling the sting of her intent.

"Then let me take him out for a ride," Corfinio suggested. "I could take him down the street for an ice cream or a donut or something."

"*No!*" she said with more force. Corfinio noticed a faint crack in her voice though, as if fear or panic were creeping in.

"Look, I was hoping we could agree on this. Everything has been going pretty good, right? No problems, no arguments." Not waiting for her reply, he soldiered on. "I thought we could move forward without getting the lawyers involved, easier and less costly for both of us."

Marsha exploded. She screamed, "*Are you threatening me?*" Her eyes were enlarged glass orbs reflecting the depths of lunacy. "I know what your plan is! You'll take him for a ride and *never come back*! *That's* what this is all about! You're trying to *take* him from me!"

Corfinio had seen these unpredictable eruptions before during their short and tumultuous marriage. She'd be fine one moment and an untethered raging maniac the next. She'd react that way because of something he said or did or something he *didn't* say, leaving him to wonder, 'Was I *supposed* to say something?' He found that any form of confrontation always made it worse, so he'd learned to retreat to a neutral corner, convinced that she was simply certifiably insane.

"I'm not *stealing* him!" Corfinio said, knowing his words were falling on deaf ears. "I just want a little more time with him, that's all."

The last of his words were drowned out by the booming slam of the front door.

"I'm guessing that's a 'no,'" Corfinio said, sarcastically addressing the door. Sighing, shoulders slumped in defeat, Corfinio decided he better call his lawyer. He drove across town to the coffee shop, dropped six coins in the only pay phone left in America, and dialed his lawyer's phone number.

Bari answered the black rotary phone on his desk on the second ring.

"Hello, Arthur Bari speaking."

"Arthur? I think we *might* have a problem."

"What happened, John?" Bari asked, exasperated, removing his glasses. He squinted hard and pinched the bridge of his nose.

Corfinio shrugged and looked out the large plate glass window of the coffee shop, staring blankly at the tortoise-like Sunday traffic crawling by. "I have no idea. One minute everything was fine, and the next, *bam!* Psycho bitch fell off the med wagon and spazzed out."

"Could you be a *little* bit more specific, John? Sharpen your analytic prose and give me something that actually describes a series of events."

"She just popped a cork because I asked for a little extra time with Michael."

"Did you raise your voice, yell or scream, *hit* anything, *throw* anything, perhaps burn rubber leaving the house? Did you *call* her anything other than her *birth* name? Was this *in* the house? Did the visit just *begin*, or did this occur at the *end* of the visit?"

"No, I didn't *do* anything," Corfinio answered defensively. "It happened just before I left ...well, *as* I was leaving. I was standing on the front porch, she was closing the door, and I swear all I did was *ask* to extend the visitation, maybe take him for a ride, and the next thing I know, the crazy train is pulling into the station."

"Okay. Where was the kid during all this?"

"Michael had already run off into the other room to watch TV or play or whatever."

"So he wasn't right there to see or hear whatever was said?"

"He wasn't there, but I would imagine anyone with ears heard whatever was said. She was screaming like a lunatic."

"That's it?"

"That's it."

"Well, if there's anything we've learned about her in the last year, it's to expect anything."

"I know what that means, but what does that mean?"

"It means she might wake up tomorrow and forget the whole thing or—"

"Or?"

"Or she'll turn this into *your* own personal Armageddon."

"Oh, great! So what do you suggest I do now?

"Wait."

Corfinio pulled the tightly clutched receiver off his ear, staring at it briefly while his blood pressure slowly climbed. He decided he couldn't continue the conversation without exploding, and he didn't want to do it in the coffee shop. With controlled deliberation, he slowly placed the phone receiver on the cradle, staring intently on the flapper as it descended, officially ending the call. He maintained a vicelike grip on the receiver, fighting off the urge to smash it violently into the rectangular wall-hung phone box. As the intensity diminished, he released the receiver, exhaled deeply, and stared at the phone for several seconds. "Wait." He repeated Bari's directive out loud to no one.

"You okay there, Johnny?" Officer Paul Young stood at the takeout counter, steam rising from the cardboard coffee cup that he slowly brought to his lips. "You look a little...agitated."

"No, I'm fine," Corfinio lied through a fake, forced smile.

"You sure? Trouble with the ole lady?" Officer Young asked, knowing full well that's exactly what it was. He had put the pieces together based on the one side of the phone conversation he heard. It wasn't that difficult to figure out after fourteen years on the force and running into the same situation a couple of hundred times. No, it wasn't difficult at all. What *was* difficult, he silently mused, was watching people's lives unravel. *It's like watching a landslide. You can see it coming, and there's not a damned thing you can do to stop it.*

"No, I'm fine, Paul," Corfinio repeated. "I just..." He paused, weighing out whether or not to divulge any of his problem but, embarrassed at his situation, decided to keep it to himself. "I think I'm just gonna go home." He offered up a halfhearted smile, walked to the door, pushed it open, and stepped outside.

11

The following week dragged by as he spent every day in nervous anticipation of being served an order of restraint. The relationship with his son, although stunted, was progressing in a positive direction. He certainly didn't want to do anything that would jeopardize his ability to see Michael, especially after not being allowed near him for such an extended period. He felt relieved as the weekend approached without a restraining order being foisted upon him and eagerly anticipated his next scheduled visitation.

Sunday morning arrived bringing fair but cooling weather, which was typical for that time of year. The early morning chill had already worn off as the temperature crept up slowly.

Corfinio hummed along with the radio as he showered and shaved in preparation for his visit with Michael. He donned worn blue jeans and a long-sleeved, gray woolen shirt and jacked the sleeves up to his elbows.

He grabbed a comb off the dresser and ran it quickly through his thick hair, sneaking a quick look at himself in the mirror. "Gotta go!" he said to his reflection, then hurried down the stairs two at a time, causing a racket that didn't go unnoticed by Mrs. Morrelli.

"*John!* Is that *you* lumbering down the stairs? I *swear*, you'll fall and break your neck one of these days! I've *told* you that a *dozen* times before!"

"Yes, ma'am!" he replied with a wink. "But I'm sure you'll mend me up and make me as good as new, and everyone will be so jealous because I've got the *prettiest* nurse in the whole county!"

"Don't you get flip with *me*, John Corfinio!" She turned to walk away but then backtracked a step. "Are you off to see your boy today, John?"

"Yeah, ten o'clock appointment."

"Well then, you'd best be off—it's half past nine. You never know what kind of traffic you'll run into, and you don't want to be late."

"That's for sure," Corfinio agreed. "Hey, Mrs. Morrelli, do you want to see a picture of him? I mean, it's okay if you don't…"

"Well of course!" she replied enthusiastically.

"This is him." Corfinio reached in his front pocket and withdrew a single photo from his wallet and handed it to his landlady.

"Ohhh, he's *such* a *handsome* little man," she gushed. "Why, *look* at his *beautiful* curly hair! And oh my *goodness*, what an *adorable* smile!"

"Thank you!" Corfinio said proudly. "I think so too, but I'm a bit biased."

She handed the photograph back to him. "You should be proud, John. He's as cute as a button! Now get yourself going," she said, shooing him out the door, "otherwise you'll be late!"

Corfinio gave a quick wave as he jumped into his truck. The drive was short and uneventful, timed to occur between church services letting out to avoid any chance of mishap or delay. The last thing he wanted was to get stuck behind a "Sunday driver." "The problem with Sunday drivers," Mrs. Morrelli would say, "is that they drive like it's Sunday!"

Corfinio arrived at the home of his ex-wife in twenty-two minutes, eight minutes early. He sat in the truck waiting for the appointed time with the radio on for distraction. The dashboard clock flipped to 9:53 a.m. as he fidgeted in his seat. He would have approached the door, but after being chastised several weeks ago by his ex-wife for "trying to extend your time by stealing mine," he opted to wait until the appointed time of ten o'clock. Annie Lennox crooned "No More I Love Yous" while he gently tapped the steering wheel, absently keeping to the beat of the melody. The DJ interrupted the fading final elements of the song, announcing that the time was now ten o'clock.

He turned off the ignition and climbed out of the truck, stuffing the keys in his pocket. Walking to the front door, he smiled in anticipation of being greeted by his son who always charged across the room and jumped up into his arms upon his arrival. He climbed the three concrete stairs to the landing, opened the metal storm door, and knocked twice in rapid succession on the windowless entry door. Ten seconds passed, but no one answered. He leaned in closer to the wooden door, listening hard for sounds of approaching footsteps but no activity within the household could be heard. His stomach clenched involuntarily in a moment of alarm, fearing something might be wrong. He turned to face the parking space where she usually parked her car and was momentarily relieved upon seeing it in its proper stall. *So why isn't she answering the door?* he thought. He knocked again but harder this time and again waited for any stirrings within. Frustration building, Corfinio's mind raced. *Could she be sleeping? Did she go somewhere? Is something wrong?* He was about to rap on the door a third time when he heard Marsha's voice speaking softly from the other side.

"Go away." It was little more than a whisper, but he heard it loud and clear.

"It's *me* Marsha. It's John." He paused, not knowing exactly what to say and not quite believing what he was hearing from the other side of the door. "It's ten o'clock," he added lamely.

"Go away," she repeated.

"*What?* What are you *talking* about?" he asked, very careful not to raise his voice for fear of escalating the situation. "It's my *visitation* time."

"I don't want you here. Just leave."

Corfinio stood there in disbelief, staring at the blank door; his gut instincts were screaming that something was wrong.

Another voice spoke from behind the door, a small voice, an innocent voice. "It's Daddy. Let him in."

"No," she answered Michael and continued, "go… away. Just go away."

His anger was rising quickly, but instead of giving in to the emotion of the moment, he simply stepped back, letting the storm door close silently, guided slowly by the mechanical closure piston. Suddenly, a pang of paranoia gripped him, and he casually looked left and right to see if he was being surveilled. An old man with a cane hobbled down the street, and four children sat on the porch across the street. It seemed no one had any interest in him that he could ascertain, but something didn't feel right. He breathed deep, turned, and walked down the stairs and over to his pickup truck.

He drove for several minutes without knowing where he was going, talking out loud to himself. "*Go away*," he said sternly into the rearview mirror. "Go away. *My ass!* I get *one* goddamned hour with my kid *a week*…ONE! And now…*now*, that—" He gritted his teeth and seethed. "That no-good…*fucking bitch* is taking *that* away from me *too*?" He ran the fingers of his left hand through his hair in exasperation and felt the sweat on his scalp. "Settle down, boy," he said into the rearview mirror. "This is getting you nowhere."

Stopping for a traffic light, he mulled over the situation and decided he should call his lawyer. *He'll fix this shit*, he thought. *He* better *fix this shit! That's what I'm paying him for.* The light changed when he suddenly realized he was only a few blocks from the coffee shop. *Yeah, I'll grab a cup of coffee, calm down a little, and call Arthur.*

12

He pulled up across the street from the coffee shop and parked, noticing two police squad cars parked alongside the building. That was nothing unusual as several of the local policemen would have breakfast there frequently and were well-liked by the local neighborhood. Besides, why would anyone question the presence of a police officer where there were doughnuts sold?

Corfinio stepped out of his truck, looked both ways for oncoming traffic along the double-lane street, and satisfied that he could cross safely, proceeded. He had reached the middle of the street when Officer Paul Young stepped out from the doorway of the coffee shop, looking in his direction.

Corfinio nodded acknowledgment, noticing Officer Young's posture was slightly rigid. "Hey, Paul. How you doing?" Corfinio said, stepping onto the sidewalk. The two men were now face to face, standing no more than an arm's length away from each other.

"Hey, John," Young replied, thumbs hooked on his belt, "I have to talk to you."

"Okay," he said, shifting uncomfortably, "well, here I am. What do you need, Paul?"

"John…were you just there?"

Corfinio cocked his head. "What? Was I just *where*?"

"Were you just at your ex-wife's house?"

"Yeah," he admitted, seeing no harm in his reply. Suddenly apprehensive, he looked over and noticed the two cops in the second car seemed to have a fascinated interest in his conversation with Officer Young. "What's going on, Paul?"

"There's a restraining order out on you, John. You're not supposed to be there at all."

"*What?*" he said in complete surprise. "That's *impossible!* Paul, I was there by virtue of a *court-ordered* visitation schedule! Look *here*…see this?"

Corfinio reached into his back pocket, pulling out a copy of the court order granting him visitation. On the advice of his lawyer, he kept it on his person whenever involved with a visitation. "Just in case it ever comes into question," Arthur Bari had advised. Like now.

"Ten to eleven o'clock on Sundays," he said, pointing a finger at the order he handed to Young. "Wait a minute, this is no coincidence, is it, Paul? How did you know I'd *be* here? *I* didn't know I was coming here!"

Officer Young continued perusing the court order, leaving Corfinio's questions unanswered.

"*Shit!* You came here to *arrest* me, didn't you?" He glanced over to the squad car that now had the driver and passenger doors opened. "Did you really think you'd need all this backup?"

"John, I'm trying to help you here. Those guys," he said, pointing a beefy thumb over his shoulder in their direction, "caught the call and were told that you'd be here. I was in the stationhouse when the call came in, and I asked the lieutenant if I could take the call… because I knew you."

"And you figured I'd be more likely to go along quietly as opposed to making these other guys earn their money?"

"Nobody wants any trouble, John, but you've violated a restraining order."

"Paul? How can I be in violation of a restraining order that was never served on me?"

"The information I got was that it was served on you two days ago."

"You know what, Paul? I want to *see* this *supposed* restraining order, so why don't we take a trip to the station and get this bullshit figured out once and for all?"

"That might be a good idea."

"You gonna slap the cuffs on me now, Paul?"

"No, John. I'm not placing you under arrest. You're just coming down for questioning."

"I imagine your two cohorts over there won't be too pleased to see that." Corfinio squinted slightly, seeing one of the officers step out of the squad car. "Is that… *Morris? Is that Bill Morris?* It is! *Jesus Christ!* I'd know that pug ugly mug anywhere. He's a no-good fucker and *everybody* knows it! A real piece of shit if there—"

"*John*," Young cut in, "please. That's why I'm here, so we can avoid any unnecessary confrontations. That's not what I want, and I don't think you do either."

Corfinio resigned himself to the fact that this was not going to end well for him at all. "Fine. Let's go and get this fiasco over with."

Corfinio climbed into the back seat of the squad car and sat there brooding. The mile-and-a-half drive to the police station took all of about twelve minutes, but neither man spoke during the short trip. There was nothing more to say until valid paperwork could be produced anyway. What he couldn't understand was if there *was* an order of restraint. What the hell was it issued for? Everything seemed to be going along fairly smooth with the visitations, or so he thought.

Arriving at the rear entrance of the police station, Officer Young opened the rear door of the Crown Vic for his passenger to exit. They entered the building and proceeded through a brightly lit corridor of painted concrete block walls, which terminated at the juncture of another perpendicular corridor. The second hallway gained access to half-a-dozen small offices and doors with no visible designation. Young stopped abruptly and pointed into a small conference room. "Wait here, John."

Corfinio walked into the sparsely furnished room—a small round conference table with four chairs, and a short run of cabinets with an ugly green countertop on one wall. There were no pictures, posters, or warning signs on any of the cream-colored walls, giving the room a stark, clinical feel. A closed-circuit camera hung like a protruding eye from the ceiling. He folded his arms across his chest and leaned against the counter, waiting for whatever or whoever was coming.

Less than ten minutes later, Officer Young returned with another policeman in tow, who was introduced as Lieutenant James Shedden. He held a sheet of paper in his right hand and was visibly agitated.

"Are you Corfinio?" he asked, a tinge of anger in his voice.

"Who *else* would I be?" Corfinio replied sarcastically, still leaning against the countertop.

Shedden stepped forward, closing the gap between the two. "Being a smartass isn't helping your case any."

"Coming at me like you're prepared for war isn't making me feel all warm and fuzzy either, so why don't you—"

"*Lieutenant*," Young broke in, "he's saying he never received the TRO, and he's got a copy of a court order allowing visitation."

"*Here's* your restraining order!" Without looking at or acknowledging Young, Shedden shoved the paper in front of Corfinio. "You've been served!"

Smoldering, Corfinio took the single page and read it through carefully. When he slowly raised his head to meet the stare of the lieutenant, he fumed, flicking the paper with his off hand. "This is *bullshit*!"

"I don't give a shit *what* you think," Shedden countered, raising his voice.

"For *chrissake*!" Corfinio stood up straight, facing Shedden, who was six inches shorter. "It's in *two* different colors of ink with *two different handwritings*!"

"*So what*?" Shedden answered defensively.

"*So what*? If this is 'legit'—*which I doubt*—then *why* does it have *today's* date on it if it was *supposedly* handed to me *two days ago*?"

Corfinio was on the verge of doing something stupid, and Officer Young could see this was headed in the wrong direction. He stepped between the two and faced Corfinio. "John, now settle down. We—"

"*Get him out of here*!" Shedden suddenly yelled. "Put him in lockup—he's in for the *weekend*!" He wheeled, furious, and angrily stormed from the room.

Officer Young sighed heavily. A thick silence permeated the room for several seconds. "John, you'll have to empty your pockets."

"Why?"

"I have to lock you up, John," he said reluctantly. "You can't have anything you can harm yourself with. I'll need you to take off your belt too."

Corfinio complied silently, knowing that it was senseless to continue. His mind raced, trying to put all the pieces together of this poorly executed setup, and it was probably his ex-wife who set the wheels in motion. He handed over his personal possessions—a pocket knife, a wallet with $112.87 in cash, and a picture of his son—to Officer Young, who then placed everything in a manila envelope. A list of the items was written on the envelope and closed with the attached metal clasp.

"Well," Young said, obviously unhappy about the entire situation.

"Yeah," Corfinio replied.

They walked to the bank of holding cells located on the lower level of the police station. Young opened the nearest cell door and motioned for Corfinio to enter. Corfinio stepped through and entered the six-by-eight cell. Over the cell door was a single lightbulb that remained on encased in an iron cage. There was an iron cot with a paper-thin mattress and a wool blanket the size of a bath towel.

"Glad I won't be sleeping on *that* tonight."

"It's either that or the floor," Young replied, closing the cell door with a modest *click*.

Corfinio turned around to face Young, stepped forward, and grasped the cell bars. "Wait, what? He said I was here for the 'weekend.' Today's Sunday."

"Today *is* Sunday, but tomorrow is Columbus Day. You won't be arraigned until Tuesday. Sorry, John." He turned and started to walk away when Corfinio hailed him.

"Hey, Paul!"

Young stopped walking and twisted his head looking over his shoulder toward the cell. "Yeah?"

"You didn't read me my rights."

"I didn't arrest you."

"Then what in the name of *fuck all* am I doing in a *jail* cell?"

"You're being 'detained.'"

13

Walking back from the holding cells, Young couldn't shake the feeling that there was something more going on than what he was being told. He didn't feel that locking up Corfinio was condoned, considering the overall uncertainty of the circumstances, but those orders came straight from his lieutenant, who for whatever reason seemed to have a hair across his ass as soon as Corfinio's name was mentioned. Young couldn't figure out why Shedden had basically come charging out of the gate like a Pamplona bull when he asked the lieutenant about the restraining order. Although Shedden was rarely in a good mood, it appeared that he had been even more agitated the last few weeks, snapping at everyone over the smallest incidentals.

He had known Corfinio for close to five years, and although they weren't "friends" per se, they had shared many conversations over coffee during that time. Young never got the impression that Corfinio was anything less than a decent guy, and he rather prided himself on being able to accurately read people, which in his line of work was paramount to his safety and ensuring the safety of others.

It sure seemed like the lieutenant had jumped the gun on this one, and there was only one way to find out why. He stuck his head around the corner of Shedden's office door and rapped twice quickly. "Got a minute?"

"What's on your mind, Paul?" Shedden sat behind his desk, still obviously miffed and the tone of his voice reflecting a level of agitation that had not yet passed.

"Jim," he began, wrinkling his expansive forehead, "what the hell's going on? Why didn't we just issue this guy his restraining order and send him on his way instead of sticking him in the can for the weekend?"

"Are you questioning me, *Sergeant*?" He emphasized Young's rank as if to remind him that he was interrogating a superior.

"No, *sir*," Young replied, acknowledging the rebuke, "but I've known this guy for a while, and I've got to say, I don't see him as a threat to *anyone*…unless *he's* threatened."

"Is that so?" he retaliated angrily. "Well, it might interest *you* to know, *Sergeant*, this 'friend' of yours tried to kick in the door to his ex-wife's house when she told him to leave."

The lieutenant seemed overly defensive, and Young could see that this conversation was getting nowhere fast.

He remained standing in the doorway, leaning against the jamb, finally deciding there was nothing more to be gained from pursuing this, but he also had considerable doubts about the information he was being fed.

Shedden pushed his chair back. "We done here?"

"Yes, sir." Young nodded and left.

*****

As he drove home the following evening after his shift ended, Young found himself contemplating the events of the previous day. He couldn't quite make the pieces fit. Corfinio wasn't the type of guy that flew off the handle easily; in fact, he was pretty tolerant to most kinds of badgering, teasing, or bullying. But on the rare occasion where conflict was impossible to avoid, the man was a whirlwind. Definitely not someone you'd want to tangle with once he crossed that line. Maybe that was it…maybe he just reached the end of his rope and finally cracked. Seriously, how much could anyone take before they finally lost it?

He approached the intersection and stopped for the sign. He paused longer than usual, mindlessly tapping on the steering wheel with his beefy fingers, staring ahead at nothing. The sun was falling quickly behind the rooftops, causing a glare on the windshield, causing him to squint painfully before reflexively flipping the visor down. He lifted his foot off the brake, letting the car roll forward slightly when he suddenly hit the brake pedal again. Straight ahead was the road home. He hit the gas, slewing the steering wheel hard to the left.

Four and a half minutes later, curiosity having gotten the better of him, he pulled up across the street from Marsha Corfinio's house, giving him a command view of the front door. He sat in the idling car, staring at the door that had suffered the barrage of Corfinio's wrath two days ago. Except the aluminum storm door didn't appear to have any damage at all. No dents, no broken glass, nothing. Surely, if a man of Corfinio's size and strength had attempted to "kick the door in" as was reported, there should have been *some* damage.

What the hell is going on? he thought and sighed heavily. He shrugged and slipped the prindle into drive when Marsha Corfinio's front door opened. A man backed out of the door, stepping onto the porch as she giggled happily in the doorway. The man smiled in return, turned, and descended the stairs, looking down at his fistful of keys as he approached his vehicle parked at the curb. Looking up, he suddenly stopped as if he had slammed into an invisible barrier. Lieutenant James Shedden's smile changed to jaw-sagging shock when he locked eyes with Sergeant Paul Young.

14

Corfinio awoke Tuesday morning to the sound of voices coming down the hallway. He couldn't tell what time it was; there were no clocks or windows to gauge the time of day. For all he knew, it could still be the middle of the night. The single caged lightbulb burned dimly under the cocoon of wet toilet paper that he had applied last night to reduce the burning glare, enabling him to grab a few hours of sleep. He swung his legs over the side of his metal cot and shook his head to clear the cobwebs, standing up slowly, waiting to see which parts hurt.

Two policemen he didn't recognize rounded the corner, approaching his cell laughing as they finished their conversation.

"John Corfinio?"

Corfinio remained silent, watching the two policemen.

"Are you John Corfinio?" pressed the taller of the two, conveying a slight level of irritation.

"You have *six* cells here," Corfinio answered, "*five* of which are empty. What do *you* think?"

"Step away from the door."

As Corfinio stepped back, the cell door was unlocked, and the two policemen entered the cell. The second officer produced handcuffs and leg irons, which were placed on Corfinio without concern for his discomfort. Each officer then took a hold of his upper arm and escorted him down to the rear exit of the police station, where he was loaded into the back of the paddy wagon. A short and uncomfortable ride later, the prisoner transport van stopped and the rear doors were opened, where he was instructed to disembark. He was again escorted by a different set of officers into the bowels of a building he was unfamiliar with and deposited in another controlled and guarded area known as the "tank."

He was in the lowest level of the courthouse building, the entrance of which was only used by the transport van for ushering prisoners in and out of court. The tank was a large holding area where the prisoners would be held until their time to appear before the judge that day. It was ill-lit, in dire need of repair, and stank of stale sweat.

Corfinio sat on the scarred wooden bench against the wall with peeling paint where he was accompanied by a dozen others awaiting the same fate. He sat there with his eyes closed, trying to block out the innocuous conversations that surrounded him.

"John!"

Corfinio opened his eyes at the sound of his name, recognizing the voice immediately. "*Arthur*? Wh...how did—"

"Doesn't matter. *Jesus*, John, you look like *shit*."

"*Really*? Wow, I thought for *sure* my weekend at the *Hoosegow Spa* would make me feel and look ten years younger! Should I ask for my money back?"

"Okay, look," Bari said, ignoring his client's obvious sarcasm, "I know this *seems* bad, but it's not as bad as you may think."

"Said the man without handcuffs."

"This is your first offense. You have no previous record, so given a modicum of good fortune and a judge that has an ounce of sense, you'll probably draw nothing worse than probation."

"How long?"

"Probably six months. Maybe a year," he paused and added, "at worst."

"You'll of course, pardon my inability to appreciate the leniency of such a 'fair' judgment," he said in mock civility, "seeing as how my crime was...*knocking on a fucking door*!"

"That may be so, but the given documentation indicates that you violated an order of restraint. So *that's* what you're being judged on."

"It was a *bullshit* order, Arthur. It was *altered* by—'

"I know!" Bari cut in, trying to keep Corfinio from boiling over. "I know, I *saw* it. It was obviously filled out by two different people at different time frames. *I know.* But I *don't* know how much that's going to matter. I can't *prove* that."

Corfinio leaned over and grabbed his head with both hands, elbows on his knees. "Fine," he said, finally resigned to his fate. "How much longer do I have to sit in this shithole?"

"Shouldn't be long. I'm going back up now. You'll be escorted to the courtroom after they send word down that your case has been called."

Corfinio nodded silently in acknowledgment; Bari motioned a thumbs-up and walked away.

Eighteen minutes' worth of an eternity crawled by before he was summoned to the gate by one of the burly attending court officers. "Corfinio, John! Let's go, you're up!"

The court officer opened the door and moved aside to let him pass and fell in step behind him issuing directions. "Straight ahead, up the stairs, turn right. Don't talk until the judge addresses you, understand?"

Corfinio didn't bother answering because as soon as he started along the directed path, he could see that there wasn't any alternative route anyway. At the top of the stairs, he turned right and found himself in the dock, a segmented area designated for prisoners off to the right side of the judge's bench. It was a Spartan area with oak benches surrounded by three-and-a-half-foot-tall oak-paneled knee walls. The top of the wall was well worn and scarred from metal handcuffs being dragged across the surface for almost forty years.

From where he stood in the dock, he could plainly see Judge Sheila M. Fleming conferring with the court clerk at the bench. Arthur Bari sat at the defense lawyer's table, shuffling pages while several other lawyers consulted with clients in the gallery section. The DA was engaged in deep conversation with the probation officer while both examined the wad of paperwork she held. Having never been in a courtroom before—at least not from this perspective—Corfinio was enthralled with the various elements of bustle and was oblivious when his name was called until the accompanying court officer nudged him.

"And you are in violation of a Temporary Restraining Order, so until—"

"Excuse me," Bari spoke up from his position at the defense lawyer's desk, "Your Honor, if I may?"

"And you are?" the judge asked slightly annoyed.

"Arthur Bari, defense counsel for the accused."

"Is your client aware of the severity of the charge and consequence?"

"Yes, Your Honor, but it remains questionable as to whether or not the order was actually served upon my client at all."

"Counselor, my information indicates that it *was* served, rendering your client as having been notified."

"Yes, Your Honor, but there seems to be some *confusion* on that point. Counsel requests to see a copy of the Proof of Service form."

Judge Fleming motioned to the court clerk to approach the bench. After several minutes of paper flipping and head shaking, the judge addressed Bari. "Counselor, that paperwork does not appear to be present, but under the circumstances, I am satisfied that the TRO was issued as specified."

"It also appears, that the Order or Restraint was 'modified' after issuance, and there is *substantial* reasonable doubt as to its validity where—"

"*Stop.*" Judge Fleming shook her head in short bursts and held up her hand, palm outward to reinforce her decision that this conversation was officially over. She glanced over to the court officer accompanying Corfinio. "Take him to County to await trial! Set no bail," she said with the authority given her by the state.

"*Your Honor!*"

"That's *enough*, Counselor."

Corfinio was dumbfounded, but he understood everything that had just transpired. The judge wasn't budging from her position no matter what Bari said. He also understood what she meant by "County." He was headed to jail.

This is just not my day, he thought to himself with a smile that belied his incredulity over the events of the past three days. As the court officer took him by the arm, Corfinio let out a nervous laugh.

Judge Fleming, already highly agitated by the proceedings, took umbrage at his reaction. "Do you find something *humorous*, Mr. Corfinio?" she scolded.

"Well, Your Honor, I *do* find it rather *sickeningly* humorous that a man can be incarcerated without a shred of proof whatsoever of *any* crime. I thought that *you*, of *all* the people in this circus, would have been smarter than *that*."

The judge stared at him wide-eyed in fury. "*You* are in *contempt of court! Thirty days!*"

On the way back down the stairs to the holding cell, the court officer snickered. "I'll bet you're sorry you opened your yap now, aren't ya?"

"Not really," Corfinio replied offhandedly, trying to carefully negotiate the stairs with leg cuffs, "but it would have been *so* much cooler if she had smashed the gavel down a few times, though!"

15

Thirty days later, Corfinio was officially released from Cambridge County Jail. He signed the necessary paperwork and traded in his prison-issue orange jumpsuit and sandals for his street clothes and personal belongings. During processing, he was instructed on what to do, what not to do, and handed a business card with an explicit instruction to call the phone number on the card as soon as he got settled. "James Pedro—Probation Officer" was centered on the card with the official county seal in the upper left-hand corner and the phone number below.

He exited the building and was met with a cacophony of noise. Blaring horns, revving engines, and the impatient whoosh of passing vehicles were the signature sounds of city traffic. The rumbling, screeching, and clacking sounds of the elevated railway train two blocks away carried clearly in spite of the audio battle.

"*Well?* Are you going to stand there like a lost and lonely tourist, or would you like suitable conveyance to a more affable destination?"

"*Arthur!*" Corfinio said in complete surprise, only then noticing his lawyer leaning against a late-model sedan chomping on a dying cigar. "What in the *hell* are you doing here!"

"Just happened to be in the neighborhood."

"But how did you know…"

"I consulted with the spectral beings trapped within the confines of my mystical crystal orb and decreed they divulge the date of your release. And *there* you have it, and *here I am!*" He ended with a flourish of sweeping arm gyrations like a magician completing a trick.

"No, really. How did you know I was being released today?"

"I called the courthouse," he said with a wink. "C'mon, let's go. I'm parked in a restricted zone."

Bari pulled into midday traffic without signaling, which resulted in several drivers gifting him curses upon his progeny and heritage and "hand signals" designating a human impossibility.

"Y'know," Corfinio began, staring idly out the side window, "I'm so screwed. No truck, nowhere to live, and I'll probably never get to see my kid again."

"Your truck is at *my* house. Mrs. Morelli *kept* your room—"

"*She did?*"

"Yeah, but I can't for the *life* of me figure out why."

"Maybe because I'm *nice*."

"You're a bastard."

"But I'm a *nice* bastard!"

"When we get back to my place, we'll discuss what the arrangements will be for you getting visitation back."

"You really think that's gonna happen?"

"It will if you do *exactly* what you're *supposed* to do, John—act like a *normal* human being."

"I'm *normal*," he said, theatrically placing his hand on his chest.

"John, *normal* people don't tell a judge they think she's *stupid*!"

"I didn't *say* she was stupid. I said I thought she was 'smarter' than that."

"*Not* a wise choice of words to the person who's deciding your situation!"

Bari slowed as he approached a yellow light signal, prompting an angry honk from the vehicle in back of him that apparently thought he could have made the light before it turned red. Neither man spoke, each consumed in their own thoughts waiting for the light to change. As the signal changed from red to green, Bari let off the brake but then suddenly jammed his foot back down again, bringing the car to a complete stop. Corfinio, shaken out of his reverie, looked through the windshield and saw the reason for the sudden stop. A man had stepped out into the crosswalk in front of Bari's car.

Corfinio promptly stuck his head out the window and yelled, "*Hey*! *Whaddya fuckin' blind*! *The light's green*!"

Bari turned to face his passenger with shock and disgust. "Jesus *Christ*, John!"

"*What*?" he snapped defensively. "Suddenly it's *okay* with you if some *retard* just walks out in front of you?"

"*You're* the retard! He *is* blind! Do you not *see* the *white cane*?"

"Well...oh," he said, mildly embarrassed but then instantly angry again, pointing his finger at the blind man. "Then he should have a *dog*!"

"*Now* do you see what I'm talking about?" Bari asked incredulously. "*This* is not *normal* behavior. You *can't* just fly off the handle every time you're met with something that doesn't *please* you. You *have* to rein it in. Do you understand me? Am I getting through that thick skull of yours?"

"So I didn't see the cane. Big deal."

"You *never* see the cane!"

The remainder of the ride continued in silence. Bari dropped Corfinio off at Mrs. Morelli's boarding house with the instruction to meet again at 7:00 p.m. at Bari's office to formulate a game plan.

They met at the assigned time, where Bari laid out how things were going to be structured.

"Now tomorrow, you are going to get in touch with your PO—"

"My what? What's a PO?"

"Parole officer. Someone should have given you a name or a card with his name on it for you to call. Right?"

"Yeah, they did." He reached into his back pocket and produced the card that was given to him. "James Pedro is his name."

"Good. Call him tomorrow. You'll contact him once a week or whatever time frame he designates as proper for you. Your probationary period is one year and, John"—Bari looked sternly at his client—"failure to contact him when you're supposed to call in is a violation of your probation. You violate probation, you go *back* to jail. Got it?"

"Mmm-hmm," Corfinio grunted.

"John," Bari began, pacing around the room like a television lawyer, "the human race has evolved to a point where a mode of communication known as 'speaking' has been devised and widely accepted by every known civilization across the globe as a way to make known the various aspects of opinion, emotion, acceptance, or denial. We call those *words*. Do you think you could extract from the inner recesses of your Neanderthal cranial cavity a few syllables—utilizing consonants *and* vowels—that would indicate a level of comprehension for what I just said?"

Corfinio rolled his eyes and held his arms out in supplication. "*Yes. Yes,* I can speak. *Yes,* I understand. *Yes, yes, yes.* Are you *happy* now?"

"Ah!" Bari turned to face his bookcase of law books and spoke as if addressing an audience. "Ladies and gentlemen of the jury, as you can *plainly* see, my client is *quite* capable and in *full*—or at least partial—command of both oratorical responses *and* comprehensive reasoning! Let the record show that he is *not* a dull-witted simian mute as was previously assumed, based on his earlier grunt-like articulation."

"Look, I'm sorry, all right? I'm just pissed off about this whole situation, that's all. It's like… I don't know, the whole thing…*sucks.*"

"Yeah, I *know* it sucks. But if you want to see your son, you're going to have to play nice, put this crap behind you, and move on. Stewing about whatever happened isn't going to solve anything. Now can we move forward?"

"Fine," Corfinio relented. "What's the plan, Counselor?"

"Here's how it's going to play out. We'll request reinstatement of visitation, which, they will grant *after* you meet with Family Services."

"Family Services? That sounds like a group funeral!"

"It'll be *yours* if you don't meet with them. You'll interview with someone from Family Services and, based on your answers and general attitude, will either *grant* you monitored visits or you may be *denied* visitation if they feel you're unstable, unsuitable, or a threat to the minor child. It is vitally important that you not reflect any type of aggression or harbor any blatant or harmful ill will toward your ex-wife."

"That part might be hard."

"Then you better give an Academy Award performance."

"Okay, then what?"

"Afterwards, the judge will ask him/her—although usually a 'her'—if she recommends visitation or not. Her *answer,* John, will be based on what feedback she gets from *you.* If she *does* recommend visitation, she will also recommend parenting classes. You need—'

"*Seriously?*" he interrupted.

"*By so doing,*" Bari continued, raising his voice above that of his client, "you're displaying that you are amenable to the will of the court in the best interests of and for the safety of the minor child. This will shine *brightly* on future requests for *extended* visitation, holiday visits, overnight visits, and *possibly* joint physical custody."

The prospect of being more than a "weekend dad" appealed to him immensely. It would never be the "family life" he had envisioned for his son, but at least this seemed to be a path in the right direction. He knew he was only one of millions of men going through the same scenario, but it didn't make him feel any better about it.

They wrapped up their conversation with Corfinio, assuring Bari that he would comply with whatever restrictions or directives were foisted upon him as long as the ultimate goal was achieved.

Two days later, as Corfinio was leaving the house for work, he was greeted by a genial county sheriff who handed him a "no contact" order. The order, issued by the Middlesex Court, stated that he was to refrain from contact in any form—phone, mail, or in person—from Marsha Corfinio and Michael Corfinio, a minor child. A distance of no less than five hundred feet should be maintained, and violation of such would result in his immediate arrest.

This came as no surprise other than the fact that it happened so quickly after his jail release. Bari warned that it was likely that the order would be issued. Still, it rankled him no end. *She just never stops,* he thought, folding the paper and slipping it into his shirt pocket. *And the worst part is, as the saying goes, "Only the good die young." She'll live to be a thousand.*

*****

The meeting with Family Services went exactly like Bari had forecasted. The meeting was conducted in the sparsely furnished interview room within the court-house, no more than thirty feet from the courtroom. Estelle Avery, a middle-aged black woman, conducted the interview with the ever-present yellow legal pad. She was completely professional and predictably somber but took Corfinio by surprise when she asked, "Has your ex-wife always been a vindictive woman?" He wasn't quite sure how to answer, fearing that she was either fishing for info or measuring his reaction to what he saw as a loaded question. He wasn't sure if there *was* a correct answer at all.

"Well," he said haltingly, "it *does* seem like she's taken on that attitude lately, but I don't know what she was like in past relationships."

Avery looked at him, searching for an undetected undertone, nodding slowly, then made a note on her legal pad. Corfinio didn't look away as she maintained eye contact with him, instinctively feeling that looking away might signal discomfort on his part or be interpreted as harbored guilt. He certainly didn't want to give that impression but couldn't help himself from displaying a slightly lopsided nervous smile. After several more seemingly innocuous questions, she called an end to the meeting.

After the meeting concluded, Corfinio searched for Bari in the bustling lobby of the courthouse. He finally spotted him standing at the bulletin board displaying which cases would be heard in specific courtrooms.

"Aha!" Corfinio said, approaching his lawyer. "There you are!"

"Well, how'd it go?" he asked without looking away from the bulletin board.

"Okay, I think. She just asked some pretty basic questions, nothing in depth. How is she supposed to make a recommendation based on what little information she collected? I don't get it...unless...oh, *shit!*"

"What?" Bari asked, finally tearing his gaze away from the board.

"What if she already had her mind made up before she even talked with me, y'know, based on whatever reports she was given in advance?"

"Entirely possible." Bari scribbled down some information from the board onto a small notebook.

"But she did ask me something that I thought was a bit odd."

"Care to share?"

"She said, 'Has your ex-wife always been a vindictive woman?'"

A surprised look came over Bari's face. "She *said* that?"

"Yeah, that's what she said."

Bari chuckled. "My friend, you've got *nothing* to worry about! She's in your corner. You'll get your visitation."

"What do you mean? How can you tell?"

"This is what she *does*, *day* after *day*, all day *long*. She *talks* to couples, husbands and wives—she's heard it all a thousand times over. She hears every story, every lie, every *excuse* that the human mind can conceive until she can spot a liar just by the way they walk."

"And this is good for me *how*?"

"She's already *recognized* the beast! She *knows*—" Bari suddenly stopped mid-thought. "John, *how* did you *answer* that question?"

"I said that she's been a bitch her whole life and everyone would be better off if she were to suddenly die."

Bari's mouth dropped open. "*John!* Please t—"

"I'm kidding! *I'm kidding*!" Corfinio quickly cut in, seeing Bari almost apoplectic. "Take it *easy*, will ya? *That's* not what I said."

Bari stared at him.

"All I said was that I didn't know what she was like before I met her."

"Are you *sure*?"

"Am I sure I didn't know what she was like, or am I sure that's all I said?"

Bari raised his eyes to the ceiling in exasperation. "*Why*, Lord? *Why* do you *persecute* me so?" He looked back disparagingly at his client and shook his head. "Come on, we're in Courtroom 3."

Bari walked swiftly through the courthouse with Corfinio following in tow while carefully dodging a score of suited lawyers and court personnel rushing to their predetermined destinations. Entering Courtroom 3, the two men took a seat in the spectator area and waited silently and patiently for their case to be called. Bari proceeded to rifle through pages and notes, while Corfinio regarded his surroundings with a critical eye.

Even though the courtroom was aged, it was apparent that in its heyday, no expense had been spared in the construction of the court of law.

"Seems like a complete waste of money for the riffraff and lowlifes that travel through here," he said quietly speaking to no one.

"True," Bari replied, not looking up from his paperwork, "but even the *dregs* of society deserve a respectable edifice in which to be judged and sentenced."

Corfinio hadn't realized he spoke out loud and was mildly surprised when Bari replied, "Oh, that's not what I meant when I said 'riffraff' and 'lowlifes.' I was talking about the judges and lawyers."

Bari sighed and was about to respond when the clerk announced Corfinio's name. They stood and walked through the gated oak railing separating the spectator area from the elevated judges' dais. The clerk motioned for them to await the judge's convenience at the table assigned for the defense. He informed them that there would be a slight delay as the judge had sent for Estelle Avery of Family Services.

Once she made her appearance, conversation ensued, deciding the status of Corfinio's visitation rights. Avery stated that she felt Corfinio didn't present a threat to the minor child and that visitation should be reinstated. However, an added stipulation specified that the visits should be undertaken at a facility designed for that purpose and aptly named the Visiting Center.

16

Two weeks later, a meeting was arranged for Corfinio to meet with Julia Polanski, the managing assistant director of the Visiting Center. Polanski, a no-frills, no-nonsense woman, was icily cordial upon their introductory meeting. They shook hands in greeting, and she invited him to sit. He refused politely, opting to stand, explaining that sitting caused him considerable lower back discomfort. The actual truth was, he found that by standing, he was less intimidated while his relative size simultaneously inspired a passive-aggressive intimidation on the other party. In this particular instance, it was a moot point as Polanski wouldn't have been intimidated by ten men his size.

"Mr. Corfinio—"

"Please," he interrupted, "John is fine."

"Very well, *John*, I'll briefly go over what you can expect from us and what we will expect from *you*. The visits with your son will be scheduled every Monday at

4:00 p.m. You will arrive *on time* and at which time you will render payment—cash or credit card, no personal checks—for the service. You'll be escorted to a room where your son will be brought *to you* for the duration of the one-hour visit. He will be accompanied by a trained clinician who will be present during the entire visit to ensure the safety of the minor child. *If,* during the course of that visit, there is any display of aggression, anger, or *any* threat to the safety of that child is perceived, the visit is *over*. Immediately. Any questions?"

Corfinio found it a little unsettling that she was neither friendly nor unfriendly, stating procedure like she was an automaton reading from a book. He shrugged it off, realizing she must have repeated these directives like a mantra over ten thousand times to ten thousand people.

"Uhh, yes, a few actually. First, where's my ex-wife during this time?"

"She will be in another area of the building, where she will have no contact with either you or your son."

"Thank God. Second, what if I'm late for the meeting be—"

"If you're late," she interjected, "the meeting will *still* terminate one hour from the assigned starting time of 4:00. You will *still* be responsible for the fee *in full*. You will *not* get extended or make-up time. Is that clear?"

"Painfully so. Third, can I bring a toy or maybe some food?"

"The room assigned to you will have various types of toys. We would prefer if you didn't. Food would be fine provided you keep it simple: candy bar, cookie."

"One last question: Is there any possibility that I'd run into my ex-wife while I'm here because I don't even want to be in the—"

"Staggered arrivals and departures are customary for *just* that reason," she cut in once again. "Our goal is to prevent conflict while offering safe child access to the visiting parent. Rest assured that the safety of *all* participants has been calculated and accounted for."

"Great. I'm glad to hear that," he said unconvincingly.

"*John*, I've pretty much seen it *all* in twenty-eight-plus years in this business. There's *nothing* new under the sun."

"Have you met my ex-wife yet?"

"No, we'll be reaching out to her later today."

"Let me know if you feel the same way after you meet her."

He extended his hand as a parting gesture, thanked her, and went home.

*****

He hadn't seen his son in almost two months and wasn't sure of the reception he'd get when they finally did meet. It was for that reason that he stopped at a bakery on the way and bought a colorful gingerbread clown cookie, knowing that the cartoonish-looking sweet would amuse his son. He also knew his son was no different from any other child when it came to cookies. What child could say no to a cookie!

Michael was brought to him, and as promised, a monitor arrived, holding his hand as they entered the room. The boy grinned, beaming like a rising sun when he saw his father, and broke away from the supervisor, running headlong into him, almost knocking him over from the suddenness of his reaction. Corfinio looked up at the monitor, and she nodded in affirmation. He hugged his boy tight and felt moisture collecting precariously on his lower lids. He looked away and quickly wiped a hand across his face.

"Hey, Mikey, look what I brought for you!" he said, handing the white bakery bag to his son.

Michael opened the bag and looked inside, an expression of pure joy spreading across on his face. "Dad! It's a giant cookie! It looks like a clown! Can I eat it?"

"That's up to you, Mikey. If you want to, you can. Or if you want, you can save it for later when you get home."

"*No, Dad!* Let's eat it *now*. Do you want some?"

The remainder of the meeting went well, and the hour passed far too quickly. He gave his son a hug when they had to part, promising that he'd see him again next week.

Corfinio continued the visits, bringing a large bakery cookie each time to Michael's delight. He tried to focus attention on different things each visit. Sometimes they would read a story, play with blocks, make shapes out of Play-Doh, or crash toy trucks. The only thing that was frowned upon by the ever-present monitor was any kind of close-contact horseplay.

Things appeared to be going well until the day he arrived and was intercepted by Julia Polanski in the main lobby. "Mister Corfinio," she addressed him, motioning for him to follow, "a word?" She led him to her office and wasted no time with pleasantries. "Your ex-wife has indicated that she doesn't want you to give the child food any longer."

"But you *told* me that was *allowed*," he lightly objected.

"She's indicated that it ruins his supper and makes him extremely hyperactive. I'm afraid I'm going to ask you to refrain from that practice in the future."

"I see," he replied, plainly unhappy about the new directive and really not understanding at all. At least not for the reason given. "What if I gave it to him when the meeting is over and he can at least take it home?"

"Mister Corfinio, no more cookies." She didn't apologize as she escorted him out of her office and handed him off to his assigned attendant.

He instinctively understood what was happening. His ex-wife saw how happy the boy was in receiving the simple gift, and it irked her no end. She tried her damnedest to forego the meetings completely and strongly resented the burgeoning relationship between father and son. This was nothing more than another ploy to sabotage that relationship.

As miffed as he was at the Visiting Center for kowtowing to her demands, he had no other option than to accept the modified terms. If he made an issue out of it, he was afraid they would see him as being aggressive or hostile and perhaps cancel his visits. That was a risk he was unwilling to take, so he bit his tongue and let it be.

Corfinio showed up at the next normal appointed time only to be told that his ex-wife had not yet arrived with his son. He was informed, again by Julia Polanski, that his ex-wife claimed that the child did not want to see his father and spent the previous evening crying and vomiting from the anticipation of being forced to go to the visit.

He thought carefully before he replied to this new information. "If you're looking for me to surrender my visits, you got another think coming, Julia. I've followed every rule and stayed within your guidelines, *and* your 'highly trained staff member' that monitors *every* meeting can attest to that. It's not *him* that doesn't want to be here—it's *her* and you *know* it. Now she's under a court order to supply me with visitation for my son, and unless you can show evidence that I've violated *any* of those rules, I suggest you inform her that she bring my son next week."

Corfinio spun on his heel and walked out the door without another word or waiting for a response.

He arrived the following week and waited impatiently in the lobby for his attendant. He paced back and forth, looking up at the wall clock sporadically. *I can't believe she's doing this. Again!* he thought. As the minutes ticked away, the more agitated he became.

"Mister Corfinio!" a familiar voice called out to him. He recognized Julia Polanski's stern command immediately. She walked toward him briskly and with definitive purpose. He knew from her stiffened body language that something was amiss.

"Miss Polanski," he said flatly.

"Mister Corfinio, I'm afraid I have some unfortunate news."

"Okay."

"It seems that your wife was involved in an accident—a *major* car accident is how she described it—*but*," she hurriedly added, "your son is *fine*."

"I'm happy to hear that," he said without displaying any emotion at all.

Polanski looked at him, quite puzzled by his apparent lack of concern for his son's health and welfare. This wasn't the reaction she expected from him. It was as if she had just told him the sky is blue. Taken aback, she repeated, "Your son is fine."

"I'm sure he is. Can I *go* now?" He stood firm, without wavering. He stared her in the eye and waited for her to answer.

"Uhh, yes…of course." She was clearly uncomfortable and a little confused with his total lack of reaction.

"Mister Corfinio, are you *okay*?" she asked, knitting her brow in concern.

"Yeah, fine. Can I go *now*?"

"Yes, yes, of course."

Polanski watched him exit the building and calmly walk to his truck in the parking lot. He started the engine and pulled out carefully, easing into late-afternoon traffic. She walked away from the entry door, bewildered.

Corfinio drove, talking to himself out loud. "Major accident…*major accident my ass!* That *fucking bitch* hasn't had an accident in her *whole life!* The *only* accident she's ever been in was her own *birth!* That no-good, lying, good-for-nothing…*fucking bitch*!" Then in a mocking tone, he said, "'Oh your son is fine.' Yeah! *No shit, lady!* That's because there *was no accident*!"

He slammed his fist on the top of the steering wheel and screamed, "Fuck!"

*****

One of the marvels of the universe was the passage of time. When enveloped in anxious anticipation, time seemed to be in a complete stall. On the other hand, engaging in gratifying experiences caused time to race forward at warp speed. Much to Corfinio's chagrin, the entire week was in perpetual slow-mo mode in anticipation of his next visitation—if it occurred at all. The days were sluggish, but the nights stood still. Normally after supper, he would retire to his room and watch something mindless on television or read. He tried involving himself in a Robert Ludlum novel but found that he couldn't keep focused and had to reread page after page until he finally just gave it up.

The week sucked, the weekend sucked, and here it was, Monday again. He debated on whether or not he should even bother going to the Visiting Center because he was positive she wouldn't show up. He checked his pocket watch and saw that it was almost three o'clock. If he was going to make the attempt through rush-hour traffic, now was the time to leave if he expected to arrive at the assigned time. He finally decided, *What the hell, I've got to go, even if it's to turn around and come back home.*

He drove to the Visiting Center mentally prepared to be met with disappointment once again. Instead, upon arrival, he was ushered into the meeting room and had a pleasant visit with his son. As much as he wanted to quiz the boy about the "accident" last week, he refrained, knowing the monitor was watching and listening, as always. He certainly didn't want her running back to Polanski saying that he was harassing the child.

Once the meeting was over, he advanced to the lobby as usual and waited for his cue to leave the building. He stood in front of the bay windows facing the parking lot, and there, right in front, was his ex-wife's car. He stepped back from the windows and almost collided with Polanski, who was returning to her office.

"Julia," he said, cocking his head toward the window, "that's her car."

They both stepped up to the window and saw a late-model Buick, polished, gleaming, and reflecting the setting sun without so much as a scratch or ding.

"*Major* accident," Corfinio said, still staring straight ahead.

Polanski's face grew dark. "Noted."

"Must be a *hell* of a body shop to get a six-day turnaround."

"I'll take *care* of it, Mister Corfinio," she said abruptly and walked away, smoke trailing from her smoldering anger.

*****

In the weeks that followed, Corfinio noticed that Michael appeared to be growing less amused with the soft and controlled entertainment that had become their practice. Even though he had been warned off any interactions involving close physical contact, he also knew that his son loved bouts of wrestling or rough horseplay. In the past, they would always play-wrestle, where his son always claimed an unchallenged victory while Corfinio would suffer a demoralizing thrashing, forever promising, "Wait till next time!"

The meteorologist on the *Nightly News* predicted fair and cool weather for the week. Unlike other parts of the country, New England weather rarely complied with the predictions of the experts. Corfinio had learned that "fair and cool" could just as easily result in "two inches of unexpected snow" or "passing showers with a twenty-degree swing." Nonetheless, he decided to bring along a small plastic bat and ball to his next visit in hopes that they might be able to take the visit outdoors. Maybe run around a little, work up a sweat instead of being sequestered away in what had become a monotonous cage of controlled behavior relentlessly overseen by an enthusiastic yet naïve sentinel. He knew the visit wouldn't be allowed without the monitor standing guard, making continual notations, but getting out of doors might refresh the general atmosphere.

Corfinio introduced the toys to the visitation clinician for approval, and was mildly surprised to be told that they would be acceptable, but they would have to maintain indoor appointments for the time being.

A slight modification of baseball was introduced to accommodate the indoor restriction. Corfinio instructed Michael in the fine art of bunting, and the boy was quite amused initially but grew bored with tapping the ball gently back from his father's underhand pitches.

Okay, Corfinio thought, *change of plan.* Looking around the room for props, he came up with an alternate. "Hey, Mikey! Have you ever played hockey?" he asked, and without waiting for an answer, grabbed two plastic chairs. Placing them three feet apart, he created makeshift goal posts for an indoor miniature hockey game. Squatting down between the chairs, he explained to Michael that the object was to get the ball between the chairs by hitting it with the bat, while Corfinio, acting as goalie, protected the goal from scoring.

Michael was eager to prove to his father that he was more than capable of learning this game. Corfinio wisely let several goals score, blaming his own inability while crediting his son's great talent and effectiveness. Trying to impress his father with his complete mastery of the game, his efforts became more furious with excitement as his father blocked several of the attempts.

When the ball lodged under one of the chairs, Michael made an excited and frantic attempt to dislodge it by shoving the bat underneath before his father could deflect it back out into the open. Instead of freeing the ball, the head of the bat struck Corfinio in the ankle, who in an instant of surprised pain, started to topple. When he felt himself begin to lose his balance, he flung his arm out in an effort to grab one of the chairs to prevent himself from crashing to the floor. Instead, coming as a complete shock to both father and child, his wildly searching hand struck Michael on the side of the head.

In spite of his frenzied maneuverings to avoid falling, Corfinio hit the floor hard. Michael was knocked aside by his father's flailing hand and began to cry as soon as the shock of the impact settled in. The monitor, who had been involved sharing time between scribbling notes on a legal pad and glancing at her cell phone, did not actually see the incident but reacted by whisking the boy out of the room within seconds, demanding that Corfinio not move from the room.

Corfinio stood alone in the room, dumbfounded by the swift and unexpected reaction of the visit supervisor. He sat down on one of the plastic chairs rubbing his ankle when Julia Polanski charged into the room.

"Mister Corfinio, I'm asking you to leave. *Immediately.*"

Corfinio stood, astonished at her demand. "What? *Why?* What do you *mean?*"

"The rules were explained to you *in detail*, and you were forewarned about making physical contact of *any kind* with the minor child. The clinician observed that you struck the child in the *head*. All subsequent visits will be *terminated.*"

"*Wait a minute!*" he objected vehemently. "That's not strictly true—"

"*Mister* Corfinio—" she said, cutting him off.

Corfinio interrupted, "It was a goddamned *accident!* I *fell.*"

"Your visit is *over*, Mister Corfinio." Polanski said sternly, her face a mask of seething anger. She stood by the door rigidly, her bony fist clutching the doorknob as she motioned for him to leave.

Silently fuming, Corfinio knew any blatant expression of uncontrollable anger would only serve to complicate matters even further. He passed by her, the pain in his ankle forgotten. Walking rapidly down the hallway with Polanski quite literally at his heels, he calculated the likely events that would follow this debacle: suspension of visitation, order of restraint, and additional court appearances.

Upon reaching the front exit door of the facility, Polanski spoke frigidly. "You'll *wait* here until I—"

"*You* can kiss my *ass*," Corfinio said cruelly, his eyes hard and cold as he stared her down.

She flinched uncharacteristically as he pushed the door open, walked through, and slammed it closed.

The next evening, after finishing a somber evening meal with Mrs. Morrelli and the other patrons of the boarding house, he was served with another restraining order and a summons to appear in court. Feeling the bile rise in his throat, he stared wordlessly at the police officer as he was instructed to refrain from any further contact with his son. His legs were leaden as he climbed the stairs to his room and closed the door.

*****

The scheduled court date arrived, with Bari entering a plea of Not Guilty on behalf of his client on the charge of "child abuse" resulting from the situation at the Visiting Center. Corfinio and Bari stood in front of the bench awaiting the decision as the judge read the charges and included documentation.

Several pages of documentation supplied from the Visiting Center included a letter from managing assistant director, Julia Polanski; an incident report written by the visit supervisor; and a letter from pediatrician Ray Stinger, MD.

Polanski's letter indicated,

> …that Mr. Corfinio was strictly prohibited by the terms of his probation from making physical contact with the child. It is of my professional opinion that he be considered volatile, having displayed an aggressive temperament during the last visitation.

The Incident report filed on behalf of the visit supervisor stated,

> During the visit, the minor child (Michael Corfinio) during the course of a playful encounter, had accidentally struck the father (John Corfinio). Mr. Corfinio immediately retaliated in anger by striking the child in the side of the head with his hand.

Dr. Ray Stinger, MD, also weighed in with gathered criteria supplied to him by Mrs. Corfinio:

> Further, it has been brought to my attention that Michael has been experiencing nightmares since the ordeal, and had been displaying periods of agitation prior to the incident. It is therefore my suggestion that visitation be suspended until such time...

After reading the documents, Judge Sheila M. Fleming decided that the violation of probation and endangering a child would be best served with a twelve-month sentence in the Middlesex County Jail, effective immediately.

17

Jail, one year ago

The jail guard walked down the dimly lit corridor of the Middlesex County Jail with Corfinio a half step behind. After being processed, Corfinio was given an orange jumpsuit and sandals in exchange for his street clothes. He carried a state-issued blanket, pillow, and towel for his personal use. At the end of the corridor, he could see the glass-enclosed officers' station with a resident officer watching various closed-circuit monitors.

To the left and right were cell doors. The door on the right led to the showers. The left door was a general population dormitory cell holding thirty inmates that was known as the Dog Pound. Fifteen sets of iron bunk beds lined the walls, and a banquet table with eight chairs sat in the middle of the large room.

As they approached the officers' station, the officer within released the locking mechanism from his control panel, and the cell door slid open slowly. Corfinio's guard walked into the cell and stopped in front of an empty bunk on the lower tier. With thumbs tucked casually into his belt and a slight nod, the guard indicated that this would be Corfinio's bunk. To Corfinio's surprise, almost none of the inmates within the cell paid any attention to the guard at all and even less attention to him.

Corfinio dropped his recently acquired belongings onto the lower bunk when he was startled by a voice from the upper tier.

"Hey, Chief," the voice said, addressing the guard, "this ain't no *old-age home*. Why you sticking this *anciano* on my stack, huh?"

The guard looked up at the slim Puerto Rican youth—no more than twenty-two—and scoffed, "Hey Felix, if you don't like your new bunkie, you can always check into another hotel!" He turned away chuckling and walked out of the cell, the gate sliding shut behind him.

Corfinio bent down and set the pillow and blanket on his bunk and sighed. As he stood, straightening out, he found himself eye to eye with Felix Segado, who had sat up on the upper bunk.

"Hey, *el viejo*, you got a name?" Segado asked mockingly, using the Spanish term for "old one."

"John," he replied, then added, "and you must be Felix."

"I seen you before, John. What's your last name?"

"Corfinio."

"What the fuck is *that*?"

"It's an Italian name."

"Holy shit! Italian! You, like, from *Rome* or something?"

Corfinio rocked his head back and forth. "Something like that."

"Yeah? You know Caesar?"

"Oh yeah, me and Caesar, best buds."

"Prob'ly true. You so fucking *old* like *dirt*. What you in for, old man?"

"Domestic. You?"

"Same, but I didn't do *nothing*. I was set up."

"I'm sure you were."

"I mean it. My old lady she come banging on my door at two in the morning, saying I'm jumping on some bitch, but I'm *sleeping*, man! I open the door to shut her ass up because you know, I got neighbors and I'm on probation. She come in and start trashing my house and hitting me and shit. So I toss her drunk ass back outside. Next thing I know, cops is taking *me* away for assault and battery!"

"That it?"

"You don't *believe* me?"

"On the contrary, I *completely* believe you. I just asked if there was more to it than that, that's all. You have any priors?"

"Possession, class B."

"Hmm, sounds like *you* made some bad choices."

"You in the same cell as me, *pendejo*."

Corfinio laughed. "Yeah, I guess you're right."

Over the next few days, Segado explained the daily routines and rituals, jail jargon, and most importantly, whom not to cross, prisoners and guards alike. They assumed an almost teacher-student rapport, and while Corfinio was grateful for the education, he knew this was never going to be a potential friendship. They were simply coexisting on a temporary basis as the need presented itself. The tradeoff was that Corfinio was physically imposing and trouble was unlikely to come at him unless it was en masse, while Segado knew the ropes and had understood jail survival tactics.

After the breakfast meal had finished and everyone was marched back to the cell, Segado wandered over toward Corfinio with a magazine, pretending to read. He stood two feet away and faced in the opposite direction of Corfinio, giving the impression that he was ignorant of his obvious presence.

"Hey, John." Segado spoke barely above a whisper, turning a page. "Some of my homies think you a pussy and want to fuck you up."

"Oh, that's *great*, Felix," Corfinio answered, lightly sarcastic, hand over his mouth. "I was *hoping* to meet some new people!"

"We going to the yard today. Maybe some trouble for you."

Corfinio sobered. "Which one?"

"Todos." Segado slowly walked away, dropping the magazine on the table as he passed. Corfinio remained standing where he was trying to wrap his head around this information. He knew that eventually, *something* had to happen or someone would have a problem with him, no matter how manufactured the reasoning. What concerned him the most was that *todos* wasn't an inmate's name; it was Spanish for "everyone."

Midafternoon, everyone was ordered to assemble in single file for yard time. After their morning "conversation," Segado had spent the remainder of the day with the other Puerto Ricans that shared the communal cell, leaving Corfinio to wonder if Segado was sharing the sentiment of the others.

Once in the yard, Corfinio scouted out the area and was pleased to find that there was an assortment of free weights and worn benches, some of which were not being used. He selected one and set the bar and plates that he knew would be suitable for a warmup routine. Laying down and stretching his arms out to reach the cradled barbell, he breathed deep and ripped off a set of ten with relative ease. He increased the weight for his second set, changing out the plates while cautiously scrutinizing the area for any impending threats. Satisfied that he wouldn't be caught unaware and sandbagged, he proceeded to lie on the bench for his second set. He reached up and grasped the barbell, lifting it off the cradle and slowly bringing it down to his chest as he inhaled a full breath. He closed his eyes and began to raise the bar when the weight suddenly increased. He opened his eyes and stared up into the face of Felix Segado, who was now leaning on the bar, forcing it down onto Corfinio's chest.

"You havin' a problem there, Gramps?" said Segado arrogantly.

Looking up into the Puerto Rican's face gave no indication as to the severity of the situation. In a sudden rush of pre-panic, Corfinio darted a glance to left and right, but no one else was within close proximity.

"You get off this bar," Corfinio said with gritted teeth and a coolness he didn't feel, "and we'll see who's having the problem."

Segado let off the barbell and laughed, but there was no mirth. Corfinio hastily cradled it back on the pegs and swung his legs over the side of the bench, rising quickly.

Segado took a step back, waving Corfinio to him. "Let's do it, *maricombe*," he said, using the Spanish invective for "faggot."

Inmates close enough to hear the exchange between the two men closed in uttering grunts of approval and encouragement. Others, recognizing the advance for what it was, moved in closer like sharks to chummed waters. The closing knot of advancing men abruptly divided into two, and from the cleft emerged a jail guard.

Corfinio's tense shoulders dropped slightly in relief seeing the guard at the forefront of the small crowd, but his relief was short lived. There stood the guard, well over six feet in height, barrel chested, and lacking any sign of a neck. What initially was a welcome sight soon turned into dismay for Corfinio when the guard produced two sets of red boxing gloves with the simple directive "Keep it clean."

With supportive howls from the surrounding assembly, Segado and Corfinio put the gloves on and began circling one another, seeking an opening. Someone on the perimeter, dissatisfied with the unhurried deliberations of the two combatants, reached in and shoved Corfinio, pushing him off balance toward the center of the designated fight area. That was all Segado needed to launch himself at Corfinio's now unprotected head. A right hook caught Corfinio on the side of the jaw, spinning him back toward the perimeter, colliding into several of the raucous, enthusiastic bystanders.

Segado, excitedly dancing in center ring at his initial coup, waved both gloved hands at his dazed opponent in invitation to return. Corfinio, infuriated that he had been suckered, yanked himself free from the tangle of limbs and crouched slightly, advancing slowly toward his adversary. Overconfident at landing the first blow, Segado charged his opponent once again, drawing back his right arm, forecasting his next strike as he advanced.

Corfinio stepped into the advance, blocking with his left, and slammed a right gloved fist in the center of Segado's sternum. Segado fell hard, a look of surprise and chagrin evident on his face. Hoots from the onlookers only served to further enrage the already wounded pride of the Hispanic fighter as he vaulted up from the floor. Blind with fury, Segado rushed Corfinio once again. The two men collided with a frenzy of wild punches and grunts, sounding far more animalistic than human. The two pounded away unmercifully at each other, oblivious to the blows each was taking, intent only on meting out the most damage to his rival.

A shrill whistle sounded above the frenzied howls of the congregated inmates clamoring for blood. The burly-chested guard reappeared, disengaging the two fighters by stepping between them and placing a paw-like hand on each of their chests. He proclaimed the fight as over and ordered the crowd of spectators to break up.

Segado and Corfinio, shaking from the adrenaline rush and breathing hard from their confrontation, leaned against a wall. Segado bit at the laces of his boxing glove, while Corfinio inspected a rising welt on his midsection.

"Is that...the best...you could do?" panted Corfinio, trying to breathe.

"I thought I was fighting...with my *sister*," answered Segado.

"Ohhh, *shit*," Corfinio complained, rubbing his side. "I'm too old...for this *crap*!"

"No shit, Gramps. What are you, like, eighty?"

"Forty," said Corfinio gnawing at his own laces. "Smartass."

"*Forty*!" said Segado, blowing air. "Man, you should be…in a nursing home!"

"Heh," scoffed Corfinio, "nursing home my *ass!* Just wait, *next* time—"

"Next time, *what?* You gonna *bleed* all over me?"

Corfinio was about to answer when another thought suddenly occurred to him. "Hey, why did you pick a fight with me? I thought you said that—"

"Let's *go*, girls," interrupted the bellowing guard, hand signaling for the return of the boxing gloves. "Playtime's over." He collected the gloves from the fatigued pugilists while both remained silent.

When he was safely out of earshot, Segado ran his hands across his forehead wiping the sweat off and patted his hands on his pant leg. "I said my homeboys wanted to fuck you up."

Corfinio waited, wiggling his jaw back and forth where Segado had planted his first blow. "Yeah…*and?*"

"I don't like a lot of people, and I don't like *you* much either, but I'm getting used to you. Even if you *are* fucked up and old like Methuselah."

"Well then," Corfinio gasped, holding his side, "I guess this is my lucky day."

Segado rubbed his chest. "It ain't over yet."

18

Current day

"Okay, so," Bari continued, "that's pretty much the situation in a nutshell. I think we—" Bari stopped short as he looked up from his paperwork and saw Corfinio with eyes closed, head against the wall. "*John?* Did you hear *anything* I just said?"

Corfinio replied without opening his eyes or changing position on the bench, "Every *boring* word, Counselor."

"Make me feel better, tell me what I said," Bari stated doubtfully.

"Word for word, or the general gist of things?"

"I'll settle for a brief synopsis."

Corfinio opened his eyes and leaned forward, both elbows on his knees, and rubbed his temples with his fingertips. "*You said*, no matter what I've done to comply with court orders, no matter how many character

110

references I have, no matter how hard I've tried to be the perfect human being they demand I be, that I *will get fucked* like a ten-dollar whore by a guy with a fistful of fifties. That about sum it up?"

"Have you ever considered a slight attitude adjustment?"

"After what I've been through in the last two years? Ahhhh, *no!* I think my 'attitude' is *completely* justified."

"*You* may think so—*and it may be so*—but if you go in there with *that* attitude…" Bari sighed deeply. "*Look*, the court wants to see that you're *remorseful* for past conduct and violations. That you've *complied* with recommended programs and satisfied the conditions of your probation."

"I *went* to Parenting Class. *Complete* joke. I *went* to Anger Management Class, *another* joke."

"Here we go," Bari said in resignation. "*Dare* I ask why *you* feel that these *proven* sociological aids are, in *your* estimation, a 'joke'?"

"Number one, Parenting Class is run by a twenty-six-year-old woman with *no* children. She also has no husband, boyfriend, or siblings. That seem a bit odd to you?"

"No, John. They're educated and *trained* for that."

"Arthur, I turn lights on and off every day. That doesn't make me an electrician."

"Oh, God! And why is *Anger Management* on the hit list of inappropriate demands unfairly foisted upon you?"

"The teacher yelled at me."

Bari laughed. "*Christ himself* would yell at you! What did you do?"

"It doesn't matter, does it? *He's* the one who's supposed to be teaching self-control, yet *he's* the one yelling like a screaming mee-mee!"

"Yeah. *What* did *you do* to provoke that?"

"I wouldn't admit that I hit, pushed, shoved, battered, brained, or berated my wife. I *never* did any of those things. Why would I admit to it? So he yelled at me, and I walked out."

"*Wait*…didn't you *complete* the Anger Management Program?"

"Nope!" Corfinio said proudly, raising his eyebrows. "Walked out of the *first* class. Actually, halfway through the first class."

"This will *not* sit well with the judge."

"When I'm wrong, I'll take what I got coming, but I'm not admitting to something I didn't do. I don't care *how* it sits with the judge."

"All you had to do was sit through *ten classes*. Would that have been so difficult?"

"Let me ask you a question: How is it that there were eleven people in Parenting Class and twenty-six people in Anger Management Class, and yet, with a sum total of thirty-seven people, there was only one—*one*—woman? How is that possible? Do you mean to tell me that 99.9 percent of men are abusive by nature, while less than 1 percent of women are classified as such?"

"What's your point, John?"

"My point? My point is *obvious!* We're *both* Italian. We *both* had Italian parents. Which one of your parents ranted and raved and nagged and complained and gave endless guilt-ridden speeches that went on for days? Was it your father? *Uh-uh*, it *wasn't.* He walked over, cracked you in the skull, and was *done* with it. Life went on. *Now* tell me which method is 'abusive.'"

"I wouldn't suggest we present your 'experimental findings' to the judge as a convincing argument for reinstatement of visitation." Bari stood up from the bench and stretched his back then readdressed his client. "Do yourself a favor—when we appear before the judge, don't even consider uttering a sound. As your attorney, I'll speak for you."

"Got it," Corfinio agreed with an exaggerated wink. "You'll take care of all utterances." He also stood and perused the large lobby now bustling with activity. "But what if the judge addresses me *directly*, should I answer or just stand there and grunt like a jungle boy?"

"If the judge addresses you *at all*, answer the question with a simple 'Yes, Your Honor' or 'No, Your Honor.' Do you understand? That's why *I'm* here, to speak *for* you, because you're *obviously* not psychologically stable enough to make intelligible responses that extend beyond 'yes' or 'no.' By the way," said Bari, casually looking around, "do you see your ex-wife anywhere? I need to talk to her lawyer before we go in."

"No, but I do see a *great* pair of legs over there attached to that woman in the gray skirt. She has that look. You know, that 'Come over here and hurt me' look. Maybe I should go over and tell her I can take her to places she's never been before."

Bari rolled his eyes, his voice dripping sarcasm, "And if she says yes, then what are you going to do, introduce her to a *travel agent*?"

Feigning insult, Corfinio whined, "Hey, y'know… that was really mean." An induced look of hurt spread across his face. "I have feelings *too*, y'know."

"Ohhh, poor Mister Sensitivity," said Bari with mock compassion, checking his watch for the time. "I'm going to see what courtroom we're in, and make a quick phone call. I shouldn't be more than ten minutes. In the meantime, do me a favor. *Try* to stay out of trouble. Just *stand* right here. Don't *move*. Don't *speak* to anyone. Don't *look* at anyone. Don't even *breathe* next to anyone else. And most importantly"—he shifted his briefcase from one hand to the other with a sigh—"no more bomb threats, okay?"

Deftly avoiding collision with bodies attached to heads buried in file folders, Bari weaved down the corridor like a roller-bladed skater and was soon swallowed in the growing crowd. For a man of such size, he moved with an amazing amount of grace and agility.

Corfinio watched as the concourse grew noisier and more crowded. From this vantage point, he could view all of the spider-like corridors emanating from the center gallery. A ceramic medallion in the center of the mosaic flooring resembled a cartography compass with the south pointer headed in the direction of the front door with the metal detection station. The line of people entering the station had no less than half a dozen patrons awaiting the examination formality. An agitated woman emptied the contents of her coat pockets into a plastic dish after walking through the portal and setting off the alarm. The remaining visitors in queue appeared irked at the additional delay, each displaying aggravated expressions, moans, groans, and eye rolls.

A door in the west corridor swung open into the hallway, and a fat man with a tie strangling his bulging neck emerged. Cracked painted letters reading "Social Services" adorned the frosted glass door. The fat man appeared annoyed as he held out a sheaf of yellow pages from his straining white shirt and announced to the noisy throng, "Richardson! Gary Richardson." Without waiting for a response, he retreated back into the sanctuary of his chamber.

Across the hall, a leather-coated teen was oblivious to a large stenciled "Out of Order" sign standing sentry over an antiquated water cooler. After several unsuccessful attempts, he stepped back and glared at the offending element as if to challenge the metal oasis to a battle of wills. Frustration proving victorious, he slammed the On button with the heel of his hand as an expression of his obvious displeasure, turned, and stormed away.

Centered in the north corridor, a wide, white Carrera marble staircase with heavily brocaded wrought-iron railings rose toward upper floors containing courtrooms and clerical offices. A small crowd of attorneys gathered in the narrow corridor alongside the left of the staircase around a bulletin board in search of names, docket numbers, and appointed courtrooms. Finding pertinent information, they scribbled notes on legal pads before running off in various directions, frequently bumping into each other without apology.

On the right side of the stairway was a bank of phone booths, no longer in service since the successful advent of the cellular phone. The telephone equipment had long been removed, leaving only the wooden stalls with a corner seat that no longer served any purpose. Corfinio smiled as he recalled that most public buildings always boasted a cluster of phone booths for their clientele's convenience. He could clearly remember the sounds of inserted coins as they dropped, pinging and clicking through the encapsulated channels identifying each coin's value. *How ironic*, he thought. *Now everyone has a phone, but no one wants to talk to anyone.*

In the central concourse, court officers strolled casually across the lobby, seemingly in no particular hurry to find their ultimate destination. Lawyers and clients conversed in low tones, leaning against walls or seated on benches, all hovering over handheld documentation relevant for their impending hearings.

Blocking the visibility of the east corridor stood a mobile coffee concession. Atop a makeshift counter, clear plastic domes revealed stacks of greasy donuts and shriveled bagels. The man behind the counter looked to be Mediterranean—perhaps Italian or Greek by the heavy accent that could be heard clear across the lobby. As each customer ordered their coffee, he asked if they needed sugar, pronouncing it "*shoe*-gah," much to the dismay of some who couldn't figure out what he was saying. An attractive woman, the one Corfinio had sighted earlier in the gray skirt, stood bewildered at the unintelligible comments being inflicted upon on her by the counter man.

"You wanna *shoe*-gah oh *no shoe*-gah?" he repeated quickly with increased volume, rapidly manipulating his hands as if the additional effort would make his thick fractured English more easily understood.

The woman stared back blankly, lost in confusion at his repeated attempts to make himself understood when Corfinio casually stepped up to the counter at her side.

"Excuse me, miss. Maybe I can help. I speak broken English," he said and turned to face the coffee merchant. "Scusi, Signore, parla Italiano?"

"*Si!* Yes, yes!" the counterman said relieved, that the verbal struggle was about to be bridged. "Inglese, eh, non c'e buono. Capisce? Engleesh…notta so good, notta so good."

Turning back to the woman, Corfinio realized by the baffled look she displayed that the Italian's rapid-fire form of broken English was as incoherent as his native tongue. "He wants to know if you take sugar…'*shoe*-gah.'"

"Ohhh, *sugar!*" the woman said in final comprehension, a slight smile appearing on her full rounded lips. "No. *No* sugar." She shook her head.

Understanding the woman's directive, the order was promptly filled, and a cardboard coffee cup was gently handed across the counter. "These stupid American women," said the counterman in Italian to Corfinio, "should stay home and make babies."

"Mmm. Di mio!" Corfinio said with a sly smile as he paid the counterman.

Both stepping away from the coffee counter, the woman was sure that a private joke had transpired between the two men.

"What did he just say?" she asked, slightly agitated. All I got out of that was something that sounded like 'American' and 'baby.'"

Not wishing to divulge the true nature of the derisive comment and hoping to avoid an ugly scene, Corfinio substituted an alternate translation. "Oh, it was nothing bad! What he said was," he smiled disarmingly, "this American woman is as beautiful as a new baby." Pleased with his off-the-cuff yet completely glib inaccuracy, Corfinio looked over coyly at the woman and awaited her reaction.

Blushing slightly at the compliment, the woman demurely dipped her head. When she raised her head again, her brows were knitted together. She remembered a further comment had been issued by Corfinio.

"Then *you* said something. What did you say *back* to him?" she asked suspiciously.

"Oh, I agreed," Corfinio answered, bobbing his head in a childlike fashion.

"You're a regular Sir Galahad, aren't you?" she gushed with gratitude.

"More like Sir *Mordred*," a booming voice proclaimed, sarcasm saturating the final syllables. Arthur Bari had suddenly appeared out of nowhere, casting an irritated gaze in Corfinio's direction.

Corfinio and the woman, surprised at the intrusion, turned to face the large man who was glaring at his client. Mouth agape, the woman simply stared at the ominous meddler. Corfinio, in an effort to salvage the shattered moment, blurted, "This is my lawyer. He—"

"Yes, and if I were *you*, miss," Bari explained, gesturing emphatically, "I'd put as much distance between myself and this man as quickly as possible. The reason he's *here* is to plea bargain out of a *stalking* charge." Bari rocked back on his heels, satisfied that his contrivance had disarmed his brazen client while at the same time instilling a sense of suspicion in the woman.

The woman shifted apprehensive glances between the two men, expecting a denial from Corfinio but getting none. He simply stood there, struggling with an uncomfortable smirk, hands now shoved deep in his pockets.

She cleared her throat, breaking the uncomfortable silence. "You know what," she asked nervously, pausing to check her wristwatch, "I'm, uhhh, *running late*, but thank you *very much* for your help!"

Without so much as a backward glance, she walked briskly toward the staircase. Corfinio watched, completely mesmerized by the perfectly shaped legs as they climbed the stairway, rounded the landing, and finally disappeared from view. Breaking out of his self-induced hypnotic stupor, he blinked several times and wagged a finger in his lawyer's bearded face. Before he could get a word out, Bari cut him off.

Eyes wide and teeth clenched together, Bari seethed, "I thought I told you not to speak, look, or breathe! Didn't I say that? *Didn't I?*"

"Is that a rhetorical question, or do I have to answer—"

"I would prefer if you would say *nothing at all.* Nothing! *Ever!* Not a *word*, not a *syllable*, not even a single *vowel* or consonant sound. Do you get my meaning, *Signor Stupido?*"

"Oh," snapped Corfinio, "so first I'm a shithead, now I'm stupid. Is that it?"

"On the contrary. They're quite synonymous. You can't be a 'smart' shithead. *Shitheads* are stupid."

"There's just no end to the personal defamatory remarks, is there?"

"Defamatory? No. How 'bout 'indicative.'"

"Y'know, if I knew another lawyer, I'd sue you for something."

"Well, this would be the *ideal* place to find one," Bari replied with a wide sweep of his meaty hands.

"True, but I bet they're all a bunch of suck bag malcontents—just like you—looking to line their pockets—"

"Here we go."

"With the blood and toil of poor unfortunates—much like myself—so that when they retire to the Lawyer's Home of Immorality and Abomination, they can all sit around and laugh—"

"Oh, Christ—"

"Comparing notes on who amassed the greatest fortune by screwing their clients over the most thoroughly, bending them over a pickle barrel while softly whispering in their ear, 'Trust me.'"

Bari grimaced at the remark. "You're not going to start *this* crap again, are you? *Wa-wa-waaaa*. Besides, what could you *possibly* hope to gain by your intervention with that woman? I mean, what kind of feeble plot was being entertained in that microscopic brain of yours?"

"I don't know…" Corfinio shrugged. "Maybe I was trying to impress her. *Maybe* it was working."

"*Impress* her?" he asked incredulously. "With *what?* Your hundred-and-fifty-dollar Morgan Memorial suit? Get a grip there, Horace! What cloud are you on? If I hadn't come along when I did—"

"And embarrassed me—"

"You would have embarrassed yourself!"

Corfinio stood silent, poised for a moment, contemplating his response but then decided to drop the issue all together. His shoulders sagged slightly in resignation as he uttered his single syllable response.

"So," he stated, fully realizing that this response would leave his lawyer without an arguable point.

Sighing at his client's overall lack of sobriety, he rolled his eyes and shook his head slowly. "Come on," he drawled, "let's go. We're in Courtroom 5." As they slowly wended their way between clumps of gathered people, Bari grumbled, "*Ha!* A *pickle* barrel! We haven't used *pickle barrels* for thirty years!"

*****

Courtroom 5 was designed as an afterthought. Because of the increasing need for criminal and civil trials and legal proceedings, it became apparent that an additional courtroom would be necessary to handle the overflow. In 1970, rather than build an addition to the courthouse, an option was exercised to utilize a large storage room on the lower level, circumventing all discussions relating to Eminent Domain concerning the adjoining properties.

In order to get to Courtroom 5, a long, circuitous journey had to be undertaken through the antiquated building. Starting at the central concourse, one had to travel to the end of the seemingly dead-ended east corridor which teed off to the left. This short hallway accessed the men's room foyer. A doorway had been cut into the stonework, which opened onto a heavily scarred cast-iron landing and stairway leading down to a lower-level storage room. Ancient file cabinets glutted with old and forgotten cases stood sentry behind a padlocked metal grating lining the pathway. Evenly spaced bronze-shrouded ceiling lights hung suspended from the ceiling, giving off an eerie luminescence. Lacking any windows or substantial ventilation, a rank, musty smell permeated the storage room. At the end of the passageway, a worn concrete stairway climbed out of the bowels of the courthouse's nether world giving entry to a wide, brightly lit waiting area with high ceilings, just outside of Courtroom 5.

Years ago, the waiting area, fifteen feet wide and sixty feet long, had been known as the Dump. It had been termed as such by police, delivering prisoners via paddy wagon from local jails throughout the county. The offenders would be "dumped" at this location, sitting on trestle-type wooden benches waiting to be processed. After processing, they would be transferred to the lower-level holding cell to further await a court appearance to determine their immediate or long-term future.

On the east side of the waiting area, a concrete stairway ran the full width of the hall, leading up to a massive set of metal-clad double doors on the worn landing. This was the entry that prisoners would formerly be delivered through in a bygone day by their police escorts. A tattered placard hung over the doors reading "Not an Exit, Official Use Only." Police and court officers still used the old entryway to gain access from the outside into the courthouse from the reserved parking lot. Once inside, the doors locked shut, denying egress.

At the west end of the wide corridor, another concrete stairway only four feet wide rose up to a landing that met a wood door with a frosted glass panel. This door accessed the foyer to the judges' chambers and was the only alternate exit from the courtroom. No sign graced this door indicating its purpose or eventual destination or that it was limited to restricted personnel. Strangely enough, even without warning signals to guard it against casual curiosity or ignorant blundering, no one ever attempted to use the unlocked door. In some inexplicable way, the door itself seemed to radiate a sense of foreboding.

Opposite the courtroom entrance, a small oak table and two chairs were placed against the south wall. This was the only reserved location for lawyer/client consultation as no other benches lined the hallway. A pen had been supplied on the table to ensure that signers would be guaranteed an appropriate tool at their disposal. Potential theft of the pen was discouraged with a short length of copper chain attaching it to the table. This precaution hardly seemed necessary as the pen had been out of ink for months.

The last surviving solitary pay phone hung on the wall scant feet from the table, denying participants at either station any semblance of privacy. Not that it would really matter; the phone was inoperable as a generous wad of gum had been stuffed into the coin slot, rendering it completely useless.

The courtroom doors were off center of the north wall, favoring the judges' chamber stairway. "Courtroom 5" was painted in neat white letters in contrast to the mahogany-stained doors. No pictures, bronze plaques, or bulletin boards adorned the wall adjoining Courtroom 5, and the dirty tan paint had begun to show signs of wear and deterioration many years ago.

In contrast to the areas outside the courtrooms on the upper floors burgeoning with activity, Courtroom 5's waiting area was stark and dreary to the point of depression. There were no windows to let in light, and one air vent rattled obnoxiously in an ineffective effort to ventilate the catacomb-like corridor. No traffic traveled through this dead-ended sector, hustling to get to alternate locations. No personnel darted from one office to another to trade gossip or discuss the game last night. No one ever accidentally stumbled into *this* corridor. Ever.

Courtroom 5 was a virtual No Man's Land.

19

Bari and Corfinio had traversed the long maze-like passage in just over two minutes. They now entered the waiting area adjacent to Courtroom 5, only to find that all available conference areas were occupied. Looking around quickly, Bari noticed two couples hovering over the oak table; two men on the stairway and a woman hummed quietly as she paced back and forth down the center of the corridor. A court officer entered the courtroom, while the pay phone held one man in thrall, totally absorbed by its inoperable state.

Bari assessed the likelihood of having a successful consultation in these surroundings as highly unlikely. The problem, he realized, was that Corfinio would develop a case of curiosity concerning the other people in the hallway. Bari knew from several previous experiences that Corfinio had a twisted gift that he could only describe as "separation.' He would outwardly appear to be completely focused on the matter at hand, occasionally knitting his brow, frowning, or nodding. But in fact, he was simply reacting to facial expressions or tonal quality while being totally absorbed in another conversation occurring inches or yards away. Not wishing to engage himself in a completely another fruitless venture, he suggested to Corfinio that they finish the remainder of their conversation on one of the audience benches within the courtroom.

"Do we *have* to go in there?" groaned Corfinio. "Why can't we stand over there by the steps that lead into the Evil Kingdom, or why can't we lean against a wall or something? I don't want to go into court yet. *You know* I really *hate* going in there. You *know* that. Especially *before* we *need* to be in there."

"Well, y'know something, John? We *need* to be in there," said Bari, bobbing his head emphatically. "Because out *here*, I can't depend on you to actually sit and listen when there's other things going on around you. You tend to lose focus on the matter at hand. We need to go over this—*in there*—so that I can have your undivided attention. So *in* we go!"

Bari walked across the corridor and entered the courtroom, tugging the heavy oak door open. Without looking back to see if Corfinio was following, he let the door swing shut.

Corfinio watched as his lawyer disappeared into the courtroom. He was trying to decide whether to follow Bari into the courtroom or to hold out and see how long it would take him to come back. He gazed around at the incidental occupants of the corridor without finding anyone interesting enough to hold his attention for more than a few milliseconds. Disappointed at the lack of potential entertainment and deciding that Bari probably wouldn't come back for him, he sighed in resignation and shuffled into the courtroom.

The large courtroom was dim and depressing. No oversized windows adorned the walls as they did in the upper courtrooms. Dusty florescent lighting buzzed annoyingly overhead, sporadically flashing a lightning-like charge of luminescence caused from a faulty ballast. The walls were paneled in a mahogany wainscoting that had the appearance of not having been cleaned in years. They held stains and layered dirt from a score of years and a thousand cases. A worn commercial-grade carpeting concealed a maple tongue and groove flooring that creaked in spite of the thick covering.

The courtroom had only two doors, the entry door which led to the hallway and a door that accessed the judges' chambers. Within the judges' chambers, a side door led to a small foyer that contained yet another door, the wood door with the frosted glass panel that stood at the top of the concrete stairway, emptying down into the same original corridor as the courtroom entry door.

Letting the door swing closed behind him, Corfinio stood for several seconds, gazing around the aged, cold, and impersonal courtroom. The judge's bench sat high on a raised dais surrounded by four smaller desks, two in front and two off to the left side. The two desks in front of the judge's bench were occupied by the court clerk immersed in rearranging the daily case load, shuffling and stacking and organizing endless reams of paper. Located against the middle of the right wall was the court officer's box, where the court officer stood talking in low tones to a uniformed policeman twirling his cap on his index finger. Seated in the audience arena were two lawyers heavily engaged in trying to hammer out a deal for their respective clients who had not yet arrived. To his immediate right, in the back row of benches sat Arthur Bari, impatiently drumming his fingers on his lap-held briefcase. Corfinio, biting his bottom lip, cautiously entered the bench and seated himself beside his lawyer.

"I really do hate this place," Corfinio said nervously, eyes darting around the courtroom.

Bari sighed. "Yeah. I know. You told me. To the point of *ad nauseam*. Now let's go over this one more time. I want to make sure that you know what's going to happen here today."

"You're the boss," Corfinio said solemnly.

"Okay, let's see," Bari said, drawing the file folder out of his briefcase bearing Corfinio's name. "We've filed yet another motion requesting the court to allow a system of visitation—"

"Arthur?"

Bari tensed at the interruption, refusing to look up from his paperwork for several seconds before finally replying, "*What*, John?"

"I know this is going to sound stupid to you…"

Corfinio's voice had an unfamiliar taciturn quality to it. Bari decided to hear him out, where normally he would have ignored the interruption.

"What is it, John?"

"Well," Corfinio began, staring ahead blindly, "I'm looking at the judge's bench sitting on that elevated platform and the desks all around it. Surrounding it all is the oak railing keeping everyone else at a distance. Over there…and there," he said, pointing in opposite directions toward each of the court officers' boxes, "are the court officers." Corfinio stopped and exhaled.

Confused by Corfinio's observation of the obvious, Bari grimaced. "What's your point, John? I mean, I hope that there actually *is* a point to your statements regarding the *blatantly* obvious."

"The whole thing, the whole arrangement. The way it's set up. Doesn't it remind you of anything? Don't you *see* it?"

"John," Bari began, effecting a slow blink and shaking his head slightly, "*what* in the *name* of Merciful Christ are you *talking* about?"

"The bench, the *judge's* bench. It's sitting up high… like it was…on a *hill*…like a *castle*! The desks are like the hovels belonging to the king's serfs, with the clerk acting as the king's adviser. The boxes are like the guard towers, complete with guards. Surrounding the whole thing is the railing keeping everyone out...a *moat*, Arthur, *a moat!* How did I not *see* this before? How did everyone *else* not see this before?"

Bari stared incredulously at his client with mounting concern. He knew Corfinio always made light of even the heaviest situations, but now his tonal quality and sudden emotional vulnerability was such that he suspected he was fast approaching critical mass meltdown. Was he losing it?

"Y'know *why* the judge is seated up so high?" Corfinio continued. "Because he's holding the *high* ground, Arthur. You can't wage a successful campaign against someone holding the high ground. Too many casualties. Psychologically and geographically, you can't win. This whole place is set up to make you feel like you're storming the castle." He paused, sitting back against the uncomfortable bench, folding his arms leisurely across his chest and looked across at his lawyer. "Kind of 'funny' in a way, don't you think?" he asked, raising both eyebrows, the slightest hint of a smile dawning at the corners of his lips.

Bari suddenly dropped the file folder on his lap, turning sideways on the bench and grasped his client by the shoulders, shaking loose his crossed arms, and looked him in the eye.

"*John!* John, *listen* to me. You have to knock off this fantasy world psychobabble *bullshit*. You *gotta* come in for a landing! You can't expect to neutralize every crisis you encounter by making it *funny*. Part of the reason you're in the predicament you're in is because you refuse to accept and deal with life's harsh realities, instead turning them into an illusion of misinterpreted social satire. *This is not good, John!* The harder you try to mold the inconsistencies of this offensive planet into a personal delusion of whimsical entertainment, the easier it is for the system to label you as an irresponsible, imbecilic, borderline wacko. 'Levity' is *not* the key to survival, John—adaptability and acceptance *are*. No matter how you want to gloss that over, *that's* the truth."

Bari released his grasp of Corfinio's shoulders and turned both palms upward in a supplicating manner in hopeful anticipation that Corfinio would confirm his disclosure as a reasonable assessment. "Is *any* part of what I just said getting through that *thick* skull of yours?"

Corfinio's shoulders sagged slightly as he dropped his head, exhaling a heavy breath. When he finally spoke, his voice was low and without the usual trace of sarcasm or whimsy. "Arthur... I *know* what reality is. Reality is, I was accused, held responsible, and incarcerated. *That's* reality. And I know what truth is too. The truth is, I didn't *do* anything to deserve that. But the 'truth' wasn't 'real' enough to dissuade previously biased mindsets. Twelve months in jail, fifteen months away from my son,

DALE DELILLO

fifteen months of my life that was a complete waste of time and energy. I didn't have any *choice* but to 'accept' my circumstances and 'adapt' to survive that ordeal, so don't sit there pontificating about 'truth' because it didn't happen to *you*."

Bari cast his gaze downward and studied the floor for several seconds before looking back at Corfinio. "No, John…it *didn't happen to me*. And I can't *change* what happened, and neither can you. But what we *can* do is put things *right* from this point forward. In order to do that, we need to approach this with the utmost in sincerity. If the court senses that you're not sincere, you're going to lose. Do you understand that?"

"I understand," said Corfinio evenly.

"Can we get on with this now?"

With a stoic look of measured indifference, Corfinio turned away. "I need a drink of water. I'll be back in a few minutes." Without waiting for Bari's approval, Corfinio abruptly stood and exited the bench, making his way hastily toward the outer hallway.

20

Stepping into the hallway, Corfinio turned to retrace the path they had taken to arrive at Courtroom 5. Passing the occupied oak table in the outer hallway with the manacled pen, the Dump doors opened at the end of the corridor. A tall, well-muscled handcuffed man stepped onto the concrete landing, followed closely by a uniformed policeman grasping his left upper arm. The sneering disheveled prisoner, framed in the sunlit open doorway, surveyed the area like he was looking over his domain. He appeared to be no older than mid-twenties with a faint stubble of beard on his chin. His sleeveless flannel shirt lay open, baring a tattooed Chinese symbol on his broad, hairless chest signifying "strength."

Once the prisoner and guard were inside, the door slammed shut behind the duo, alarming everyone in the hallway into a momentary startled silence. As one, heads turned to face the cause of the commotion. A thin smile spread over the prisoner's face, realizing that he was the focus of their attention and in some apprehension. His reverie was broken when his accompanying attendant nudged him forward.

"Let's go, Felix. Down the stairs. Door on the right."

"Don't be pushin' me, man," warned the Hispanic in a loud voice, "else you be lookin' for a police brutality charge in front of witnesses."

"You can take it up with the judge," responded the policeman indifferently, taking the Hispanic by the upper arm and escorting him down the stairs.

"*Felix!*" mumbled Corfinio under his breath. He immediately recognized the young Hispanic from their time spent in the Middlesex County Jail.

*****

Six days ago, a group of men met in the dark recesses of shadow to discuss a business transaction that could not be held in plain view of the law-abiding citizenry. The purpose of the meeting was to make a "buy." Four of the men were the sellers and the remaining two—one of which was Felix Segado—were the buyers. During the course of discussion, the "business associates" apparently had a severe difference of opinion, resulting in Segado being shot in the thigh. His buying partner and the cocaine merchants quickly dispersed immediately after the shooting, leaving Segado bleeding on the sidewalk.

Police had been dispatched to the scene, following an anonymous caller reported hearing gunshots. Unable to flee the scene successfully, Segado was picked up by the police and escorted to the local hospital, where they questioned him at length concerning the incident. He insisted that he was simply taking a walk when he was shot by four unidentified men in an automobile for no apparent reason. No, he didn't know them, and no, he had never seen them before. The police searched him and found a switchblade knife in his possession—strictly against the terms of his probation. He was placed under arrest and held in the local hoosegow until his arraignment could be scheduled.

*****

Today was his arraignment date.

As an escorted Segado passed Corfinio in the hallway, they made eye contact nodding a silent greeting of acknowledgment. No other visible sign was exchanged, and the police escort was ignorant of the salutation or that the two men were familiars.

Corfinio watched as Segado and his attendant entered the courtroom and disappeared from view behind the swinging doors. *No shit!* Corfinio thought. *It didn't take long. What has it been, six, seven months since he got out? And here he is, right back again.* Shaking his head, he turned into the hallway leading to the concourse.

The memory of jail did nothing to improve his already gloomy mood. It was a situation and a time he wished he could just forget, but something would always trigger the memory. He explained to Bari once, "I'm not trying to pretend it didn't happen. I just don't find any pleasure in remembering it." He tried to shake it off as he continued his trek through the maze-like corridors.

He walked slowly through the lower-level storage room containing the antiquated and half-forgotten vast collection of files stored in rusting metal cabinets. He stopped in mesmerized awe, gazing at the hundreds of metal filing cabinets holding thousands—*hundreds* of thousands of file folders—containing snippets of people's lives that couldn't be resolved amicably or without legal counsel. *How did we get so fucked up?* he asked himself out loud.

He resumed his short journey climbing the metal fire escape-like stairway and entered the men's room foyer that had become a necessary detour to access travel toward Courtroom 5. Glancing at the scarred bathroom door with initials carved into the oak panels, he decided to forego his trip to the coffee counter for water, choosing instead to use the immediate facilities.

Stepping inside, a pungent odor of disinfectant assaulted his nostrils. Approaching the worn marble counter, he leaned over the basin with a flat palm on each side and studied his reflection in the mirror for several moments.

"Man! *You* look like shit!" he said aloud to his reflection, taking note of the soft, puffy skin under his eyes. "You really ought to try sleeping at night. You'll never win any beauty contest looking like this!"

Reaching out, he turned the worn, knobby white porcelain handle, blasted the cold water and shoved both hands under the faucet. Cupping his hands, he filled them with water and gulped down the contents, reaching for a second handful to splash his face. The cold water stung his eyes as he wiped his palms down his face, flicking off the final drops into the basin. Blinking the excess water out of his eyes, he reached out for the paper towel dispenser to his left, spinning the creaking handle of the metal-enshrouded paper holder rapidly to obtain extra toweling proved fruitless as the container was empty.

Naturally, he thought, *why would there be paper towels in the dispenser? That would mean someone in this hellhole would have to do a job that actually resulted in a positive effect. Oh, but I bet there's paper towels in the bathroom the judge uses. Wouldn't want to piss him off, now would we?*

Disgusted, Corfinio pushed one of the stall doors open and reeled off about three feet of toilet paper to dry his face and hands. Tossing the wad of paper into the trash barrel, he turned to face the mirror once again. Stray bits of toilet paper clung to needle-like whiskers that evaded the morning's shaving strokes. Picking off the flecks of paper, he assessed himself once more.

Nope. Didn't do any good, pal. You still look like shit...

"Y'know what I need?" he asked his reflection out loud. "I need gum. My mouth feels like Beau Geste just stomped his feet off on my tongue."

Reaching into his right jacket pocket, he suddenly froze.

He slowly withdrew the gun.

Staring down, the .38-caliber Saturday Night Special lay flat in his hand. The barrel glinted from the overhead soffit lighting as he slightly shifted his right hand. Deliberating, he wrapped his thumb around the dimpled walnut pistol grip and carefully placed his index finger through the trigger guard. Keeping the gun low at his side with elbow cocked, he pointed the revolver at his reflection.

Squinting, teeth clamped, he squeezed the trigger.

Instantaneously, with a loud *snap!* the projectile's path ended, buried in Corfinio's reflected abdomen. The plastic yellow dart wobbled slightly but remained fastened to the mirror.

Grinning, he reached out and removed the dart with a *snick* as the suction cupped dart released its hold. Dropping the dart into his left pocket, he again looked down at the gun cradled in his right hand.

Wow. Works pretty good! Michael's gonna love this.

Corfinio had bought the dart gun in a drug store last week after attending an early morning funeral. Amazed at the realistic appearance of the toy, he decided then to buy it as a gift for his son. The stop-and-go traffic on the ride home afforded him an opportunity to peel open the blister wrapping and inspect it for rough edges or burrs. Satisfied that the toy offered no element of potential marring to the boy's soft skin, he absently stuffed the gun into his suit pocket, and there it remained.

The bathroom door suddenly thumped open, startling him from his reverie. An overweight, sour-faced court officer sporting a military haircut approached from his left. Corfinio's heart stopped as he realized that he was still holding the plastic gun in his right hand. Rigid, he dared not move for fear the palmed gun would attract the attention of the uniformed patron. Instinctively, he clutched the gun to his right thigh, concealing it from view. Trying to appear as casual as possible, Corfinio edged the revolver slowly into his suitcoat pocket, patting the flap down neatly.

The fat, disheveled officer tugged at his waistband with a struggle and unzipped as he walked to the urinal on Corfinio's left side.

"Hey, how you doin?" asked the officer staring blindly into the ceramic wall issuing a sigh of relief as he began his business.

"Oh, uh…just great," said Corfinio nervously. *Terrific!* he thought in a flash of momentary panic. *If this idiot catches sight of this thing, he'll shoot me deader than a cold ham.*

"Don't even try washin' your hands," offered the officer, shaking his head, digging in under his overhanging girth. "There ain't no paper anyway."

"Uhhm, yeah. So I see," Corfinio agreed. He stared at himself in the mirror attempting to appear as nonchalant as possible, while his heart pounded heavily. He saw that he had suddenly developed speckled beads of sweat breaking out on his forehead. He hastily blasted the cold water tap, cupping both hands under the spout. He splashed the cool water on his face then ran his hands back through his hairline. Flicking his hands in an unsuccessful attempt to dry them, he gently patted his palms on his upper thighs. Using both semi-dried hands, he straightened his tie, sneaking a nervous glance down at his reflected right side to see if the gun showed a bulge and was relieved to see that it did not.

"I gotta tell ya," the cop began again, "that damned maintenance guy they hired is as useless as eatin' soup with a fork." He smiled, pleased with his own metaphor. "He's a real winner. Jamaican, *Mon.* Never fills the paper towel holder. I swear he takes the rolls home and wallpapers his house with it. Son of a bitch." He sighed as the stream of urine splashed the back of the urinal. "The one before him was no better either. Jamaican sons-a-bitches, all of 'em. They don't wanna work. We wouldn't have this problem if they'd hire on some Americans instead of these chatterin' monkeys. Know what I mean?"

"Can't say I'd be too enthusiastic if I was making four bucks an hour and had to deal with a bunch of ingrates." Corfinio leaned closer to the mirror in an attempt to get a glimpse of the officer's name badge in the reflected surface. "J. McCorken" was inscribed on the brass plate in capital letters.

"Hey, the inmates come with the territory," explained McCorken, "and we got *plenty* of them!"

"*Ingrates*—I said 'ingrates,' not *inmates*," Corfinio corrected.

Slightly self-conscious over his gaffe, McCorken shrugged and sneered, "Whatever."

"But you know what," asked Corfinio with a wry grin turning from the mirror to face the fat man, "maybe you're right, Officer *McCorken*. I bet there'd be *reams* of paper towels in here if someone just hired some *real* Americans. Like maybe…" Corfinio rolled his eyes toward the ceiling as if he were searching for just the right answer. "A boatload of keg-sucking potato pickers."

McCorken flashed an ominous scowl in Corfinio's direction, yanked up his zipper, failing to flush the urinal. He now faced Corfinio, who casually turned back to peruse his mirrored image. "You're a real wiseass, aren't cha?" McCorken sneered as his pockmarked face flushed in hostility.

Corfinio unbuttoned his suit coat, ran his thumbs around his waistband, and methodically rebuttoned his coat. "There again, what do I know? I'm just a poor, uneducated ginzo meatball. I wouldn't have a *clue* as to the true nature of upstanding Irish-Americans."

"Goddamn *right*, you don't!" McCorken replied through gritted teeth, clenching his beefy fists.

The restroom door creaked open as a well-dressed elderly man shuffled in and tediously made his way to a stall. The timely interruption momentarily doused McCorken's mounting irritation.

McCorken stared malevolently at Corfinio while entertaining thoughts of brutal physical aggression. "Hey, *asswipe*," he breathed the words in venomous contempt, "if I were *you*, I'd watch myself."

"And if I were *you*," Corfinio replied, pleasantly finally turning to face his adversary, "I'd wash my hands."

McCorken backed his way toward the door. "I ain't servin' your supper." He scowled, storming into the hallway. The door made a soft *thump* as it closed behind him.

21

Corfinio returned to the courtroom and entered the bench where Bari sat patiently waiting for his client to return. The yellow legal pad remained on his lap laying on the opened file folder bearing Corfinio's name. He watched as Bari intently scribbled notes with a ball point pen, circling words and highlighting others with under-lining and arrows.

The activity in the courtroom had increased in Corfinio's short absence. In addition to the ever-present court officers, several of the benches in the spectator area were beginning to fill with new arrivals. The court clerk had arrived, taking his station at the table located in front of the judge's bench and was rifling through a stack of folders, calling out the names of the scheduled appearances. As each name was called out, plaintiffs and defendants acknowledged their presence with a raised hand or a mumbled admission of "yes" or "here."

"Has he called our name yet?" Corfinio asked, leaning forward on the backrest of the bench in front of him, draping his arms over the top. Waiting for Bari's reply, he scanned the new arrivals as well as the various personalities working the courtroom area.

Bari nodded affirmative without looking up from his legal pad. "Yes, they already called us. Which is in itself *amazing*." He paused, pushing his sliding glasses further up the bridge of his nose. "I fully expected to *not* hear our name *at all*. *That's* the way things usually go around here. Paperwork gets lost in the maze of institutionalization *quite* frequently. I sat waiting for a roll call for *six weeks* one time without ever hearing my client's name."

"Six weeks," Corfinio repeated, letting the wild exaggeration lie. "Hey, Arthur, doesn't it seem like the guy calling out names is a bit on the pompous side? Look at him. It's almost as if he's *sneering* out the names as he calls them."

Bari looked up from his legal pad and grunted in the direction of the court clerk and shook his head. "Pompous *and* arrogant. This is his *shining* moment of glory in his otherwise mundane and trivial existence. He's in *total* control right now. He's the Official Name Caller-Outer, and by *God! No one* is going to take that assignment away from him!" Bari chuckled at the mockery he created then added, "Do you see what he's doing now?"

Corfinio wasn't sure what he was missing at the urging of his lawyer. He didn't see anything unusual; the court clerk was talking in low tones to an impeccably dressed man with his hair styled perfectly. "What," Corfinio asked puzzled, "what am I looking at?"

"See that guy he's talking to? Mister *Slick*? Well, Mister Slick wants to get out of here real quick, so he's kissing the clerk's ass so he can get his hearing moved up in line. Mister I Am the Judge's Official Name Caller-Outer realizes that *this* is his power position and has at his disposal one of two options to exercise. He will either accept the deal with a wink or an unctuous smile while mentally cataloguing Mister Slick for a future favor, *or*, if he doesn't think he can get anything *out* of Mister Slick, he'll adopt a face reflecting remorse and sadness, shake his head forlornly, and Mister Slick will miss his tee time."

"Seriously? That doesn't really happen, does it?" Corfinio asked, honestly surprised. "I thought everything was first come, first served. You get your name on the list and wait your turn."

"Watch."

As Corfinio and Bari watched, the court clerk listened intently, knitting his brow as if trying to grasp a difficult concept while Mister Slick animatedly posed his request. There was a brief lull in their conversation as each man waited for the other to give the proverbial inch. Mister Slick leaned in closer, whispering to the court clerk, who then smiled thinly nodding his head. The clerk reached over to the hefty stack of file folders sitting on the corner of his desk, lifting one out from the cluster, and placed it on the upper right-hand corner of the table. Mister Slick smiled back and winked, mouthing a silent thank-you as he backed away from the clerk's domain.

"See?" Bari said in complete satisfaction at having forecasted the entire scenario. "What did I tell you? Looks like Mister Slick gets to go golfing today."

"Are you—" Corfinio said a trifle too loud, causing Bari to instantly shush him. Corfinio hacked on the rebuke and continued in an agitated grumble, slightly more than a whisper, "*Well then*, why can't *we* do that? I *certainly* don't treasure the thought of sitting around *here* all blasted day!"

"Three reasons," said Bari, closing his eyes and leaning back against the bench.

Several seconds elapsed without a word being spoken.

"*Well?*" Corfinio demanded in a loud whisper.

"Number one," Bari began, without opening his eyes, "I don't make deals with shit-sucking, power-hungry, insignificant rat turds like him. Number two, we're in no particular hurry *anyway*, and finally, number three, I don't golf."

"Maybe I should have enlisted the services of Mister Slick."

"You couldn't afford him."

"I can't afford *you*."

Bari frowned. "Is *that* her?" he suddenly asked looking over Corfinio's shoulder, straining his eyes through his heavy black glasses.

An attractive woman in a green dress walked alongside a man who was apparently her lawyer. She was well aware that she had captured the attention of several of the men in attendance but feigned ignorance. Her lawyer ushered her into the second-row bench across the aisle, where she instantly began primping.

Corfinio stiffened involuntarily and turned around slowly in the direction Bari was tipping his head toward and immediately recognized her. Even though her back was to him, there was no mistaking that it was his ex-wife.

"Ah, *shit!*" Corfinio bowed his head on his chest for a moment and wiped his hand over his face. "That's her," he said venomously.

"Are you *sure*?" Bari asked. "She's not facing this way. It's been a while since you've seen her…"

"Not long enough. But that's her all right. I'd know that bitch if I was a blind man in a dark room. Besides, she's wearing that perfume that I *hate*. I could smell that crap from New Hampshire. *Look* at her, she's the only person in the world who gets all dolled up and buys a new dress to go to court so she'll get a favorable decision from the judge. *Christ!* Always with the mirror."

"Hey, *you* married her," Bari reminded him. "Y'think she's tapping her lawyer? He's got his arm on her shoulder." Bari nudged Corfinio with his elbow several times and winked exaggeratedly.

"Naw," Corfinio said assuredly, "she's going for the drama. Gotta be the eternal victim. That's her whole thing."

Bari shuffled his paperwork into the folder and stood up. "I have to go talk to her new lover boy," Bari said with a wicked smile. "I'll be right back."

Corfinio watched as his lawyer approached the second bench on the opposite side of the aisle. Leaning in but not entering the bench, he excused himself for the interruption and introduced himself as counsel to the defendant. The opposing lawyer extended a hand while Corfinio's ex-wife turned her head in disgust, folding her arms across her ample chest. The two representatives talked in somber tones for several minutes before Bari returned to his client.

"I was right!" Bari said with gleeful satisfaction. "He's *definitely* screwing her!"

"You're full of shit," Corfinio said. "What did he say?"

"Well, John," Bari replied, the smile fading from his bearded face, "they're holding the line on no visit/no contact."

"Consistent."

"They also have signed statements from the Visiting Center and DSS reinforcing the decision. You might want to read these." He handed Corfinio the two documents.

Corfinio scanned the paperwork quickly. His face turned pallid as he read the contents of the document from the Visiting Center, indicating that he was termed "abusive, at times highly volatile, recommend psychiatric evaluation." He flipped the report on the bench and quickly scanned the contents of the DSS report. The report included a demand for an order of restraint as well as a request to the court to abolish visitation and/or contact with the minor child. As he completed reading the legal forms, his ashen pallor diminished only to be replaced immediately with a furious reddening.

"This is all *lies*, Arthur. How can they make these accusations without a shred of evidence? I never so much as raised my *voice* in front of my son. This is a load of crap!" Corfinio's hand trembled from anger as he handed the paperwork back to his lawyer. "I did every goddamned thing they told me to, and they're *still* trying to hang me out to dry. What are they basing 'highly volatile' on? I never *once* displayed any emotional outbursts. The only person I ever expressed *any* anger or hostility toward was that DSS *bitch* when she *insisted* that I must have done something to my son. How the hell am I *supposed* to act when they're sitting there making accusations against me without any foundation *at all*?"

"Unfortunately, John," Bari said with a sigh, "what they say carries significant weight with the court. What they say—*especially DSS*—matters. They parade around, waving a huge banner stating that they perform their duties to best effect the security and protection of *all* the children in the world. It doesn't matter who gets in the way or how many contingent casualties there are—or *who* they are—they must *save* the children. That's the shroud of fanaticism that they cloak *everything* with: 'Protect the children.'"

"Protect the children," Corfinio venomously spat. "Look, I'm all in favor of protecting children, but at what cost? What about the collateral damage? What about *that?* They can't boast, 'Oh, we saved the children, but we accidentally burned the city down and killed thousands of adults.'"

"As long as the children are saved, that's all that matters to them."

"Apparently, *facts* have very little effect on the decision-making process." Corfinio gritted his teeth, barely able to contain his frustration. He knew Bari was right. He had heard it all before.

"Facts are incidental information, minor inconvenient points to employ when useful to them and toxic drivel when it works against them," Bari explained. "What matters here is what *they say* the facts are. And if the facts don't line up with their *professional* opinion, then the facts must be wrong. But, John, you have to remember one very important thing here."

"Yeah, and what's that?" Corfinio asked with disgust.

"No matter what is said today, *no matter what*, you *have* to remain calm. You cannot—absolutely *cannot*— show any anger or attitude *at all*."

"Just *how* am I supposed to do *that*? *Especially* when what they're saying about me is complete *bullshit!*" Corfinio asked between clenched teeth.

"You *have* to, John. I know you're frustrated, but the court doesn't like it when you get emotional. Especially when that emotion is anger. Then everything that Polanski and DSS is alleging is proven out, and you lose."

"*Lose*? Seriously? There's no way for me to *win!* If I get upset and, *God forbid*, actually 'emote,' then I prove their point and *I lose*. If I remain calm, then I'm a heartless bastard who needs a psych evaluation—oh, and guess what? *I lose!* Well, y'know what I think about that? They can *all* kiss my ass!"

"John, an emotional outburst in front of the judge will get you nothing but a contempt ruling, and you'll end up in the same position as that guy over there." Bari pointed a finger in the direction of the prisoners' box to the right of the judge's bench, where Segado sat handcuffed with his jailer in close company.

Corfinio exhaled, exasperated, realizing that his lawyer was only looking out for his best interests. "Fine, *whatever*," he said with resigned disgust, "I'll be the model defendant. This sucks, Arthur, but I swear to God, next time…" he trailed off, gnawing on his lower lip, reigning in his inner rage.

"Next time?" Bari asked with a tinge of apprehension.

"Next time, I'm hiring a lawyer that knows how to lie. The truth doesn't mean jack *shit* around here."

"All rise!" The court clerk made the loud announcement by rote as the judge exited his chambers and entered into the courtroom.

The courtroom chatter diminished immediately upon hearing the pronouncement of the judge's entry, standing as instructed by the court clerk.

Adorned in his honorary robes, Judge Gerald L. Thompson, a remarkably opinionated man well past middle age, carried himself with an air of confident pretentiousness. His mass of thick, silvery hair gave way to a pasty complexion punctuated by piercing blue eyes. It had often been said that to look into the eyes of Judge Gerald L. Thompson was like looking into the eyes of Medusa, whose legendary stare could turn a man to stone. It certainly was a fact that no man felt comfortable keeping eye contact with the judge, whose penetrating stare seemed intent on burning the soul out of anyone displaying even the slightest hint of arrogance or contentious behavior. Judge Gerald L. Thompson was a respected and feared man on both sides of the law.

In the prisoners' box, Segado remained seated in spite of the directive to "rise." His accompanying jailer grabbed him firmly by the upper arm in an attempt to bring his prisoner to a standing position. Segado, still handcuffed, twisted his upper body away forcefully from the grasping officer, encircling both feet around the legs of the chair, successfully thwarting the jailer's intention.

A soft, swishing sound accompanied the judge's stiff, military-like movements as he purposefully strode toward the elevated dais. Taking his chair with great precision and pageantry, he cast an appraising stare out at the audience for all of two seconds before directing his attention to the small pile of paperwork stacked neatly in front of him. An almost imperceptible nod toward the clerk indicated that he was ready to proceed.

"The Honorable Judge Gerald L. Thompson will be presiding over the events today. Be seated," commanded the clerk, shifting his attention back to his orderly stack of labeled file folders.

Everyone sat as they were instructed with the exception of Segado, who chose this moment for a further moment of defiance. Never having stood as demanded by court etiquette, Segado decided instead to now stand in a show of defiance of the "Be seated" directive.

Having been a court officer for almost twelve years, his jailer anticipated this exact response and leaned heavily on Segado's shoulder, forcing him to maintain his seated position. Despite his valiant and strenuous attempt to stand, Segado couldn't overcome the downward pressure exerted by the court officer, thereby ending his failed coup. Having no choice but to remain seated, he looked up over his shoulder with scorn into the face of his oppressor, now displaying a thin-lipped smile that did not extend itself beyond a purely mechanical facial expression.

Judge Thompson was aware of the minor drama occurring to his right but ignored the blatant disrespect. He knew the court officer had the situation under control and the handcuffed prisoner didn't pose a threat to the safety of anyone but himself. But he also knew that he would reward Segado's display of belligerence with a marginally harsher sentence than was warranted. Judge Thompson was a man who was long on memory and short on tolerance, especially when rude or argumentative behavior occurred in his courtroom.

"What do we have today, Pete?" Judge Thompson's voice carried a coarse tone not unlike that of someone who had just arisen from a deep sleep or, in Thompson's case, the result of a forty-year, three-pack-a-day smoking habit.

Peter Masters, the orderly court clerk, approached the bench without looking into the steely blue eyes of the judge carrying several folders of information. He explained each one briefly, handing them off to the judge, who swiftly examined each one with an experienced eye, picking out the most pertinent information.

"We've got *Sweetman v. Sweetman*—she's requesting additional child support," Masters said, handing off that folder to Thompson and producing a second.

"Uhm, *Hollister v. Quinn*...non-payment of child support—"

"Mm-hm."

"*Corfinio v. Corfinio*, reinstatement of visitation—"

"Mm."

"*Segado v. State of Mass*, and *Jankowicz v. Talbot*, 209A."

"Seems like a light load. That it?"

"The rest are defaults, sir."

"Good. If we're lucky, we'll be done with this by noon," said the judge with a tight-lipped smile. "Any preferences, Pete?"

"Yes, Sir. Counsel for Sweetman requested a first hearing because—"

"Fine," Thompson interrupted, not wishing to hear the particulars. Rubbing the palm of his hand over his eyes, he added, "I can't stand that bastard anyway. The sooner he's out of my courtroom, the better I like it."

"Yes, sir," the clerk replied, relieved that he would not have to make apologies to counsel for Sweetman.

"While you're at it, put the visitation case up after Sweetman. I want that one out of the way too. Let's deal with these first and end the day on an easy note." Judge

Thompson leaned on his elbow, cradling his chin in his hand, his forefinger patting his upper lip. He squinted his eyes slightly, furrowing his wrinkled brow as if contemplating some weighty measure and added, "Oh, and uhhh, Pete?"

"Yes, sir?"

"Let's hold *that* one for *last*," the judge said, moving only his eyes in the direction of the prisoners' box where Segado sat involuntarily. "I don't think he's going to miss any appointments."

"Yes, sir," agreed Masters with a smirk as he annoyingly tapped the collection of folders with his pen. "I'm sure his social calendar is empty today."

22

"*Sweetman v. Sweetman!*" the clerk announced, looking toward the audience in a less than concerned manner. Noticing several people standing awkwardly in confusion, he waved them in with a scant hand gesture and a look of annoyance at their unfamiliarity with the process. "Approach the rail," he said in a tone that bordered on disgust. He handed Judge Thompson the appropriate folder and turned back toward the plaintiff and defendant waving impatiently for them to approach the railing.

Judge Thompson gave the contents of the folder a full two minutes of attention, gleaning necessary information with a practiced eye. He then leaned back in the tall leatherette, crossing his arm across his chest and looked to counsel for the plaintiff. "Counselor?"

The plump woman was conservatively and tastefully outfitted, but her finger jewelry indicated her weakness for flashy baubles. Her hands waved about animatedly as she spoke, leading one to wonder if she was showing off her jewels or had a penchant for dramatics. Her energetic gesticulating and flashing trinkets became irrelevant distractions once she began speaking. The tone of her voice sounded like someone with a nasal head cold. Making matters worse, she also suffered from a slight speech impediment, conveying a painful assault upon the eardrums.

"Yes, Your Honor," began the pudgy lawyer, "m-m-my client is seeking an increase in support p-p-payment by the defendant—Mister Sweetman—and with the documentation supplied…" she droned on.

Corfinio watched soundlessly as the words carried across the nearly empty courtroom. He had always been enthralled with the machinations of courtroom proceedings. He had questioned Bari several times about the obvious tediousness of courtroom demeanor, seldom experiencing any outbursts or moments of high tension or drama that he had become familiarized with through Hollywood productions. Bari pointed out that in reality, cases were won and lost through minor points of drab and clinical questions and answers. The difference, Bari explained, was that Hollywood was trying to "sell" something, while in reality, the defendants and plaintiffs were trying to "buy" something. More time, more money, more leniency. Buyers, he claimed, don't need barkers.

Without looking away from the proceedings, Corfinio leaned toward his lawyer and whispered, "Why does she want more money? If she can afford a lawyer with a fist full of knuckle-busting rings like those, she must have a nice little nest egg already."

"Doesn't matter," replied Bari. "The state says she's entitled to 28 percent of his income for child support. It's pretty cut and dry."

"Then what are they here for?" Corfinio questioned. "What's she looking for, a Christmas bonus? She probably already has the house, the car, the kids, *and* a pipeline to his bank account."

"You have an awful lot of strong opinions there, John," said Bari, giving his client a sidelong glance. "It *could* be that Mister Sweetman there is paying substantially *less* than he should. Has *that* ever occurred to you?"

The monotonous tone of Mrs. Sweetman's lawyer slogged on, continuously highlighting that her ex-husband's income was well in excess of half-a-million dollars a year. Without changing the tone or pitch of her laborious vocal patterns, she cited that the current payment status was far from accurate and requested that it be taken in consideration for reassessment.

The judge casually flipped through the paperwork on his desk, assuming a detached look of concern resting his chin on a fisted hand. Without changing the position of his head, he shifted his penetrating gaze toward the well-dressed lawyer of Mister Sweetman. "Arguments?" The single word resounded with authority, delivered more as a demand rather than as a request for counsel for the defendant to take the floor.

The judge's unnerving demeanor was not lost on Corfinio. "Tell me *this* guy doesn't have a control problem! About the only thing he *hasn't* done is jump up and yell 'I am the law!'" Corfinio mimicked the judge's rasping voice, contorting his facial expression into that of a madman.

Against his better judgment, Bari let a stifled laugh escape. His broad shoulders shook as he tried unsuccessfully to cover the laughter with a cough. He bowed his head down and pinched the bridge of his nose as the moment overtook him. "Yeah, really," he said between coughs continuing with his own mimicry, "you will present your arguments *now!*"

Corfinio and Bari were startled when a voice from behind them sounded. "You guys want to keep it down?"

Looking over his right shoulder toward the cause of the sudden intervention, Corfinio sobered immediately. Staring down at him was the pockmarked face of the court officer, James McCorken, whom he had met briefly in the men's room.

"*You!*" snorted an equally surprised McCorken, recognizing Corfinio from their earlier confrontation. "I already warned you once today, you'd do well to keep your trap shut while you're in here." McCorken tugged at his sagging beltline and glared at Corfinio. "Got it?"

Corfinio turned on the narrow bench and faced the pig-faced court officer, snapping a mock salute from the brow. "*Javol*, Herr Capitan!"

"Smartass," McCorken growled, backing away from the bench to resume his position to the left of the entry door.

"What was *that* all about?" Bari asked in a barely audible whisper looking down at his lap. "Do you *know* that guy?"

"Yeah," Corfinio replied, slowly turning to face his lawyer. "He was one of the models at the Beauty Academy. He's pissed off at me because I accidentally gave him a facial with muriatic acid."

"What's with the attitude?"

"His or mine?"

"*His*, you blithering idiot!" Bari hissed between clenched teeth.

"Who can say?" replied Corfinio in a childlike manner. "Maybe he's just jealous of my manly good looks and effervescent personality."

"And you're sure you've never had a run-in with this guy before? Because it sure sounded like he'd met you at an earlier occasion."

"Nope. Never saw him before today."

"You're *sure?*" Bari persisted, instinctively knowing that there was more to the story than Corfinio was letting on.

"Absolutely," Corfinio said, emphasizing his answer with a quick nod. "I *swear*, I have *never* laid eyes on that repulsive excuse for a human being before today. That's the truth."

Bari still wasn't buying into it. "You'll of *course* forgive me if I tend to somewhat doubt the credibility of *your* account, based on the many instances of your convoluted versions of truth that I've had to sort through in the past."

Corfinio pantomimed a hurt look, placing his right hand on his chest, allowing his lower jaw to drop in equally feigned shock.

"Oh, don't hand me that crap, John. I *know* there's more than what you're telling me." Bari decided not to pursue the issue, knowing full well that he wasn't going to get anything more out of him. He sat back and ran his fingers through his thick mass of hair and sighed heavily, growing slightly agitated about the length of time it was taking for the judge to make a decision on the Sweetman case.

"Hey, Arthur!" gasped Corfinio, elbow-nudging his lawyer several times. He sat forward leaning on the bench backrest, squinting a little as if trying to focus on something he was not quite sure of, his brows furrowed. "Look at the judge for a minute...who does he look like? Who does he remind you of?"

Bari stuttered, bewildered, "I-I don't know, John… who?" He rolled his eyes skyward, anticipating nothing more than a nonsensical response.

"*Look* at him!" Corfinio insisted, visibly excited. "Somebody famous. Somebody you *know*."

"John, I don't know."

"*Yes*, you do! Come on, *guess*!"

"Oh, sweet Jesus," Bari mumbled. "Uhhh, Judge Wapner?"

"*What*? Seriously? He doesn't look *any*thing like Wapner! Are you even *looking* at him? Someone *more* famous."

"Uhm, Ronnie Cox?"

"*More* famous," he whispered harshly.

"I don't…pshhh! *John!* I don't have a *clue*."

"Fast Eddie Felson," Corfinio said with deliberate satisfaction. "Paul Newman."

Bari studied the judge for several seconds. "Wow… you're *right*," he agreed in sudden realization. "He *does* look a little like Paul Newman!"

"How do you like *that*?" he exclaimed triumphantly. "Fast Eddie! Butch Cassidy! Cool Hand Luke! No *shit!* This is *sooo* cool!"

23

While Bari and Corfinio were engrossed in deep debate over Judge Thompson's Paul Newman-like countenance, "Mr. Slick" was making arguments on behalf of Mister Sweetman.

"So you see, Your Honor, the amount of income can't be taken at face value. The amount, while correct, is a reflection of gross income *before* taxes and liabilities have been assessed against that total. In order to ascertain an accurate account of net income, these liabilities must be deducted, reducing the amount to a more appropriate net income. I have supplied the court with the paperwork reflecting an accurate accounting along with Mister Sweetman's 1090 Form from the previous year. I—"

"Hold on, Counselor," the judge interrupted, his left hand held palm outward. "Pete, do I have that here?" he asked Masters.

As the tidy court clerk scurried to approach the judge's bench, Bari nudged Corfinio and whispered, "Looks like *Slick* is making some headway." He continued speaking in low tones after the warning issued by Officer McCorken. He had no intention of attracting further attention from the already irritated court officer.

"Hm? What do you mean?" asked Corfinio, shaken from his stargazing reverie.

"*Slick* there," he said, tipping his head in the direction of the attorney, "is pointing out that Sweetman's income is the result of a DBA. It's not a personal net."

"So what does that mean?"

"It means he's probably taking home a hundred and fifty, two hundred K max. His support will be assessed on that total instead of the half a mil that they cited."

"Soooo…what does that work out to?"

"Mmm, somewhere around seven, eight bills a week."

Corfinio's eyes rounded in genuine surprise as he slowly turned his head toward his lawyer. "For *child* support?"

"Yup. That's the way it works," Bari stated flatly, reaching up to squeeze the bridge of his nose.

Corfinio sat silent for several moments. "You know, I could *be* that man's son…for only…say, *four hundred* a week."

"There's only one problem with that, John."

"What's that?"

"Once he got to know you, he wouldn't want *you* for a son if you paid *him* four hundred a week. Besides, I don't think he'd want a forty-two-year-old son."

"Are you kidding me? There's a *definite* advantage to having a forty-two-year-old son! No diapers to change, no bed wetting, no bad report cards, and I can cook for myself. What's not to love? It's a definite plus."

Bari leaned back against the bench, squeezed his eyes shut, and reached up to pinch the bridge of his nose again. "Yeah," he sighed, "but there's always a mess to clean up after you, John. There's *always* a mess."

The sound of the judge's voice halted Corfinio's intended response.

Judge Thompson's graveled baritone voice carried clearly in the quiet courtroom. "Based on this information, I don't see any reason to increase the amount of support due. However…" his voice trailed off.

"What did he say?" Corfinio asked, straining to hear the judge's explanation.

"I didn't hear him," Bari replied, shrugging his massive shoulders.

The next intelligible comment they heard was that of Mr. Slick thanking the judge.

"Well, apparently," Bari said with a satisfactory sigh, "Slick will make his tee time. Which is more than I can say for us. We'll probably be here for the next two hours."

As the Sweetmans and their respective attorneys filed past Bari and Corfinio's bench, the court clerk Pete Masters immersed himself in stacking and shuffling items on his desktop. After sixty seconds of tiresome and exacting deliberation, he selected a folder. Facing toward the uncrowded audience, looking down at the folder held in his hand, he read off the names with considerable difficulty. "Cor-Corn-Cornfa-nif-ee-oh? *Cornfanero v. Cornfanero*," he said in final resignation, eliciting an exaggerated eye roll from Corfinio.

"*Oh God!* Could he have screwed it up any worse? It's not that difficult a name to say," Corfinio complained to his lawyer, who groaned in reply.

"Come on, that's us, no matter how bad the enunciation," Bari said, rising off the bench. "I guess we got lucky, Mister *Cornfanero*. Looks like we won't be here all day after all."

"Yeah," Corfinio said, suddenly feeling very tense, exhaling a deep breath. "Lucky us. Time to 'go to the chair.'"

Stopping as he was exiting the bench, Bari glanced over his glasses at his client's remark and looked inquiringly at Corfinio.

"What?" Corfinio asked, seeing the puzzled look on Bari's face.

"Time to go to the chair? What's *that* supposed to mean?"

Corfinio presented a weak grin. "That's what they call it in jail. When it's your turn to go up before the judge, it's called 'going to the chair.'"

"Hmm," Bari grunted, "how quaint."

Ahead of them, they could see Marsha Corfinio rising from her bench, accompanied by her overattentive lawyer. The court clerk noticed both parties in movement and waved them forward. "Approach the rail." Turning away from the involved parties, he placed the folder squarely in the center of Judge Thompson's desk.

Judge Thompson was slouched back casually in his leather chair. Extending his right arm, flipping the sleeve of his gown over the edge of the desk, he grasped the manila folder. He opened the cover and perused the contents, quickly scanning down each page, gleaning necessary information. After completing the task, he placed the folder down on the desktop, leaned forward and addressed his court clerk. "Pete, there's a note in here that says Mrs. Avery from Family Services wants to be present at the hearing. Call down for her, will you?"

Masters stumbled over himself in an effort to expedite the judge's request. Snapping up the receiver of the phone that sat on the upper left-hand corner of his neat and concise tabletop, he dialed one number that would access the Family Service Office located off the courthouse lobby. Speaking clearly enough to be heard by the contingents of the Corfinio hearing, he spoke with deliberation and not without his usual smug indifference while addressing someone he considered to be his inferior.

"Mrs. Avery? Judge Thompson has advised me to inform you that the Corfinio hearing is now at hand. Would you please come to Courtroom 5?" Without waiting for a response, Pete Masters hung up the phone and turned to face the judge. "She's on her way, sir."

Corfinio bent sideways from the hip, hands clasped in front of him, leaning toward Arthur Bari and whispered, "What is *she* coming here for?"

The burly lawyer shrugged. "I don't know for sure yet, but it's not unusual for the judge to ask for Family Services to give recommendation regarding child visitation. We'll know for sure which way she's leaning when she gets here." Casting a suspicious glance at Marsha, Corfinio's lawyer revealed a smug half-grin on his face. Bari knew that look. He had seen it before, usually when one side had a piece of unshared information that would be critical to the judge's decision. A twist in the pit of his stomach amplified the suspicion that they were about to be sandbagged. He wisely decided not to share this trepidation with his client, instead saying, "Let's just wait and see."

"Great," Corfinio whispered back, never releasing the eye hold he had on the rumpled carpeting, "just what I need...more anxiety."

Judge Thompson leaned back in his chair, locking his hands together on the crown of his head. "Why don't you relax for a moment?" the judge said to the ceiling, slowly shifting his gaze downward toward the assembled parties. "I've sent down for Mrs. Avery from the Department of Family Services. She expressed an interest in being present."

"*Avery?*" Corfinio whispered to his lawyer. "Isn't she the one that I talked to before, from last year? I think it is…yeah, I'm sure of it. That was her name, Avery. She's the one who endorsed visitation for me. This is good, right?"

"A lot has happened since then," Bari warned. "Don't get your hopes up. Let's wait and see what she has to say."

"Y'know," Corfinio said disparagingly, "you *really* need to work on your 'supportive' role."

While Corfinio uncomfortably shifted from one foot to the other, he glanced nervously around the courtroom. To the far right, parallel to the judge's bench, Segado sat handcuffed in the prisoners' box with his attendant blue-uniformed police officer. To Corfinio's immediate left stood his ex-wife's lawyer, David Goldman, a heavyset, balding man fast approaching middle age, exuding an air of competence and arrogance, and to his left, Marsha Corfinio.

Although David Goldman was representing his ex-wife, it was Marsha Corfinio whom he feared. He had been married to her and discovered through many prior events that she had a penchant—an absolute *talent*—for exaggeration and drama when it suited her. He had long suspected that she harbored an undiagnosed case of either bipolar disorder or a mild form of schizophrenia. She could be flying high and happy one moment and then instantaneously change into a raging, screaming psycho-path because he didn't answer the way she expected him to. It was like being on a round-trip roller-coaster ride from hell. He never knew which version of her would greet him when he arrived home from work each day.

Looking over his shoulder, five other people were seated in the audience benches. Standing at the entry door, Officer James McCorken was engaged in conver-sation with another court officer Corfinio had not pre-viously noticed. An irritating tapping sound drew his attention to the desk of Pete Masters, who stood hov-ering over his neat piles of manila file folders, flipping a pencil between his middle and index fingers on the wood desktop.

"Hey," Corfinio leaned slightly forward, looking around Bari to get the attention of Masters, "you pro-nounced my name wrong."

"Excuse me?" Masters looked up from his desk, surprised at the unexpected intrusion on his vacuous thoughts.

"You said 'Cornfanero.' It's *Corfinio*."

"Let it *go*, John," Bari whispered loudly, stepping forward a half step to block Corfinio.

Corfinio leaned back and looked around the back side of his lawyer and continued his spiel. "'Core,' like apple *core*, 'fee' like a price you pay—"

"*Shut up, John!*" Bari growled barely above a whisper.

"'Nee' like the joint in the middle of your leg, and 'o' like the fifteenth letter of the alphabet. Cor-fi-ni-o. *Corfinio.*" He smiled at Masters, who stood staring in absolute disbelief of the audacity displayed. "Just trying to help you with your pronunciation there, Mr. *Mustard.*"

Pete Masters didn't respond to Corfinio except to glare at him with unabated animosity. He didn't take well to being corrected, especially by the likes of court clientele. He made no secret that he felt most of them were hardly better than the dregs of society and, in most cases, treated them as such.

Bari also scowled at him with clenched jaw, barely moving his lips. "Would you *please* just *shut up!*"

Corfinio looked at his lawyer standing rigidly with eyes opened wide, directing his incensed glare in hopes of silencing his client through pure willpower. Corfinio retaliated by staring back and opening his eyes as wide as he could in parody. Bari turned away and sighed in exasperation.

Corfinio exhaled noisily and resumed his uncomfortable stance, waiting impatiently for the arrival of Estelle Avery. Looking up at the clock, he swore that it hadn't moved at all, or at least it felt that way. He reached up and fumbled with the tie knot at his throat, feeling restricted and anxious with anticipation. As he tugged at the necktie, a bead of sweat rolled down the center of his back, causing him to hunch forward slightly, forcing the white cotton shirt against his flesh to absorb the tickle that caused him to involuntarily shiver.

Large cast-iron radiators lined against the walls hissed in contempt at the prolonged delay. The suspended fluorescent light tubes continued to buzz annoyingly overhead as if to draw attention to the fact that they were incapable of supplying the room with even an adequate amount of light. Though the courtroom was large, it had a distinct tomblike quality. Perhaps it was because it lacked ventilating windows—or any windows at all—that gave it a quality of suffocating enclosure.

Everything about this place, Corfinio scowled silently, *screams gloom and doom.*

The courtroom doors creaked open to allow Estelle Avery access. She paused momentarily, holding the door open with her right hand while another woman entered behind her. Both women approached the rail wordlessly and took positions to the far left of Marsha Corfinio and her attending lawyer.

Corfinio recognized Avery immediately. She had interviewed him over a year ago when he had initially requested visitation. He felt that her positive recommendation to the court for visitation may have been the deciding factor for the judge allowing that to occur. He breathed a small sigh of relief seeing someone who would hopefully be in his corner. The way things had gone up to this point, he felt he needed all the help he could get.

Avery's hair was pulled back into a severe knot, in contrast to her loose-fitting blouse and sweater. In her capacity as a Family Services interviewer for the courts, her job was to ascertain the likelihood of filed allegations as being true by each of the involved parties and supply a recommendation to the court. She once remarked that her job was not unlike that of a kindergarten teacher, trying to segment wild fantasy from actual fact during a vilification process. The only difference, she claimed, was that children—unlike the adults she was forced to contend with—tended toward using actual elements of the truth from time to time.

Judge Thompson removed his hands from his head, leaned forward, and flipped both sleeves of his gown with a swift twisting motion of his arms. "Let's begin," he commanded. "Mrs. Avery." He made a nodded salutation with his flat gravely monotone, shifting his position to face the small group of people on his right.

"Judge Thompson," she replied just as succinctly, "I—"

"Excuse me, Mrs. Avery," Thompson interjected. Redirecting his penetrating gaze toward the woman accompanying Estelle Avery, he asked, "And *you* are?"

Adjusting her eyeglasses with an air of confidence, the blond, thirtyish woman dressed in a business suit and large rimmed glasses met the judge's stare with an iciness of her own that clearly indicated that she would not be intimidated by Judge Thompson's attitude or reputation.

"Donna LaTrina, Your Honor." She spoke clearly, precisely, and not without a liberal dose of superiority. "I'm the head coordinator for Family Counseling at the DSS Center that handled the allegations of abuse on behalf of the minor child, Michael Corfinio. I'm here at the request of Mr. Goldman to make recommendations for the continued revocation of visitation."

"Unbelievable," Bari mumbled, closing his eyes, slowly shaking his head from side to side. "Unbelievable."

"Weeell," drawled Judge Thompson, sitting forward, leaning on his crossed arms resting on the bench. "Why don't you just hold tight for a moment, Miss… *LaTrina?*" he asked, pronouncing it correctly. "I'll get to you in a moment. Mrs. Avery, what have you got to report?"

"Your Honor, I have met with each of the parties at length, and my recommendation at this time"—she paused—"is to recommend that visitation be reinstated. In my estimation, Mr. Corfinio poses no threat to the safety of the child, and I have considerable doubt as to the validity of the allegations, again, based on my assessments of the personalities during the interview process. It is my opinion that a permanent visitation schedule be instituted by the court allowing Mr. Corfinio a definitive schedule to follow. I don't think that, left alone, the two parties can agree to a schedule that would be 'supported' by either side."

Judge Thompson nodded, pursing his lips. "Thank you, Mrs. Avery." Then with a barely noticed grimace, he shifted his line of sight to Marsha Corfinio's lawyer. "Mr. Goldman?"

"Yes, Your Honor. Uhh, we are requesting that visitation *not* be reinstated because of the extremely volatile nature of Mr. Corfinio. The minor child has been through countless hours of counseling, and it is their opinion as well that any form of visitation should be revoked. A *complete* revocation of visitation, Your Honor, because Mr. Corfinio's destructive and abusive temperament can only result in situations that would be conducive to a compromise of the child's safety.

"As documented by *this* report—which I believe Your Honor has—the Visiting Center indicates that on the last visit involving Mr. Corfinio and the minor child…on March 9, an altercation evolved, which resulted in an injury *to* the minor child, instituted *by* Mr. Corfinio."

Goldman instituted arm waving and stabbing motions toward the documentation to insure the severity of his argument. At each sentence, he leaned forward on his toes to emphasize further points, augmenting his speech with emphasis on selected verbiage.

"*Earlier* documentation—in a complaint filed by Mrs. Corfinio with the police department—indicates that Mr. Corfinio had struck the child on several occasions as witnessed by Mrs. Corfinio. These actions resulted in Mrs. Corfinio filing an order of restraint at the suggestion of the police department against her husband on behalf of the minor child.

"A mode of visitation had been instituted by the court after a motion had been brought to bear to allow visits and nullify the order of restraint. The visitation allowed for one-hour visits at the child's home, monitored closely by Mrs. Corfinio herself, in which Mr. Corfinio could visit the minor child in a safe environment.

"During one of the visits, Mr. Corfinio *struck* the child once again in a moment of frenzy and was immediately expelled from the premises. Fearing for the safety of her child and herself as well due to the abusive nature of Mr. Corfinio, a subsequent order of restraint was issued against Mr. Corfinio.

"One week after that incident, in *spite* of the warnings issued against proposed visits, in an act of *pure defiance*, Mr. Corfinio attempted contact once *again*. This led to his immediate arrest and subsequent term of sentence.

"Since that time, Your Honor, the child has been complaining of bad dreams in which he states that his father is chasing him and trying to hit him repeatedly. The child has *no* desire to see his father and is, quite frankly, in fear each time his father's name is even *mentioned*. *Any* contact with Mr. Corfinio at this time is repulsive to the child, and he has stated on several occasions that his father is mean and calls him names.

"Therefore, Your Honor, for the continued safety of the child, we request that a 'no visit, no contact' order be instituted and remain in place...for the *safety* of the child."

Judge Thompson grunted as Goldman completed his well-rehearsed diatribe against the defendant. Sitting forward, scanning the contents of the folder displayed on the bench, he pointed a lanky finger at the attorney and asked, "Is there an order of restraint in effect at this time, Counselor?"

"Uhh, yes, there *is*, Your Honor," Goldman replied, effecting a rolling finger wave while adding, "which we are requesting the court to—"

"Reign it in, Mr. Goldman," Judge Thompson interrupted, leaving Goldman's rolling finger suspended in midair. "You've made your point."

"Yes, Your Honor, but—"

Goldman had stopped midsentence when Judge Thompson directed a baneful stare in his direction. Goldman felt his blood thin as the icy-blue eyes bored into his own.

"I said, that will be *enough*, Goldman." The words were spoken in a barely audible whisper, but they carried to the far corners of the courtroom. Segado was nudged heavily by his armed keeper when a snicker escaped him.

In order to stifle a like response, Corfinio cleared his throat, keeping his head pointing down toward the floor.

"Miss LaTrina," Thompson said, lazily looking toward the young blonde woman, "you have something to report as well?"

"Yes, Your Honor," she said carefully but without sign of intimidation. "The Department of Social Services has had cause to interview Mr. Corfinio on two separate occasions.

"The first occurred after the initial report of abuse was filed by Mrs. Corfinio two years ago. The DSS investigation supported those claims of abuse based on documentation supplied by Mrs. Corfinio—who was witness to the abuse—the child's pediatrician, recommending that visitation be suspended, and the DSS interviewer.

"The second abuse charge was also supported by DSS based on the reports filed by the Visiting Center's monitor, who was present at the time of the incident, which led to the second restraining order against Mr. Corfinio. During one of the monitored visits, Mr. Corfinio apparently had become enraged with the child and struck him in the head, causing an immediate cessation of visit and the removal of Mr. Corfinio from the visiting program.

"During each interview conducted by DSS investigating the charges of abuse against Mr. Corfinio, we have found Mr. Corfinio to be somewhat volatile in nature and a potential danger to the welfare of the child.

While he has not admitted to striking the child, he has indicated that should the occasion call for a mode of punishment, striking the child—in his opinion—is entirely suitable.

"We feel that this is 'bad parenting,' and until Mr. Corfinio is educated in better parenting and enrolled in an anger management class, we recommend that he be restrained from further visits."

Looking somewhat bored with the proceedings, the judge raised his head from the paperwork, passed a glance toward LaTrina, mumbling a statement of thanks for her report.

"Thank you, Miss… *LaTrina*. Okaaaay," he drawled, scribbling notations, "Counselor?" He nodded in the direction of Arthur Bari.

"Your Honor." Bari spoke the words as a definitive statement rather than as an address. "I would like to respond to Mr. Goldman's statements, starting with the most recent concerning the latest issuance of an order of restraint, which was apparently issued by the court but *never* served upon my client. I only discovered this morning in speaking to Mr. Goldman that we had been *sandbagged* with yet *another* restraining order.

"First, the timeline of his accrued information is non-sequential.

"Secondly, regarding the events occurring at her home where she alleges that my client struck the child, there were *no* filed police reports of this nature nor were there *any* medical records indicating any sign of physical abuse to the child. There was also *no* court-ordered monitor *during* the visit to either support or deny Mrs. Corfinio's claim. If my client posed *such* a formidable threat, then why weren't charges of neglect filed against Mrs. Corfinio by DSS for placing the child in a hostile environment? And yet my client was assumed guilty of violating a restraining order that had, in fact, *never* been served and in itself was suspect in its preparation by having been *obviously modified*, leading to my client's first incarceration period without benefit of arrest or set bail.

"Third point, the so-called documented visit at the Visiting Center was the *last* incident that led to Mr. Corfinio's secondary and—I'd like to add—*totally unjustified* incarceration period. The 'altercation' Mr. Goldman refers to was reported by the visit supervisor, who by her own *admission* stated that father and son had been involved in *playing*. There was *never* any subsequent investigation of the incident, and my client was *never* questioned as to his version of the event.

"The letter offered by Dr. Ray Stinger suggesting revocation of contact should also be considered nothing more than hearsay based on the fact that *all* of the information supplied to him was volunteered *by Mrs. Corfinio*. His decision was *not* the result of his own investigation or assessment, *nor* does he indicate at *any* point prior that he has noted or observed *any* form of abuse—*psychological or physical*—to the child."

Bari paused, taking a breath, knowing he was becoming more agitated but desperately trying not to come across as overly aggressive or dismissive of the severity of the situation.

Judge Thompson appeared unruffled at the rising level of sentiment, now leaning on his hand with thumb under chin and forefinger sitting high on his cheek. He may have appeared composed, but he was weighing everything carefully, noting the several discrepancies in declared information.

Thompson spread out the paperwork on his desk calmly with his off hand while still leaning on the other. His steely blue eyes shifted from the paperwork to Bari. "Has he completed the required parenting and anger management classes?" he asked Bari directly then looked over toward Corfinio briefly.

"Yes, I—" Corfinio started to answer.

"*Yes,* Your Honor," Bari quickly interjected, drowning out Corfinio's reply, "he *has* completed parenting classes"—Bari paused apprehensively—"but he has not completed the anger management class."

"Why not?" Thompson asked calmly, not removing his hand from his face, redirecting his attention to Corfinio.

Corfinio drew in a deep breath, but before he could answer, Bari cut him off again. "*Your Honor,* during the initial session of the anger management class, an admission of guilt is considered *mandatory* in order to begin the 'healing process' of managing abusive behavior, whereas my client has *always* maintained his innocence in that regard. Admitting guilt in the program would be inconsistent with his 'not guilty' plea in court."

Bari held his breath, knowing full well that the judge could stop the proceedings and demand that Corfinio comply with the former court-ordered anger management program before moving forward.

Judge Thompson sat silently, staring at Bari for several seconds. As if in slow motion, he removed his hand from his chin and nodded almost furtively. "Okay... I'll allow it."

Bari stifled a sigh of relief, while an irritated out-breath emanated from DSS agent LaTrina, making the victorious moment all the sweeter.

"If I may, Your Honor, one last point."

"Go on."

"My client has complied with all requirements and demands of the court, including parenting classes, supervised visitation, probation and child support, and *has also* complied with *several* requests for interview by DSS and Family Services. These programs were also understood to be compulsory for *Mrs*. Corfinio *as well*, including parenting classes, which she *blatantly* blew off as not necessary, stating that she did not require parenting classes. *Additionally*, she violated visiting procedure several times, *including* withholding visits during ordered timeframes. It has been noted from the Visiting Center that she did not fully comply with the set arrangement so ordered by the court. If my client had taken that position, he would have been held in contempt of court. We feel it only fair to request that Mrs. Corfinio be held in contempt of court on these issues and held accountable, otherwise it's as if she thumbs her nose at the court saying, 'Na-na-na, na-na, naa!'"

Upon hearing the playground taunt issued by his lawyer, Corfinio bowed his head, raising a hand to his mouth in an attempt to disguise his stifled laughter with a phony cough. Almost immediately, a secondary and more disquieting thought struck him. He thought, *Oh crap! What if the judge finds that remark disrespectful or inappropriate?* He quickly stole a glance in the direction of Judge Thompson, fearfully anticipating a scolding retort at Bari's remark.

Thompson seemed oblivious to the comment, never raising an eyebrow or showing any sign of distraction as he scanned several pages on his desk. Instead, he turned to address Goldman. "Is that true, Counselor? Your client hasn't completed any of the programs indicated as suggested?"

Goldman was completely taken off guard by Thompson's query, rather expecting an admonishment to his adversary for the audacious "na-na" comment.

"Your Honor," he began, searching for an explanation that would appease Thompson, "a parenting class would be a redundancy, as she has been engaged in parenting since the birth of the child. Up until this moment, no one has ever questioned her integrity as a capable mother nor has she been deemed to be an inappropriate parent by any of the agencies. Additionally, Your Honor, she is the legal custodial parent and is averse to leaving him in any child care facility for reasons of safety and financial restrictions."

Thompson frowned. "That's pretty weak, Counselor. Being a parent doesn't automatically instill the ability to be a good one. I shouldn't have to be the one to point that out to you." Redirecting his attention to Marsha Corfinio, he continued, "You are to enroll in a parenting class. Mrs. Avery"—he paused, identifying her with a nod—"will be kind enough to supply you with a list of locations that offer those services. Understood?"

Marsha Corfinio stiffened, a look of surprise evident on her cosmetically enhanced features. "But I...no, I don't understand! I—"

Thompson cut her off quickly. "I don't care. You have thirty days to sign up for classes, otherwise this court will find you in contempt."

Corfinio couldn't help himself, a sneaky half-smile forming at his ex-wife's reprimand.

"Mr. Corfinio," Thompson began, shifting his attention once again, "while Mrs. Avery has advocated strongly for resumption of visitation, it would appear there are a host of others that do not share her confidence in your ability to maintain a stable profile. The

Visiting Center report states that you struck the child, as does the initial police report."

"Your Honor—" Corfinio attempted to interject, but Thompson ignored the interruption and continued on.

"You have been in violation of two restraining orders, and the Department of Social Services states repeatedly that you have been argumentative and confrontational during their interviews. It would appear your comportment leaves much to be desired, so if I must err, Mr. Corfinio, I must err on the side of caution, and for that reason, I am denying the reinstatement of visitation until such time that the court feels you have made sufficient progress to be entrusted with the care and safety of the minor child. That will be all."

24

Corfinio stood rooted to the floor, staring blankly at the judge. He felt a twisting in his gut that threatened to empty the contents of his stomach. His leaden legs were in direct conflict with the swimming feeling of light-headedness, but his building rage was all-consuming.

"No!" he finally blurted out between gritted teeth. "No, Your Honor, *no*, that *can't* be all! You can't *do* this!"

"*John!*" Bari urged desperately, grabbing him by the arm. "*Stop*," he pleaded. "Come *on*, let's go!"

"*Let go of me!*" Corfinio said savagely, pulling away from Bari's grip. "*Judge…*"

Thompson stared emotionlessly down at Corfinio. "I said that will be *all*, Mr. Corfinio." With a condescending wave of his hand, Thompson turned away and motioned to the court clerk, Pete Masters, for the next case.

"*Why are you doing this?*" Corfinio took a step toward the judge's bench, raising his voice accusingly. "I don't deserve this!"

"John! *Stop!*" Bari demanded, again tugging at his arm. "Have you lost your mind? Come on! *Stop!*"

"*Mr. Corfinio!*" Thompson reprimanded. "*Officer!*" he shouted, pointing toward Officer McCorken standing by the courtroom double doors. "*Get him out of here!*"

"I did everything I was supposed to do!" Corfinio's voice grew louder and angrier, shoving an arm in the direction of his ex-wife and Goldman. "*They lie*, and *I'm* the one who *pays the price?* What kind of kangaroo court *is* this?"

"John! For Christ's sake! *Stop!*" Bari pleaded in vain, trying desperately to get Corfinio to discontinue his rant but was instead rewarded with a forceful shove from his enraged client.

Estelle Avery, Donna LaTrina, Stephen Goldman, and Marsha Corfinio were all in a genuine state of shock at the sudden turn of events, clustering together like cattle in a rainstorm, mesmerized by the developing commotion.

Felix Segado sat in his chair, mildly amused by the turn of events and chuckled, adding Spanish invectives to the growing discordance. He was rewarded immediately with a sharp jab in the side by the accompanying officer, which only elicited further verbal abuses directed at the cause of his pain.

Officer McCorken smiled evilly as he quickly approached the front of the courtroom drawing near the two men. Pushing Bari out of the way, McCorken took firm hold of Corfinio's arm as he continued his verbal assault on Thompson, whose face had become a crimson mask of fury.

"Officer! Remove this *maniac*!" Thompson demanded, abruptly standing while pointing an accusing finger at Corfinio.

"*You* should be removed! *Not* me!" Corfinio bellowed at the judge. "You *blew it! It's all there in front of you*—" He was cut short by the wincing pain in his shoulder as McCorken twisted his left arm up behind his back.

With an obvious and vicious pleasure, McCorken savagely increased the pressure on Corfinio's arm while attempting to turn him toward the exit doors. In an effort to decrease the cause of the painful restraint, Corfinio turned his left shoulder toward McCorken, but at the same moment, McCorken shoved his knee into the back of Corfinio's legs, causing him to buckle. Corfinio went down on his right knee, head turned slightly to his left, and saw that McCorken was reaching for his nightstick.

In those fleeting moments, everything suddenly seemed to move in slow motion, where every movement was like a single frame of celluloid, made all the more relevant by the crystal-clear resolution of reality. His heartbeat did not quicken. There was no sudden rush of adrenaline; everything simply "happened" as if by second nature without conscious thought or threat of panic. The fight-or-flight response to the situation was an instantaneous and uncontrollable physiological reaction. The warrior mindset permeated his entire being as "fight" mode took control.

As McCorken's left hand pulled the ebon polycarbonate club free from his hip, Corfinio's right hand instinctively reached into his suit jacket pocket. In one fluid motion, he twisted to his right, bringing his right hand up, now gripping the plastic pistol as McCorken raised his arm with full intention of bringing the bat down on Corfinio's unprotected head. McCorken froze, night stick held high above his head as Corfinio jammed the plastic pistol deep into the soft, pulpy flesh of his exposed throat. Several panicked screams came from somewhere behind them, but neither man was aware of anything except their own drama being played out only yards from the judges' bench. Both men shared an instant vile hatred for the other while locked in an unblinking dead-eyed glare.

Corfinio spoke in a whisper, his voice raspy. "Drop it. Drop the bat."

"Fuck you."

Corfinio shoved the gun deeper into McCorken's throat, causing him to gag reflexively. "You ain't Ted Williams, and I'm not a surgeon. Drop the bat, and I won't give you a tracheotomy."

McCorken face was flushed bright red from the rush of adrenaline, his arm noticeably trembling from its lofty position above his head. A bead of sweat crawled agonizingly from his temple down the side of his cheek.

"Slow," Corfinio instructed.

McCorken brought it down slowly, dropping the baton when his arm was at full extension to his body. Corfinio kept the gun pressed up into McCorken's throat, hoping that the fat man wouldn't realize that the weapon was a plastic toy. Considering the position he was in, it was unlikely he'd be giving that any consideration at all.

"Good. Now drop the belt."

Judge Thompson's graveled voice interrupted the tense drama. "You're done for, Corfinio, do you hear me? *Done for!*" Turning toward Segado's jailer, he shouted, "Are you going to just *stand there* like a toy soldier, or are you going to *do* something?"

Corfinio never broke eye contact with McCorken, ignoring Thompson's interruption. He instinctively knew the other officer wouldn't do anything at all while Corfinio had a gun to McCorken's throat. Corfinio jiggled the gun in McCorken's throat. "Go ahead...drop the belt."

McCorken slowly pulled the belt flap back, disengaging the buckle, and let the belt slide carefully to the floor. Corfinio reached over slowly and dragged the belt toward him. He unclasped the lock on the holster with his left hand, allowing the Glock to pull free. He made sure McCorken saw him flip the safety off as he raised the weapon, backing away slowly, lowering the plastic gun from his throat. McCorken was now standing between Corfinio and Segado's police escort.

Corfinio kept the Glock pointed at McCorken and motioned with the plastic gun toward the tactical belt lying on the floor between them. "Cuffs."

McCorken breathed heavily from the exertion of the failed attempt to restrain Corfinio and was sweating profusely. Bending over slowly with difficulty because of his girth, he unsnapped the buttoned leather loop that held the metal-hinged handcuffs.

"Both sets," Corfinio commanded, again motioning with the plastic gun. The second set of handcuffs were in a flap pocket secured to the belt. McCorken flipped open the flap and removed the second set of cuffs. Corfinio stuck the plastic gun in his waistband and held out his left hand, issuing curt instructions. "Give me one. Put the other one on."

"I'm gonna break every bone in your goddamned body."

"You ain't gonna do jack *shit*, fat boy. Put them on."

McCorken took the hinged handcuff and deftly attached it to his left wrist.

"Stop," Corfinio ordered. "Turn around." McCorken turned his back to Corfinio, facing the prisoners' holding area, where Segado and his escort sat and stood respectively behind a low railing. "Spread your legs apart and lean forward." He watched him carefully as McCorken opened his stance and leaned forward slightly.

"Right hand," Corfinio demanded, knowing full well that this position put McCorken at a major disadvantage, now being posed totally off balance. If McCorken tried any heroics at this point, he'd fall flat on his face. He sincerely doubted that McCorken would attempt any show of bravery; the man just didn't have it in him. McCorken was a lot of bluster and braggadocio when he was in control, but when the tables were turned, he was nothing more than a bully with no balls. Like now.

Corfinio clamped the remaining cuff on McCorken's wrist after threading the single metal strand through the rear belt loop. He squeezed the cuff until he heard the single strand teeth engage with a *tk-tk-tk* that blurred into one sound.

Segado's police escort moved slightly sideways in micro steps, trying to get directly behind McCorken's bulk to conceal his movements. Under ordinary circumstances, he was never to leave his prisoner unguarded or left alone for any reason even if he needed to use the bathroom, but this situation couldn't even remotely be considered "ordinary circumstances." He thought if he could get in a position where his movements were shielded from Corfinio's view, he might be able to draw his weapon and end this debacle. His entire body was as tense as a coiled spring wire; the nervous tension that permeated the room was palpable. He inched his way nervously, holding his breath as he moved with cautious stealth until he was satisfied that he was hidden from Corfinio's view. His hand edged slowly toward his holstered weapon as he watched McCorken clasp the handcuffs on his own wrists. But his movements did not go unnoticed.

"*Five-O!*" Segado yelled suddenly, causing Corfinio look up immediately in his direction. Corfinio knew instantly that Segado was warning him of something and it involved the transport deputy.

During their time in Cambridge jail, he and Segado never bonded to the point of friendship, but Segado, being a frequent visitor to the institution, had schooled him in the jargon and protocols employed by the inmates. It wasn't from any sense of duty or compassion on Segado's part; it was simply an extension of survival mode, an "us against them" mentality. If the inmates were involved in something that would be considered illicit activity, a well-placed lookout always announced "Five-O" when a guard was approaching. Most of the time, the guards would rattle their keys or approach noisily to tip off their immanent arrival as warning, especially if they suspected the unlawful goings-on was no more than a minor infraction. Filling out pages of paperwork was a tedious job that was nothing more than a waste of time, which they chose to avoid if at all possible.

"Hey, *Barney!*" Corfinio shouted, further startling the officer. "You don't want Fat Boys' brains all over your nice, clean uniform." He toggled the weapon in an up-and-down motion. "Raise 'em." He took one step forward, grabbing McCorken's cuffed hands and lifting, causing McCorken to lean forward involuntarily and wince from the sudden discomfort. Corfinio urged him forward slowly, gently, not really knowing what his next move would be should the deputy try something sudden or brazen.

The deputy hesitated, mentally calculating the chances of failure or success when Segado's feet smashed into the base of his spine, causing him to crumple in a heap. Even though he was bound in leg irons as well as being handcuffed, Segado had raised both feet off the floor from his seated position and drove them as hard as he could into the deputy's back. Before the fallen officer could recover, Segado rapidly leaped off the chair, awkwardly penguin-stepping to the slightly dazed constable. Straddling the man's neck with his leg irons, he twisted his legs viciously, tightening the chain like a metal noose. Though still muddled and disoriented by the blind attack, the deputy reacted to the cold steel tightening around his throat, clawing at the chain, trying to loosen the intense pressure of the strangling choker while Segado grinned down at him sadistically, cursing his ancestors and progeny.

Shocked by the sudden turn in events, Corfinio shoved McCorken forcefully toward the prisoners' holding area, where he collided with the low railing. With his hands locked behind his back, there was no hope of avoiding the inevitable collision exacerbated by the momentum of his own obesity. He hit the rail stumbling and teetered precariously for an instant before finally crashing hard to the floor. The sturdy oak railing held firm while McCorken groaned heavily.

"*Segado!*" Corfinio yelled, but the Puerto Rican was lost in determination, deaf and blind to all around him. Corfinio switched the gun to his left hand, stepped in closer, and brought his arm back to deliver a roundhouse right to Segado's unprotected face, knocking him over sideways to land in a heap on the floor, completely unconscious.

"*God damn it!*" Corfinio flicked his right hand violently as if to ward off the pain of the impact, flexing his fingers automatically to feel if anything was broken. It certainly felt like he had broken something on Segado's granite head. Glancing down at the purple-faced, choking deputy gasping for air, he reached over and disengaged the now slack leg irons loosely wrapped around his throat with his throbbing right hand, although with some difficulty. He struggled to regain his breath, still unable to speak from the brutal near strangulation he suffered from Segado. Corfinio unfastened the deputy's service belt, pulling it out from under him while he continued wheezing, unable to put up any defensive resistance to being stripped of his arsenal of weaponry.

"You brought this on yourself, Barney," Corfinio scolded, using the insulting vernacular in reference to Barney Fife from the *Andy Griffith Show*. He persisted with the reprimand with a sincere hint of remorse as he stuffed the Glock in his waistband, checking first to make sure the safety was still engaged. "Maybe you should have been watching your prisoner instead of trying to play hero and this wouldn't have happened." He took one of the two sets of handcuffs off the service belt and held them out to the policeman still lying on the floor, holding his bruised, discolored throat. Noticing his brass name tag, he addressed the officer, D. Kennedy, "You okay to sit up, D. Kennedy?"

Deputy Kennedy struggled to express an intelligible response but choked immediately, his damaged throat rejecting any attempt at vocalizing a coherent reply. He coughed painfully several times, a genuine look of distress apparent and, with considerable effort, managed to sit up.

"Good," Corfinio congratulated him. "Here." He offered the handcuffs to Kennedy. "Take these."

Kennedy again tried to speak, but the attempt only resulted in a coughing jag, accompanied by wincing pain and a contorted grimace.

"Don't talk, D. Kennedy." Corfinio turned back to where McCorken had fallen to the floor less than ten feet away, hands cuffed behind him. He had managed to roll onto his side but was failing miserably in his valiant efforts to raise himself off the floor. Corfinio was somewhat amused, thinking that McCorken looked like a beached turtle flipped on his back. Returning his attention to Kennedy, he asked, "Can you make it over there?" pointing toward McCorken.

Kennedy nodded, finally taking the cuffs from Corfinio.

"Okay, D. Kennedy, I want you to lace that cuff to Lard Ass over there and then put the other on your right hand. Understand?"

Kennedy nodded, sighing in resignation, humiliated and embarrassed that he was being held hostage with his own weapons. He did as Corfinio instructed so that the two policemen were latched together, sitting on the floor back-to-back in misery.

McCorken was breathing hard from the challenge of maneuvering into a sitting position. Red faced from the exertion, he stared up at Corfinio and cursed belligerently, "I *swear*, I'm gonna *fucking* kill you." Tossing his head in the direction of Segado still out cold, he added, "You *and* your fucking partner over there."

Corfinio looked at McCorken sitting uncomfortably on the floor, sweating like he had just run a marathon in the heat of summer. A thin smile formed as he chuckled. "Heh-heh…yeah. Not today."

"*Fuck* you."

"Officer McCorken," Corfinio said lightly, acting astonished at the remark, adding a touch of derision and an air of triviality to his voice, "*that* is a *very* poor way to express yourself. *Surely* a man of your *worldliness* and *high education* can convey your thoughts in something marginally better than *base* profanity."

"*Eat shit!*" McCorken raged.

"Well, *there* you have it," Corfinio answered with mock disappointment. "I was wrong!" Turning away from the trussed-up duo, he faced Judge Thompson and addressed him sarcastically. "Judge, I would like to file a formal complaint against this man, Officer McCorken. He has used excessive profanity in this court, which I believe is a contempt charge. *And* he has *threatened* my life, which I find *reprehensible* coming from a man charged with *upholding* the law!"

Thompson eyed Corfinio calmly as he sat in his leatherette, trying to assess just how close this man—*this lunatic*—was to potentially turning his courtroom into a shooting gallery. He certainly didn't want to antagonize him to the point of no return—if it hadn't already reached that point. Thompson had seen it all during his long tenure on the bench: yelling and screaming, crying and pleading, shock and anger, threats and acquiescence, but never a situation that had the potential to turn deadly. He briefly entertained the thought of informing this madman that he would spend the remainder of his days in a six-by-eight federal prison cell for this passionate stunt but immediately decided against it. What if that was what finally pushed him over the edge? The sudden realization of the situation came upon him like a revelation. He wasn't insane; he wasn't going to purposely hurt anyone. Corfinio appeared to be eerily calm, which was in itself upsetting. He already *had* the opportunity to exact and abet injury on *both* officers McCorken and Kennedy at the hands of Segado but instead *aided* in their *safety*, *disabling* Segado! As Thompson digested the situation, maintaining eye contact with Corfinio, he nodded slowly, almost unperceptively, and decided to let this play out.

"What is it exactly you're looking for here, Mr. Corfinio?"

"Well, Judge, I sure would like for you to hear the truth of this matter instead of the bullshit you've been fed. It would be nice if *some*one—*anyone*—would tell the truth for a change."

"Hmmph," Thompson grunted, silently agreeing, "that would be...*novel*. But I'd like you to do me a small favor first."

Corfinio squinted a little at Thompson, tilting his head slightly in question.

"Why don't you secure your prisoner?" Thompson said, looking over at a still-prone Segado.

"He's not 'my' prisoner, Judge. *None* of you are 'prisoners.'"

"Oh, is that so? Then what would *you* call it?"

"No, Your Honor, you're simply being...'*detained*.'"

25

Corfinio walked back to where he had discarded Kennedy's service belt and removed the second set of handcuffs. Using the key, he released the single strand, allowing the cuffs to open, and proceeded to where Segado lay on the floor, just beginning to stir. Corfinio quickly latched one end of the cuffs to the hinge on Segado's handcuffs and grabbed hold of the leg iron chain securing his ankles. He tugged hard drawing Segado's legs up into a fetal position and then attached the other end around his leg iron chain. He had no sooner secured the second cuff when Segado suddenly jolted hard against the metal restraints, but they held firmly, holding him in a trussed-up position not unlike that of a calf about to be branded.

Trying desperately to shake off the cloudiness that pervaded his semiconsciousness, Segado struggled to release himself from his confinement. His jaw ached from the terrific impact of Corfinio's roundhouse blow, and his head throbbed horribly. He tried to rub his aching jaw only to find that his arms wouldn't raise beyond his bent knees from the restriction put upon him by the joined restraints. He squinted through a hammering headache at the restrictive manacles, and as the pounding abated, his vision cleared enough to realize an attentive form standing above him.

He recognized Corfinio and, with sudden total clarity, recalled the events leading up to this moment. He spat viciously, launching a gob of spittle that landed on Corfinio's pant leg. "Esta *muerto!*" Segado said with uncontrolled anger, resentment, and hatred, not only furious that his former cellmate didn't back his play but also that *he* was the one responsible for his current situation. "You're *dead! Dead!* I'll kill you for this…you wait."

Corfinio stared down at Segado trussed up like a prized hog and sighed heavily. "Seems to be the overwhelming opinion today. Almost makes me wish I bought a better life insurance plan."

He turned away and walked the six steps back to the judge's bench. Looking up to face Thompson's grizzled countenance, he spoke. "Judge, all I want is for you to hear the truth. The *truth* about what happened—*what really happened*—not the load of crap that all these agencies fed you and the *blatant lies* that *he*," he said, pointing an accusing finger in Goldman's direction, "spews forth like…like *water* from an endless fountain."

"You're hell bent on having the 'truth' be told, Mr. Corfinio, but I want you to understand something. At the end of the day, it won't make a *damned* bit of difference. Do you understand what I'm saying to you?"

Corfinio nodded. "I do, but it matters to *me*, Judge."

"So what's *your* version of the truth?"

"Well now, y'see, that's just it. I don't want to tell *my version*, and I don't want *them*," he said, pointing accusingly toward the cluster of personalities that had testified against him, "to tell *their version*. I want the manipulation of the facts to *stop* and just lay it out there for all to see, warts and all. *Then* you can make a fair judgment." He glared at his ex-wife with venomous hatred. "And it starts with *her!*"

Marsha Corfinio shrank back into the folds of her lawyer's protective embrace, mustering up the most convincing fear-stricken look of horror and victimization complete with fright-induced shivering. DSS Representative Donna LaTrina gathered in protectively, patting Marsha Corfinio gently on the back, trying to allay her obvious fears.

Marsha Corfinio had mastered that ability long ago once she realized the power it held to advance her own cause. Do you want sympathy? *Cry.* Do you want protection? *Cower.* Do you want an ally? *Plead.* Do you want to eliminate an irritating husband? *Accuse.*

Unfortunately, Corfinio had also fallen for those well-practiced antics. It took about a year for him to realize his gullibility after witnessing a series of orchestrated dramatics, but by then, they had already married. He had hoped that these displays were isolated events and not a psychotic personality disorder.

The marriage didn't start out bad. In the beginning, she was always professing her undying love for him, starry-eyed and devoted. Once he realized that her admissions of love and devotion were issued as an early introduction to her latest material desires, the words became nothing more than meaningless drivel. He recognized that the marriage was destined for failure once her tact changed to aggressive hostilities. She became hateful and vile, threatening divorce every time he failed to yield to her demands. She would fly off in fits of destructive rage, bombarding him with any household item within reach until he sought refuge outdoors. Usually, he would go for a short drive, giving her time to calm down before he would return, only to find her sprawled out upon the bed in total exhaustion.

After the conclusion of each episode, she would be serene and pleasant, which he found equally as disarming, but considering the former alternate option, he didn't want to complain. Besides, the makeup sex was indescribably marathon in scope and imagination. What he was mercifully unaware of at the time was that she hinted to friends that the "knock-down, drag-out" arguments would ritually end with her being beat and raped. The actual truth of the matter was, the arguments never escalated to the point where he became physically aggressive. Once she started throwing things, he ducked for cover or left the house. Her ultimate objective was to get pregnant so that she could keep the child, get rid of the husband, and collect a check. In her mind, this was the easiest road to attaining "sole independence." She never told her husband that she had stopped taking birth control pills, so when she announced that she was pregnant, he was far less than thrilled at the circumstance. Marsha deftly used his underwhelming reaction as the basis for the latest demand for divorce. Before the week was out, she served him with divorce papers, demanding weekly support and the first of many restraining orders. Her continual allegations of assault, battery, and intended rape had to be continued in order to keep up the facade of being eternally victimized by this monster. Otherwise, her bogus claims would be obviously transparent if she willingly allowed him within close proximity of her and their child.

And so she wore the cloak of deception with confidence, having practiced it to perfection as she stood effectively quivering in the courtroom, convincing herself and some others that she was indeed a helpless, defenseless victim.

The *British Journal of Social Psychology* had conducted several studies on the effects of an individual who displayed a tearful countenance. "Research found that the mere sight of tears promotes the willingness to provide support to the person shedding the tears." The conditions prompting a tearful response mattered greatly as did the percentage of people willing to offer support.

Stepping away from the clustered group offering patronizing support to Marsha Corfinio, Estelle Avery offered neither support nor sympathy. Avery, Head of Family Services for the Massachusetts Department of Children and Families, was frequently called upon by the court for her input and reports involving child care, abuse, and neglect in cases where children were involved in custody disputes and terms of visitation. Her professional advice was always taken with substantial consideration as her assessments were rarely off target.

Born the second of nine children to Magritte and Justin Proctor, her protective and maternal instincts toward her siblings became obvious at an early age. She proved to be an excellent student, consistently making the Honor Roll and Dean's List through elementary and high school, which lead to a substantial scholarship to UMass Amherst, where she earned her master's degrees in both social work and mental health counseling, as well as a bachelor's degree in psychology. When she interviewed for a job at DCF, she was more than a little apprehensive due primarily to the overbearing political atmosphere of affirmative action dominating hiring practices. She knew she was qualified for the job, but she wanted it based on her qualifications rather than the color of her skin or her gender. It became such an issue for her that she vocalized her concerns to the interviewer. "Mr. Zalinski, if I'm being offered this position because you have to meet a specific quota of minority hires, then you'll have to excuse me for refusing this offer."

"Miss Proctor," Zalinski started, leaning back in his chair, hands folded across his stomach with his thumbs tapping each other, "please forgive me for not being more transparent. I'm the regional director for DCF, and quite frankly, I haven't conducted an interview in over eight years now. The reason I'm here with you today is because you're the best candidate that's come across my desk. I need qualified people based on education and experience. I didn't know you were black until you walked through that door."

She rose quickly through the ranks and established herself as a no-nonsense, hardworking team member, issuing accurate assessments and defusing potential catastrophes through her ability to read human frailties.

Although the current series of events seemed to indicate that she had erred in her evaluation of John Corfinio in a major way, she remained confident and steadfast with her assessments.

"John." She spoke quietly, addressing Corfinio, standing alone, noticeably removed from the group of Marsha Corfinio supporters. "John, this isn't the way."

Corfinio faced her calmly without animosity or anger. "Mrs. Avery, all due respect—and I do sincerely appreciate all you tried to do for my cause—but I've been trying it the 'right way,' and well, heh…" he said with a sweep of his arm, "here we are! *This* is where it's gotten me!"

"I know it's frustrating, John, but—"

"But what? If I'm just patient, everything will work out? You *know* better than that. The system is *broken. You* know that better than anyone. *You're* the one who has to sit down with all the *liars*," he said, glaring at his ex-wife, "and *manipulators*," he added, stabbing a finger at Goldman, "and then try to figure out how to make *him*"—he flipped a backward thumb over his shoulder toward Thompson—"make the right decision!"

Thompson retorted immediately and defensively, "I make my decisions based on *the law*!"

Corfinio spun around to face Thompson. "Then *you* should make a decision based on what's 'right' or 'wrong' because the law's *not working*!"

"*You* don't understand the law."

"Sure I do. It's a control device used against those who stand against a common moral principle…unless it's a person of high political or social importance, then all bets are off."

"The law applies to everyone equally."

Corfinio looked at Thompson questioningly. "I can't—*won't*—believe you're actually that naïve. What's that saying, 'Justice is blind'? Maybe you ought to take the blinders off and see who's *really* tipping the scales, Judge." Shaking his head rapidly in faux disbelief, he turned away from Thompson and walked toward the seated duo of Kennedy and McCorken. Pointing down at McCorken, he asked, "Do you trust this man, Judge?"

Thompson sat indifferently without answering.

"Judge, is it against the law for me to call this man a bigoted, bloated bag of bluster? Now I know it's insensitive, insulting and degrading, but have I broken any actual laws in saying that?"

"Yes," Thompson stated flatly.

"No shit, Judge?" Corfinio looked genuinely surprised.

"*No shit*, Mister Corfinio. Slander."

"Slander, huh, how 'bout that?" As if mulling something weighty over in his mind, he spoke deliberately. "Okay, so let's say 'hypothetically' that Officer McCorken claims I said that to him. Would you believe him?"

"I'd have no reason to doubt him or question his word."

"Are you basing your belief on the fact that I just said those words and therefore find it extremely credible that I would actually say such a thing or the fact that he's an upstanding member of society, a representative of the law and therefore above reproach?"

"Like I said, I'd have no reason to doubt him."

"What if I told you *he* made a similar comment in reference to someone? Would you believe me?"

"Why should I?"

Corfinio went wide-eyed as he pointed accusingly at Thompson, repeatedly stabbing his finger angrily in midair. He cried out like a victory song, "And *there* you have it!" He turned toward the empty jury box and addressed imaginary jurors with a dramatic flair worthy of praise. "Ladies and gentlemen of the jury, *I beseech* you to recall these very words issued forth from yonder judge, 'The law applies to all equally!'" Spinning on his heel back to face Thompson, he accused, "That's what *you* said! *Your words,* Judge, *your words*! You can't *make* that decision based on the personalities delivering the message if the law applies equally!"

Thompson didn't react to the accusation nor did he lose his obvious composure. "Mister Corfinio, I didn't say that I *wouldn't* believe you. I asked why I *should* believe you."

Corfinio skittered back to stand in front of a savagely red-faced McCorken, and with palm held out flat as if presenting a treat to a dog, he indicated the seated officer. "Because this man...this"—he paused, stumbling for the right words—"this worthless piece of *shit* shouldn't be allowed an opinion *at all!* He's belligerent, arrogant, inept, bigoted, racist—"

"*Fuck you!*" McCorken exploded. "*Fuck you, you fucker!*" McCorken attempted to kick out at his accuser with his rubber-soled shoes but instead only managed to almost topple himself over. He screamed out, "*I'm not any of that shit!*"

"Oh, and did I mention he's a filthy slob as well? Were you aware, Your Honor, that *this* man that you hold in such *high* regard doesn't wash his hands after he pees?"

"*You fucker*—" McCorken shouted over Corfinio, sweat once again popping out visibly on his forehead. He squirmed about, frantically trying to free himself, but being cuffed to Kennedy thwarted his every effort.

"If you shook hands with him, you might as well be grabbing a fistful of fat man genitalia. I would *not* recommend it."

"Pete," he screamed at Masters, "*help me up!*"

"*And* he *hates* Negros."

"*Uncuff me!*"

"Or was it Jamaicans…yeah, I can't remember now—"

"*Piece of shit*—"

"No, it *was* Jamaicans. *Definitely.* I remember now!"

"*Aaaarrrrgggh!*" he screamed, spittle dribbling from his mouth.

"He apparently feels—by his own admission, I might add—that only pasty-faced white people are true 'Americans,' while all others should be cast aside. So—"

"*I never said that!*"

"You know what I think, McCorken? I think this all comes back to your childhood. Yeah. I think you were a fat little kid that everyone taunted, right?"

"*Fuck you!*"

"Oh, I'm getting closer… I think in gym class you were embarrassed because you had a little dick—"

"*Fuck you!*"

"And the kids made fun of you—"

"*Not true!*"

"And you never had a girlfriend because of your little dick—"

"*Uncuff me, you fucker!*"

"So you turned into a *big* dick to compensate."

"*None of this is true!*"

"It's true. You hate the Jamaicans because you *know* it's true what they say about black guys…so every time you see one of the cleaning crew, it reminds you that you have a scrawny, little dick."

McCorken continued struggling against his metal bonds to no avail, grunting and cursing loudly while Corfinio droned on.

"But y'know what? They came here same as you and I, so they—'

"*They don't belong here!*" McCorken screeched. "*And neither do you, you fucker! You dago, wop bastard!*"

Corfinio raised an eyebrow, the corners of his mouth turning up in a hint of a smile, satisfied to a certain extent that he had exposed a part of McCorken's secreted bigotry. He turned away from McCorken in disgust, who was now totally drained of energy, chest heaving in deep draughts of breath, rivulets of sweat running down his swollen, mottled face. Corfinio twisted to his left to once again face Thompson directly and sighed heavily. "Well, Judge, think you should believe me now?"

26

Pacing back and forth slowly in front of the bench, Corfinio looked over at Pete Masters still standing in semi-shock near his work station. Masters inhaled sharply, precariously on the verge of breaking as Corfinio stopped suddenly and stared at him.

"What's the matter, Pete?" Corfinio asked with a tilt of his head. "You nervous?"

Masters didn't respond; he was truly rattled by the performance that had just taken place. He actually *couldn't* respond, so he simply nodded fearfully.

"Is that a yes or no, Pete? I can't tell if you're nodding 'yes' or if that's just you shaking all over." He didn't expect a reply and didn't wait for one. "Y'know, Pete, maybe you're shaking because you drink too much coffee. Do you drink a lot of coffee? All that caffeine's not good for you, Pete. You should *really* take better care of yourself. Switch to decaf. You seem a little tense, Pete.

Are you tense? Maybe you should sit down. Would you like to sit down?"

Masters swallowed hard, trying to muster up some saliva, but his mouth was starchy and dry, his breath coming in a short staccato as he nodded slowly with concentrated effort.

"Well, go ahead then. Sit. I want you to relax." Corfinio actually sounded sincere in his efforts to get Masters comforted. "Go ahead," he prompted, waving toward a chair at the clerk's desk, nodding approvingly as Masters pulled out the chair and sat apprehensively. "Good...*good*," he said, flashing a quick smile. "Now I can continue without having to worry about you having a heart attack. I'm in enough trouble already without having to worry about being charged with murder because you decided to drop dead. We wouldn't want *that*, would we?"

Turning away from a visibly shaken Masters, Corfinio walked slowly toward the cluster of Marsha's support team when Thompson's voice cut through the pervasive tension. "Are you *done* yet, Mister Corfinio?"

Without looking back at Thompson, he answered, "Not yet, Judge. I was hoping to see if I could persuade my *lovely* ex-wife to offer a particle of truth on this whole matter, and then we can all go home...*well*," he added with an intended scoff, "*you* guys can go home. *So...* whaddya say, Marsha? Care to embrace the untapped reservoir of truth you've deftly avoided your entire life?"

He stopped ten feet short of the quartet when Donna LaTrina broke her empathetic embrace of Marsha Corfinio and took a menacing step forward. "Why can't you just *leave her alone*?" she scolded. "Haven't you done *enough* damage today?"

"Haven't *I*—" The look of shock on Corfinio's face was genuine. "*Look* who's calling the kettle black! *You're* a fine one to accuse *me* of doing irreparable damage! I'm *here*—" he said pointing to the floor then sweeping his arm across the expanse of the courtroom, "we're *all here* primarily because of *your* bogus report!"

"How *dare* you!" she snapped indignantly. "My report was *accurate* in its findings *and* in its recommendations!"

"Accurate? *Accurate?* What kind of crack are *you* smoking? The only thing 'accurate' about that report was that it accurately reflected the *bullshit* lies you were told. Maybe if you had done a little *research* instead of simply banding together like a coven of witches around a caldron, you'd have discovered some actual *facts*. But oh-*ho!* We wouldn't want anything like *facts* to get in the way of a predetermined lynching, now *would* we?"

LaTrina stood mouth, agape at the accusation of a falsified report. "You're *insane*," she mouthed barely above a whisper, seething in barely controlled anger.

"Judge," Corfinio addressed Thompson without breaking eye contact with LaTrina, "I'd like to question

Miss LaTrina as a witness. Can I borrow the witness stand?"

"Oh, for Christ's sake," Thompson said, rolling his eyes in disbelief, "how much *further* do you intend to carry on with this fiasco?"

He turned to face Thompson. "Just until you hear the truth, Judge…just 'til you hear the truth."

Leaning forward, Thompson rubbed the palms of his hands over his eyes and exhaled deeply. "Miss LaTrina? Do me a favor," he said with obvious exasperation, "take the stand so we can be through with this lunatic and his idiocy."

"Your *Honor*?" she said, staring at him incredulously.

He stared back at her, shifting his glance momentarily toward the witness box and then back at her again as if instructing her on what to do based on sheer willpower and eye command.

"I can't *believe* this! *Why* are you giving *in* to him?"

"Hmm…seeing as how he's holding every firearm in the room, it seems like the prudent thing to do at the moment. *Take* the stand." Thompson's glare was never to be taken lightly.

In a demonstrative huff, she stomped her way like an angry child to the witness stand, plopping down hard having been totally humiliated. Her normally sallow complexion was now flushed crimson, and her green eyes shot thunderbolts in Corfinio's direction.

Corfinio paid no attention to her spoiled child-like antics as he began pacing again, deep in thought, tapping the gun gently on his temple when he turned toward Masters seated at the clerks table. "Pete? Do you have one of those…uhhm, what do you call those typing things?"

"Stenotype machine," he replied nervously.

"Yeah, *that's* it! Do you have one of those?"

"No, we don't," Masters answered reluctantly. "It's usually only used in jury-based trials."

"Pete," he said shaking his head in displeasure, "I gotta tell ya, Pete, so far, you've been a *total* disappointment today. Your usefulness is *definitely* on the decline here…how about a tape recorder?"

Masters shook his head apprehensively, feeling his stomach tighten, unsure of what Corfinio's reaction might be.

"Okay, how about a pad of paper? You must have paper of *some* kind, right, Pete? Maybe a pen? Pencil? Crayon? *Anything* you could write with?"

"Y-yes… I-I have a pen and a legal pad."

"*Ah! Perfect!* A *legal* pad! How apropos! I love it, a bit archaic in this computer generation, but it'll have to suffice. Now, Pete, I'm going to need you to do something for me, okay? I need you to write down some things that I'm going to talk about with Miss LaTrina. Can you do that for me, Pete?"

Mesmerized, Masters watched as Corfinio tapped the barrel of the gun on the oak desk several times as he spoke. He knew he couldn't capture the entire exchange *verbatim*, but he hoped he might get enough to satisfy the gunman.

"Pete?"

Glancing nervously upward from his seated position, he saw Corfinio standing with a sly smile, patiently awaiting his answer. "Uhm, yes... I can...do that."

"Atta boy, Pete." Corfinio nodded and gave Masters a wink. Turning back toward the witness box, he assumed a more serious attitude. "Miss LaTrina, I'd like to discuss your report. Do you have it with you?"

"No, I left it over there," she said haughtily, pointing her manicured hand back toward where she had been standing earlier.

Corfinio sighted her folder sitting on the floor, some of the contents of which had spilled forth. "Mrs. Avery? Would you be so kind? I'd ask Goldman over there, but he'd probably alter the contents before it made it over here."

Mrs. Avery calmly collected the file folder and the loose pages and brought them to Corfinio, who thanked her for her cooperation. She immediately resumed her position away from Goldman and Marsha Corfinio to stand nearer Arthur Bari.

Corfinio set the folder down at the table occupied by Masters and scanned the pages quickly until he found what he was looking for. "Miss LaTrina, your first report on the allegations of abuse against one John Corfinio—that's *me,*" he said, pointing his thumb at his chest, "are widely supported based on documentation supplied by Marsha Corfinio'—that's *her.*" He pointed over at his ex-wife. "Is that correct?"

"Yes," she replied icily.

"Would you tell me what the nature of the abuse was that was 'witnessed' by Marsha Corfinio?"

She stiffened and folded her arms across her chest in agitation. "It's *in* the report." She refused to look at Corfinio.

"I'd like for *you* to tell me if you don't mind…and even if you *do* mind, I'd like you to tell me anyway."

She huffed, looking angrily at Thompson for some form of rescue from this demand. Instead, he stared back at her dead-eyed and nodded succinctly once.

"Mrs. Corfinio witnessed *you* hitting the child in the head. *Several* times, not just once."

"Were there *other* witnesses to these incidents?"

"No."

"So let me understand…even though the visits were court-ordered *monitored* visitations, there were *no* other witnesses?"

"That was how it was reported to us."

"That there were no other witnesses?"

"Yes."

"I see. *And yet* DSS never charged Mrs. Corfinio with neglect in exposing the child to a continual, hostile, and—*according to your report*—'potentially dangerous' environment, did they?"

"We did not find Mrs. Corfinio to be neglectful," she answered defensively.

"Of course not," he said, rolling his eyes and continued sarcastically, "she's a loving, doting mother."

"She's—"

"Let's move on." He cut her off. "I don't see a pediatrician's report here. I would have thought there *would* be one. Miss LaTrina?"

"There was no report at that time. But he wrote a letter recommending that visitation be suspended."

"No report? Well, I'm confused, then what exactly is he basing his 'recommendation' on?"

"I don't know," she said disgustedly, adding with more than a touch of animosity. "Maybe he saw bruising or some evidence of the brutalities *you* inflicted on him."

"If it was that obvious, then there *should* have been a report indicating such, correct? Yet I see nothing *here* that looks like a police report was filed by his office..." LaTrina remained silent. "Your Honor? Aren't doctors *required* to report instances of child abuse or neglect?"

"They are."

"Miss LaTrina, it's beginning to look like either (a) Doctor Stinger failed in his obligation to report these alleged incidents or (b) there *wasn't* any evidence of physical abuse to be seen."

"That doesn't mean it didn't happen."

"No, but without evidence of *any* kind, the information that was supplied to you from *Mrs.* Corfinio *should* have been somewhat suspect. I *believe* the 'burden of proof' is on *you*, not me!"

"The child *also* told us that *you hit him*!" she cried out furiously.

"According to your 'investigation'—and I use that word *extremely* loosely—you've got three people, Marsha Corfinio, Doctor Stinger, and Michael Corfinio, all making abusive treatment claims while *they themselves* are beyond reproach of *any kind*. Meanwhile, the alleged abuser is *never* called for questioning, *never* approached for a statement, and *never* considered to be as honest and upright as his accusers. Is that about right?"

"If the shoe fits…"

"Did it ever occur to you in *any* capacity that *maybe*, just *maybe*, *one* of them or *all* of them might be lying?"

"Why would they lie about *that*?"

"Maybe you should have asked that question two years ago."

"Why would a two-and-a-half-year-old lie?"

Corfinio stopped slack-jawed and stared at her for several seconds before bursting out in laughter. Stunned appearances were shared by all at his seemingly inappropriate reaction to her question.

"Oh, wow." Corfinio finally got himself back in control, wiping a tear of laughter from the corner of his eye. "Why would a two-and-a-half-year-old lie?" he mocked. "Gee, I don't know—maybe because it's deep rooted in our DNA! You don't have to *teach* someone to lie. *It's a natural instinct!*"

"I don't believe that! That is *not* true!"

"Oh, *really*? Here, let me help you out then. When a witness is called to the stand in a trial case, they are sworn in, correct?"

LaTrina refused to answer, hatefully glaring at her inquisitor.

"You don't have to answer. It's okay. Anyway, until recently, when someone was sworn in, they would be required to place their left hand on a Bible and raise their right hand in a form of submission. Then the bailiff would ask, 'Do you swear to tell the truth, the whole truth, and nothing but the truth, so help you God.'"

"I'm *familiar* with the process, Mister Corfinio," she stated condescendingly.

"I'm sure you are, but have you ever *really* examined the full ritual? I don't think you—"

"*Oh my god!*" LaTrina cut him off, impatiently rolling her eyes. Again, she implored Thompson, "Your Honor?"

"Where *are* you going with this?" Thompson interjected. "Is there a point?"

"*Absolutely*, Judge. I'm going to establish that everyone in this goddamned courtroom is a liar and that their word has no more weight than mine."

Thompson tapped his fingers lightly, absentmindedly, as he studied Corfinio carefully. He still felt certain that there was no mortal threat to anyone's safety even in view of the events that had already transpired. It would only be a matter of time before someone either accidentally stumbled upon the circumstances here or Corfinio completed his mission of transparency. Intuitively, he felt that this desperate man only wanted to be heard, and having accomplished that, he may surrender himself. A long shot? Perhaps, but he preferred that option over the former as an unexpected interruption by an intruder would no doubt have the potential to be disastrous… *and* messy. He decided the short-term goal would be to keep him on as much of an even keel as possible in collecting the information he was so determined to prove. Besides, until some form of the cavalry came to the rescue, there was no point in poking the tiger.

Thompson squinted at Corfinio, who stood patiently, awaiting his reply. "Do it quickly."

Satisfied with a nod to Thompson, Corfinio faced LaTrina once again and picked up where he left off. "So it may interest you to know that raising the right hand was not an indiscriminate selection any more than shaking one's hand is generally done with the right hand. Did you know that, Miss LaTrina?"

She stared through him grimly without acknowledgment.

Corfinio continued, "In days of old, when warriors met on the road, they would offer peaceful salutation by displaying their right hand, weaponless, to prove that they offered no harm. This practice extended itself to the act of taking oath. When one took an oath, swearing allegiance, they raised their right hand, offering it—*believe it or not*—as *collateral* should they break that oath. The right hand being dominant, the intention was to be truthful about your intentions by either a display or by submitting it for removal should you be shown to be dishonest. Amputation is largely frowned upon today, so instead we move toward more…'civilized' punishment.

"*But first*," he added dramatically with an emphatic forefinger pointing skyward, "we must ensure that all precautions and warnings have been overt. Hence the 'oath.' *First*, placing the hand on the Bible. *Why?* Because the Bible is widely accepted in this land of Christianity as the Word of God, and a lie would make you guilty not only of a civil crime but also a moral crime. *Second*, 'Do you swear to tell the truth?' *Why?* Because even though you're expected to tell the truth with your hand on the Bible, you might decide otherwise, so now you're expected to 'swear' truthfulness in order to give assurance that you will indeed tell the truth. *Third*, 'the whole truth.' *Why?* Because we as human beings tend to delete parts of a narrative so that we don't self-incriminate. A survival tactic that is, quite frankly, perfectly understandable yet also not acceptable when searching for elements of the *entire* truth. *Fourth*, 'and nothing but the truth.' *Why?* Because again, we as frail humans tend to make logical excuses for our lies in an effort to be seen by all others as less guilty, condoning our verbal digressions as acceptable.

"Lastly, 'so help you God.' *Why?* Because if you lie without fear of repercussion of punishment from the court, you will be accountable to God himself for your transgressions.

"Are you still with me so far, Miss LaTrina?" Not waiting for an answer and knowing full well that she had no intention of answering anyway, he stepped back and took a breath. "Here's the *best* part. No matter *who* sits in that chair—doctor, lawyer, policeman, grocer, drug addict, hero, or heel—*no matter who they are* in the sociological order, they *all* have to take…that…oath. Isn't that right, Your Honor?"

"That's correct."

"So you see, Miss LaTrina, the court, in its *infinite wisdom*, not only treats *everyone* in *that* chair as an equal but has also come to terms with the inexcusable fact that no matter *who* sits there, they are *still* inclined to lie. By nature."

"That's…that's just *bullshit!*" LaTrina remarked defensively, visibly agitated taking offense to being schooled by someone she considered little more than an uneducated, unsophisticated inferior.

"I was counting on you saying that." Arching an eyebrow, Corfinio smiled thinly and turned his head to face Judge Thompson. "Your Honor, would you please be so kind as to explain to Miss LaTrina what 'perjury' is?"

"Lying under oath."

Turning back to face LaTrina, he raised both eyebrows twice in quick succession. "Wow," he said, barely above a whisper, "lying under oath...*lying* under *oath*!" His voice slowly increased in tempo and volume. "Even after *swearing* on a Bible, *swearing* to tell the truth *without* embellishments and with the knowledge that the *Lord God Himself* may well *smite* thee down with a bolt of *divine wrathful lightning...*" Corfinio's arm-waving performance was similar to that of a fanatical Baptist Minister delivering a sermon to a sinful congregation. He stopped abruptly, exhaling in dramatic exhaustion, dropping his arms to his side in conclusion. His voice dropped to a flat monotone. "They *still* lie."

Corfinio watched LaTrina's reaction carefully. He knew she would never admit that he was right, but he could plainly see that she realized the truth of his theatrical performance.

"People lie to get themselves out of trouble," she said, anger prevalent in her tone. "A child of *two* doesn't have the sophistication to contrive a lie of that magnitude."

"Do you actually *have* children of your own, Miss LaTrina?"

"No, but—"

"I didn't think so."

"I work with children every day!"

"Spoken like a woman whose birth canal has never been challenged!"

"*Excuse me?*"

"Only a woman who *never bore a child* would make such an *absurd* comment. It's *always* different when they're your own. They act differently toward you, and you act differently toward them. Now *that's* an absolute *fact!*"

"It doesn't matter! Why would a child of that age say that you hit him if you didn't? *He's* speaking the truth!"

"I just told you why—people are liars by nature. It's no coincidence that both civil laws and moral laws have made lying a crime. People have to be taught *not* to lie!"

"He's *two* years old! I'd believe *him* before I'd ever believe *anything* that *you* have to say!"

"Even if he was prompted? Or threatened?"

"What…that's *ridiculous!*"

"Is it? You don't think it's possible that his mother would instruct him to lie? Is that what you're saying?"

She fidgeted, becoming more agitated. "*Yes!*" she blurted.

"Wouldn't you agree that parents routinely lie to their children?"

"Of course not!"

"Have *you* ever lied to the children you work with, Miss LaTrina?"

"*Never!*" she yelled back, insulted by the implication.

"Oh, *come on*! Are you telling me that you *never* told *one child* to leave cookies for Santa?"

"I…it's—" Flabbergasted and tongue tied, she searched for the words to refute his outrageous statement but came up short.

"Judge." Corfinio suddenly turned away from LaTrina, which only further infuriated her. "I am requesting that *all* of the testimony given by Miss LaTrina on behalf of DSS be thrown out—"

"*Your Honor*—" LaTrina objected, trying to talk over Corfinio.

"As unreliable information. *Clearly*, if she believes in *Santa*—"

"*You bastard! That's not the same!*"

"Her *entire* testimony must be regarded as unrealistic and the accuracy highly suspect based on her toehold in some kind of la-la land where Santa and the Easter Bunny coexist in *her version* of reality!" Corfinio spun on his heel to face Masters, who was scribbling furiously on his yellow legal pad. "Are you getting all this, Pete?"

LaTrina jumped up from her seat and grabbed the rail of the witness box, knuckles white as she screamed at Corfinio. "*That's not the same as lying!* Every parent tells their children—"

"*It's either the truth or it's a lie! You don't get to pick and choose!*" Corfinio whirled back to face LaTrina and yelled, cutting her off, pointing his finger at her accusingly.

He leaned in closer, and she reacted instinctively by backing up a step prompted by uncertainty and fear. The chair hit her in the back of the knees, causing her to sit hard involuntarily. She could see that his eyes reflected a deep-seated anger that he had thus far controlled, but his tolerance was wearing thin. Her heartbeat pounded heavily in her chest, evidenced by her blouse collar fluttering faintly at her throat.

"It's not that simple," she said between gritted teeth, torn between fear and anger.

"*Only to you!*" he snapped back at her and then suddenly stepped back, lowering his accusing finger, cursing himself silently for having lost control for the moment. "Only…to you," he repeated in a calmer tone.

LaTrina sat back in the witness chair, grasping the oak armrests, mustering the energy to speak again. "Mister Corfinio," she said and paused while regaining a portion of her lost poise, "society as a whole has recognized and accepted the virtue of the 'white lie.' That is *much* different than outright lying."

"I couldn't agree with you more," Corfinio stated flatly, assuming control of his emotions once again.

"But…"

"*Outside* this courtroom. But not…in…here." He emphasized each word with his gun hand by pointing toward the floor. "The *law* does *not* recognize the difference between a white lie, a feel-good lie, a defensive lie, or a blatant lie." He looked over at Thompson. "Back me up on this, Judge."

Had it not been for the current circumstance, Thompson would have found the entire confrontation between the two almost amusing. Instead, he huffed. "Yes, Mister Corfinio, you are correct. Recognizable lying by any faction of the court process is not looked well upon."

"And that is equally true for false information on a document or legal statement as well, isn't that right, Judge?"

"Correct."

"And that is *also* subject to either fines, a conviction, or even a sentence if proven to be a more serious offense. Isn't *that* also correct, Judge?"

"How long do you intend on beating this dead horse, Mister Corfinio?"

"Just until I can push him over the finish line."

LaTrina stood, eager to remove herself from the witness stand.

"Miss LaTrina," Corfinio addressed her politely, "don't go anywhere yet. We still have another item to discuss."

With a look of agonistic disappointment, she faced Thompson once again and silently implored him to release her from this nightmare. His only response was a simple nod toward the chair she had just vacated. Dejected, she sat as instructed, shoulders sagging in a reflection of mental exhaustion.

Corfinio returned to the table where the case file remained opened. Flipping through several pages he found the report filed by the Visiting Center. "Now regarding this second allegation from the Visiting Center—"

"Which was witnessed by someone *other* than Mrs. Corfinio!" she interrupted, leaning forward in the chair, eager to point out that *this* witness had no personal stake in making the allegation.

Looking up from the paperwork, Corfinio remained quiet for several seconds. "Yes…that's true." He returned his attention to the report. "But as I'm reading her report here, there seems to be, something…*missing*."

"You mean like *your arrest*?" She cocked her head, spewing vitriol from each word uttered.

"Miss LaTrina, did you ever actually 'meet' the woman who wrote this report?"

"Why would that matter?"

"I'm just curious. Personally, I'd like to eyeball someone to see how they react when being interviewed. Everyone's got a 'tell,' as they say in gambling circles. Body language is a dead giveaway for something you're trying real hard to hide or not to say. You may have spotted that if you had actually taken the time and interviewed her in person."

"We had the report written by a competent employee of the facility, who was in this case also the witness. We didn't require anything further. Her assessments were also signed off by Julia Polanski, the admin for the facility."

"Ah yes, stone-faced Julia."

"Do you have a derogatory name for *everyone*, Mister Corfinio?" she scolded.

"Apparently you've never met *her* either." Staring down at the floor, Corfinio wandered casually away from the table on an indirect path toward the witness stand. "You obviously have a great deal of faith in this woman's accounting of the events that day."

"Why *shouldn't* I? She's a *highly trained clinician* for the facility." LaTrina's ire was apparent as was her obvious distaste for the entire proceeding. She felt like *she* was the one being accused unfairly of incompetence, and she resented it badly. Her brusque answers reflected her disdain, and her hateful glaring increased it emphatically.

"Good question!" Corfinio announced to the assembly, arms outstretched, turning slowly and deliberately in a 360-degree circle like a victorious combatant in the Roman Coliseum. He stopped when he faced LaTrina once again. "*Yes*, why *shouldn't* you have faith in this

'mystery' woman's ability to relate an event that she has been *highly trained* to handle!"

"And just what is *that* supposed to mean?" she asked, pulling a snarky expression. Then waving a hand to dismiss her previous question, she continued with a huff, "Y'know what? I don't *care* what you mean. These facilities have impeccable standards and qualifications."

A broad smile broke out across Corfinio's face. Once again, he turned and pointed toward the court clerk. *"Pete!"* he called out enthusiastically and began pacing back and forth. "Write this name down, 'Cindy Beamer.' Twenty years old, two years Boston College, studying for a master's in social work. Three-point-two-point grade average. Hired on at the Visiting Center on a part-time basis only three-and-a-half months prior to the 'incident' involving John and Michael Corfinio. Broke up with her boyfriend two weeks earlier, loves pancakes, Bon Jovi, and yellow unicorns, *and*—"

LaTrina leaped from her seat, "Just *where do you get off* collecting *personal* information on someone?" She turned toward Thompson indignantly, hands on hips. "Your Honor, is that *legal?* He can't *do* that, can he?"

"That would depend entirely on how and where he got the information. Mister Corfinio?"

"People just *looooove* to post their whole lives on Facebook for the world to see. Is it still 'personal infor-mation' if it's freely posted *by her* on social media?" He waited for an answer, looking first to Thompson then to LaTrina. Neither spoke. "Yeah, I didn't think so." Looking out of the corner of his eye toward Masters, he asked, "You keeping up with all this, Pete?"

"Yes sir," he answered timidly, keeping his head down while continuing to scribble feverishly. "I-I got it."

"You're a good man, Pete. Keep up the good work. Maybe I'll hire you on full time!" He snickered at his own put-on and faced an irritated LaTrina, who remained standing. "Miss LaTrina, please, sit. You look like you're about to *bust wide open* from a cerebral aneurism or something. Sit please."

LaTrina glared at Corfinio with unmitigated hatred. Her left eye twitched, and her lip quivered slightly, but she sat back down, albeit slowly.

"Okay!" Corfinio announced. "Now *where* was I... *ah yes!* The infallible Cindy Beamer, lover of pancakes, Bon Jovi, and unicorns—*yellow unicorns*—I want to get it right. So oddly enough, Miss LaTrina, it would appear that Miss Beamer, the 'highly trained clinician' would appear to be little more than an immature part-time undergraduate who seemingly 'forgot'—a mere *oversight*, I'm *quite* sure—to mention in *any capacity* in her report that she was juggling time between mandatory note taking and forbidden scrolling on her personal cell phone." He held his hand up, palm outward. "Now before you get all defensive, saying there's no proof of that, maybe you should ask for her phone records from that day and see if the phone was in use at the time of the...'incident.'

And when you find out that it *was*, I'd say you'd then *have* to admit that she couldn't *possibly* have witnessed the events in a completely unbiased and dedicated manner without interruption or outside influence while she was simultaneously engaged in searching for pretty flowered scrunchies on Hair-we-are dot com!"

LaTrina's boiling point was at its apex. "You think you're so goddamned smart," she seethed.

"No," he said, bowing his head. "It's actually the complete opposite—it's *you* who thinks you're so goddamned smart." He paused. "Miss LaTrina, I want to ask you a question, but I want you to think about it before you answer, okay? I'm not trying to trick you, I'm not trying to embarrass you, and I'm not trying to anger you. I just want you to think for a moment before you answer, that's all. Will you do that for me...please?"

She stared back at Corfinio silently.

"You supported reports and recommendations given by Mrs. Corfinio, Dr. Stinger, and the Visiting Center. I think I've given you substantial reason to reassess your decision. You may not agree, but you have to admit there are several...*inconsistencies* that may warrant further attention. Would you, given all those uncertainties, still firmly support those reports?"

Several seconds elapsed in silence. "Abso-*fucking*-lutely."

Corfinio sighed disappointedly, shoulders drooping a little at her reply. He kept his position in front of the witness box, turning to face Thompson. "Judge, once again, I'd like to request a complete revocation of the supplied documentation against me."

"Why?"

"Because it's obvious that Miss LaTrina is incapable of making a rational decision, at least in this instance. She's basing her decision entirely on pure emotion."

"Considering the circumstance, Mister Corfinio…" he said, letting the sentence trail off then presenting an upward facing palm toward Corfinio.

"Mmm, yeah. I can see where that may have had an effect, but Judge, what about my Sixth Amendment Rights? Whatever happened to 'innocent until being proved guilty'?"

"The evidence supplied to this hearing *is* evidence of guilt. If you disagree with that, then you have the right to appeal. Although I might strongly *suggest* that it be done using legal counsel…instead of a firearm."

"I *disagree*, Judge! *Without* the firearm, no one would be listening *at all!*" He paced quickly back and forth in front of the bench, his ire gradually increasing. "Why is it on *me*? Why is *my* character always being called into question? Why is *me* that always has to prove I didn't do anything wrong while the *accuser's* word is accepted beyond a shadow of a doubt? Their professional credentials shouldn't allow them to make accusations that they can't prove just because of their societal standing! This might come as a shock to you, but the highest-ranking officials in this country have proven to be far bigger liars than the people that pick up their *garbage*. And let me point out the obvious here, Judge—that DSS report 'proved' *nothing*! They're crying wolf, and you *bought* it!" Corfinio smoldered. "This isn't 'evidence'! This is nothing more than hearsay! If it *was* evidence, they'd have something concrete to back it up with instead of a bunch of 'he said, she said' bullshit. The *problem* here, Judge, is that the court *choses* to believe what 'she said' and discard whatever 'he said.' *That*...that is *not* an unbiased judgment!"

He wiped the sweat from his forehead with the back of his gun hand and stepped over to the witness box. He tapped the gun barrel on the rail twice, leaned in toward LaTrina, and with great effort said softly, "When I fuck up, *I pay*. When *you* fuck up, *I pay*?"

"Are you quite finished harassing me?" LaTrina glowered hatefully at her gun-toting captor.

Corfinio took a full step backward away from the witness box, sweeping his free hand in a presentative fashion. She exited the box and returned to rejoin Marsha Corfinio and her accompanying lawyer. Corfinio walked absently back to the desk where Pete Masters sat flicking his pen hand to relieve the onset of cramping. He gathered up the DSS report he had splayed across the desk earlier, tucking it all neatly within its folder. Before closing the top flap, he read her signature at the bottom of the page and snickered.

"Miss LaTrina, among all the accusations that you've leveled against me here today, I *certainly* wouldn't want to add 'stealing documents' to that list." He handed her the folder politely, which she received without comment. "I didn't know your first name was Donna. Donna LaTrina. That's kind of an interesting name…very apropos actually. In Italian, 'Donna LaTrina' means 'woman of the bathroom.' And what you're holding there," he said, pointing to the folder, "is something we would call *merda*. Do you know what that means? No, of course you don't. *Merda* in Italian means 'shit.'" He stared her down, waiting for some kind of retaliation, but she offered nothing. "The Bathroom Woman delivers *shit*… and there you have it."

27

Attorney Robert Johnson poked his head into the doorway of Family Services. "Hey, Maria," he greeted the lone occupant casually, "have you seen Mrs. Avery?"

"Hey, Bob," she said returning the succinct greeting without raising her head from the paperwork she had splayed out in front of her, "I think she's still over in Courtroom 5. She said she wouldn't be long, but…"

"Great. When is she due back?"

Maria Cortez flipped her shoulder-length hair back from her face and glanced up at the wall clock. "Wow, I didn't realize it, but she's been gone almost an hour. Why, what's up?"

"She's supposed to meet with my client for mediation. Is there any way to reach her?" Johnson asked.

"She's in Courtroom *Five*," she said with the expectation that everyone who walked into the courthouse knew that Courtroom 5 was practically incommunicado by misdesign.

"Okay?"

"Judge *Thompson's* presiding," she said folding her bare arms across her chest, once again expecting the answer to be self-explanatory.

Johnson's shoulders sagged with disappointment upon hearing her reply. "Oh, *Christ*! Does he *still* make everyone shut their phones off?"

"Only the ones who refuse to dump them in the basket by the door." She was referring to a small wicker basket that was placed on a small table by the courtroom entry doors. Most people refused to give up possession of their phones, opting to instead shut them off completely. Judge Thompson had made it abundantly clear that if a cell phone interrupted the proceedings, the owner of such would forfeit their place in queue for the day, to be rescheduled for an alternate date.

"Maria…" Johnson said pleadingly. "Can't you just run down there real quick and let her know we're here?"

Cortez looked up from her seated position at the table covered with paperwork and narrowed her eyes evilly as she scowled at the lawyer.

"*Please*. Please, please, please!" Johnson begged.

"*Bob,*" she scolded, "I *hate* that place. You *know* I hate that place. I have to walk through that *creepy,* dirty storeroom and practically walk *through* the men's room—*ughh*!"

"Maria, I *know*," he said apologetically, "but we're on a time crunch here. *Can* you…*please*…?" Johnson hunched over, hands clasped tightly together as if he were praying, a painful expression of pleading obvious on his comically contorted features.

She let out a long-winded breath and rolled her eyes. "Have I ever told you what a total pain in the *ass* you are?"

"*Yes*. Yes, you have," he conceded good-naturedly.

"*And* have I ever told you that of *all* my brothers-in-law, I despise *you* the most?"

"*Every* time I ask you for a favor." He gave her a wink and a gleaming smile as she good-naturedly shoved him out of the doorway.

Cortez entered the busy concourse and walked briskly toward the east corridor. She traversed the long hallway quickly, almost noiselessly in her crepe-soled shoes. Arriving at the end of the corridor, she drew in a large breath and held it as she approached the men's room foyer. It did little to stifle the antiseptic odor emanating from within. She blew out a huge gust of air after passing through and stepping out onto the cast-iron landing overlooking the enormous storage room. She descended the stairs without hesitation and involuntarily shivered once she reached the lower level.

The dimly lit area always reminded her of a horror movie setting. All those ancient file cabinets with musty-smelling contents and spider webs stretching from the long-stemmed bronze ceiling lights only enhanced the overall feeling of trepidation. She gathered her arms tightly around her chest, scurrying as quickly as she could to exit the storeroom. Only steps from the exiting concrete stairway, a brilliant flash of light exploded just over her head. With a sharp intake of breath, she suddenly shrank back in shock. The sharp burst of light was followed immediately by a noticeable dimming. Looking up fearfully, she exhaled in relief and snickered softly, realizing that one of the ceiling light bulbs had simply burned out. *Nothing like creating your own drama,* she chastised herself and climbed the short set of concrete stairs, turning left into the spacious and brightly lit corridor leading to Courtroom 5.

The corridor was cold and empty, and she could hear raised echoed voices coming from within the courtroom. *Uh-oh,* she thought to herself, *someone's not having a very good day.*

Cortez took the last remaining steps, approaching the courtroom doors, tiptoeing silently. Peeking through the thin gap between the doors revealed only a sliver of Judge Thompson slouched lazily in his high-backed leatherette. Gently pushing the door forward about a foot, she stuck her head inside to see if she could spot Estelle Avery.

What she saw instead shocked her into frozen immobility. Her dark-brown eyes widened in absolute astonishment at the sight she beheld. Her hand rose quickly to her gaping jaw to stifle the sudden gasp of breath. Tremors immediately racked her entire body as she backed slowly away from the door, letting it close softly and silently. Stepping unsteadily toward the right side of the door, she staggered against the cool plaster walls, raising both shaking hands to her mouth, trying to control the rapid pace of her breathing. "Omigod, omigod, omigod," she whispered to herself. Taking several deep breaths, she closed her eyes and pushed off from against the wall. Her legs were still unsteady as she inched toward the access hallway she had arrived from, looking back over her shoulder apprehensively. She descended the four steps into the dismal storeroom and stopped, listening. Hearing only the murmur of muted voices from Courtroom 5, she broke into a frenzied run.

*****

Maria Cortez burst into the courthouse's bustling concourse and stopped short. Still shaking from the adrenaline rush, she looked about desperately, frantically searching for a law enforcement uniform yet finding none. At any given time during the course of an average day, there would be an almost constant flow of uniforms—local cops, state cops, probation officers, bailiffs, or sheriffs—but at that moment, none were within sight. "Oh God,'" escaped her lips softly.

"Maria!" Robert Johnson came from behind and touched her shoulder.

She recoiled immediately, letting out a contracted shriek, catching the casual and somewhat jaded attention of those within close proximity.

"Maria, did you—" Johnson's playful mood dissolved completely once he saw the wild-eyed, frantic look of anxiety upon his sister-in-law's face. "Maria! What's *wrong*?" he demanded, grabbing her arm.

She tugged weakly, trying to wriggle herself from his firm grip. "Let me *go*…" she said with an angry tone. "I need *help*," she said slightly louder.

"What—"

"*Let go! They need help!*" she said, slightly louder the second time.

"Hey, buddy!" A rasping baritone voice attached to a monster of humanity stepped up behind Johnson. Frowning ominously, he glared. "Maybe *you* should try another dance partner. *I'm* free!"

Johnson turned to see a granite-faced, leather-clad tower of a man directly behind him standing no less than six feet five and could not have weighed less than 320 pounds. He paled instantly. "What—? No, it's not—"

"It never *is*!" The behemoth of a man stepped forward, driving his baseball mitt sized palm into the center of Johnson's chest, knocking him backward several feet before colliding into an inattentive passerby. Both men, caught off guard by the unexpected impact, flailed aimlessly for two seconds before crumpling awkwardly to the floor in a heap of tangled limbs.

Lawyers and clients, courthouse personnel, and incidental visitors all stopped or slowed at the sudden outburst, unsure of what exactly was going on. Some scurried on quickly, unwilling to discover the cause and hoping to avoid any fallout from being too close. Others, curious or perhaps fascinated with the potential for bloodlust, crowded in closer.

Maria continued her plea, pointing in the direction of the corridor leading to Courtroom 5. This was to be misunderstood completely as circumstances placed Johnson and Maria's misguided giant protector in the same general direction. "They need *help! Please!*" She stamped her foot down in frustration, pointing her arm rigidly toward the corridor. "*He has a gun!*"

The concourse formally devoid of police presence only minutes prior was suddenly swarming with lawmen from every branch of law enforcement. Several of the arriving cops took in at a glance what appeared to be a mountain of a man threatening two helpless victims on the floor cowering in fear. They approached from three different directions, hands on batons or service revolvers, and closed in quickly. One of the officers yelled out to the big man, "Come on, Sky! Back off now, down on the ground, hands behind your back!"

Quincy "Sky" Bluford was a semi-pro wrestler who had many more victories outside the ring than within. He was well-known to local law enforcement for habitually enforcing vigilante justice in his rough-and-tumble community, which the neighbors fully appreciated being the immediate benefactors. But while the neighbors loved him, local law enforcement had a different opinion having to deal with the trail of broken bodies that was hard to ignore, no matter how well meaning.

Sky turned at the shouted command, obviously confused by the attention that was misdirected toward him. "Who, *me*?"

"*On the floor!*"

"I didn't do nothin' wrong! I was just trying to protect the girl from this...*pervert* over here." He eyeballed each of the officers surrounding him now with batons in hand and noticed several more were working their way toward him. He raised his hands slowly and began to descend into a prone position on the floor.

Johnson separated himself from the tangle of limbs, apologizing repeatedly to the muddled, disheveled mess of a man that shared this minor catastrophe. He stood up quickly in the confusion and attempted to offer explanation while two of the officers quickly patted down and handcuffed a still protesting Sky Bluford.

Two other policemen were involved in trying to calm an obviously shaken Maria Cortez, who was becoming more agitated in spite of their attempts.

"It's okay," said the taller of the two, "just calm down, miss," he continued patronizingly.

"*No!*" she replied, her frustration and anger increasing. "The guy with the gun—"

"He doesn't *have* a gun," the short cop interjected.

"*That's not the guy!*" she practically screamed in the short cop's face. "*You f—*" She stopped herself before the curse was completed. Cortez's face was a mask of wrath as she pointed to the large man prone on the ground. "*It's not him!*" Then she redirected her aiming finger toward the east corridor. "He's in Courtroom 5!"

Both cops looked at each other in confusion. The taller cop spoke. "*Who's* in Courtroom 5?"

"*The guy with the gun!*"

28

Thompson broke the temporary silence. "While this has all been *very* interesting and quite entertaining, Mister Corfinio, I think it's time you wrap up. We've all got better things to do, and you've got a cell to check into."

Corfinio turned to see Thompson leaning lazily on his elbow. "Not yet. I want *her*," he emphasized, nodding in the direction of his ex-wife, "to come clean once and for all. I'm sick and tired of this goddamned charade she's been playing and getting away with. And quite frankly, *Judge*, you should be sick of it too. Especially since *you're* the one—you and your broken system—who has enabled it to continue.

"The entire system is so heavily stacked in her favor that I've already been assumed and judged guilty before anyone even knew my name, much less the validity of any 'crimes' I've supposedly committed. And *why? Why*, Judge? Because it's not about justice at all! *Is it?* It's about keeping *your* ass out of a sling, and *fuck me! She* runs around screaming that I beat her, and instead of putting the burden of proof on *her*, you throw *me* in a cell! *Why?* So just *in case* it's true—even though there's *no* witness, *no* physical proof, *no* medical report, *no* police report— heh, well…we can't take *any* chances, so just *in case it's true…just in case*, you can throw your hands up in the air and say that *you* did what you had to do to protect this poor, innocent victim." Corfinio stopped for a breath. "Well, guess what? *News flash! This just in! She's* not the *victim!* And she is *far* from innocent! When the *fuck* are you going to wake the fuck up, huh? *She's* the problem! *She's* the manipulator! *She's* the one playing you like a five-dollar fiddle! *Her!*"

With his final accusation, Corfinio pointed his gun arm in the direction of his ex-wife without turning around to face her, directing all his wrath toward Thompson. Thompson sat immobile, seemingly unfazed by the angered rant, and answered with only one word, tipping his head toward Marsha Corfinio.

"Her?"

Corfinio turned to face his ex-wife, who stood huddled in the protective embrace of her lawyer, while she sobbed into his lapel. "Oh, for *Christ's sake!*" he roared, furious, rolling his eyes skyward. "Would someone *please* give this two-bit drama queen an Academy Award!"

Marsha clung onto Goldman like she was trying to crawl into the protective encasement of a harboring cocoon while he embraced her tenderly.

Corfinio scoffed at the touching scene before him. "Cut the 'daddy' routine, Goldman." Raising his voice mockingly, he imitated a cartoonish version of the lawyer's unspoken attitude. "'There, there. Don't you worry, Daddy's gonna protect you from the big, ugly man.' Get a grip, Goldman. You'll be singing a different tune when this over. The only money she's got is the child support she gets from me and all the money she can steal from welfare."

Goldman stiffened, obviously offended at the mock and the implication. "Your Honor," he started to protest, "I think we've had—"

Thompson interrupted immediately, "Shut up, Goldman."

"*Yeah!*" Corfinio added. "*Shut up*, Goldman!"

"*Mister* Corfinio…"

"I have a question for you, Judge. If I requested a restraining order because I feared for my personal safety from *that* woman, would you issue the order?"

Thompson remained silent.

"Let me help you out—you *wouldn't*. You'd sit there and probably tell me that I should go home and try to 'work it out.' *Why?* Because you'd refuse to admit that she has the ability to do me physical harm, *that's* why. You'd look at me and you'd look at her, and you'd sit there in your aura of pontification and decide that this was a frivolous request. Isn't *that* right?" Corfinio once again began pacing back and forth in front of the bench. "*Isn't that right!*"

"Given your size and stature Mr. Corfinio, one would have to assume, and rightfully so, that *you* would be far more capable of causing bodily injury than someone of a more…diminutive stature."

"So you *admit* that the court has biased attitudes against men or *anyone* based solely on a visual image?"

"That's not what I said."

"I'm pretty sure that's *exactly* what you said! Here's something you may want to take into consideration with your concept of 'diminutive stature.' Ma Barker, notorious Public Enemy number 1, was only 5'3". Lizzie Borden, highly suspected of murdering both parents with an axe, 5'4". Bonnie Parker, with thirteen notches on her gun, was only 4'11". It would *appear*, Judge, that size does *not* indicate a lack of capacity for violence, does it?"

"You can't assume that all women are of the same mettle as Bonnie Parker, *Mister* Corfinio."

"And *you* shouldn't assume that all men are O. J. Simpson, *Judge!*" Corfinio was visibly agitated, still pacing nervously back and forth. He wiped his forehead with his off hand and looked toward Pete Masters.

Masters caught the glance and went wide-eyed. "I'm getting it all, I am!"

Corfinio nodded his approval, unable to keep from smiling faintly. "I'd like to ask my ex-wife a few questions, Judge. You don't mind, do you?"

"Would it matter?"

"No, not really."

Without any feeble attempt to hide the sarcasm, he answered, "Well then, by all means, continue."

Corfinio ambled over to where Marsha stood embraced by her lawyer and alongside a doting Donna LaTrina. As he slowly approached the trio and true to melodramatic form, Marsha shrank further into the protective embrace of her protector. "Oh, *come on*, Marsha, stop already with the theatrics. It's getting old…and predictable. Don't start quivering and quaking, or the next thing you know, you'll be peeing all over Goldman's $300 Oxfords. I'm just going to ask you a few questions."

"*Why?*" LaTrina butted in with a sneer of disgust. "Are you going to badger *her* on the stand too?"

"Was I talking to you? *No*, I *wasn't* talking to you! When I *was* talking to you, *you* didn't want to talk, but *now*, you've got *plenty* to say! Well, isn't that too bad! In case you didn't get the memo, this is *my* shit show, so shut the *fuck* up!"

He stopped, boring a hole through her with a deadly stare. Breathing deep, he continued in a quieter, calmer tone, "I'm sorry, Miss LaTrina, I didn't answer your question, did I? 'Am I going to badger her on the stand?' No. I reserved *all* the badgering for *you*." Corfinio spoke in a pleasant voice, a charming, bright-eyed smile spreading across his face. Cocking his head to one side, he lilted, "Now don't you feel special?" He glanced over at the witness stand and thought for a moment. "No, no witness stand for Marsha. That would only appeal to her flair for emotional dramatics." He looked back at the clerk's desk and called out, "Hey, Pete, do me a favor— slide that extra chair over here, will you? You don't need it right now, right?"

Masters looked up, startled at having been the focus of Corfinio's attention once again. He was still more than a little uneasy with the situation even in view of the fact that the gunman had never posed any direct threat to his safety. "Yes, sir—oh, I mean *no*, sir, I don't need it," Masters stuttered, stumbling around a bit in trying to release the chair from its sudden entanglement with the desk leg. Yanking and twisting the chair in his panicky state only served to raise the entertainment value. "Yes, sir, I...it seems—"

"It's okay. Calm down," he said reassuringly, closing the distance between himself and the clerk. "And listen, Pete, you don't have to call me 'sir,' okay? In fact, you know what? I think...that with *all* that you and I have been through today, I think we've formed a real *bond*. From now on, *you* can call me John!"

Masters's mouth fell open, not knowing how to receive this news. He shot a despairing look over at

Thompson only to see that the judge had rolled his eyes back and was shaking his head a little from side to side.

Corfinio grinned at Masters's obvious discomfort, grabbed the chair, and dragged it over toward the trio. He pushed it the last remaining three feet toward his ex-wife with a terse command. "Sit." He motioned toward the chair absentmindedly with his gun hand, not intending for it to be intimidating, but it could hardly be taken otherwise.

She clung tenaciously to Goldman, who whispered reassurances that everything was going to be all right as he gently guided her down into the chair. LaTrina stood in back of Marsha, alternately stroking her hair and rubbing her shoulders.

Surveying the trio, Corfinio felt the hate and the indignation emanating from each of them reserved expressly for him. There was something else too, fear and trepidation. After several silent moments, looking from one face to the next, he scowled without apology. "Sucks, doesn't it?"

He turned away from the threesome and scanned the courtroom. Masters was still scribbling away at his desk, McCorken and Kennedy were still linked together back to back, Segado was lying in a fetal position with his back to Corfinio, while Estelle Avery stood beside Arthur Bari near the jury box.

"Mrs. Avery? I'm sorry," he uttered with genuine sincerity. "Would you like to sit as well? Here." He indicated the small swinging door leading to the jury box. "Please sit down."

She nodded politely and stepped carefully into the enclosed space, grateful to finally sit.

"Arthur, you should sit down too. I don't want you getting all lightheaded and not paying attention to what's going on here. After this is over, you should get a copy of Pete's notes. You're going to need them so you can figure out how to get me out of this mess."

Bari stared at him in total disbelief. "John, there are moments when you simply *astound* me! You're *not* 'getting out of this mess.' You're *going* to end up in a federal prison. There *is* no way out of this."

Corfinio looked solemnly at his lawyer. "Why do you *always* have to be so negative, Arthur? You're downright depressing. Every interaction with you should come with a bottle of Prozac. I don't want to talk to you anymore."

29

Maria Cortez sat uncomfortably in the duty room, anxiously answering questions from the lieutenant deputy sheriff.

One of the three deputies that had manned the x-ray scanner at the courthouse entry had taken her as a handoff from the local boys in blue that intercepted her when she burst into the main concourse frantically screaming about a man with a gun. The deputy had called for an immediate lockdown of all exit doors and placed a radio call to the lieutenant, who had arrived on the scene in less than seven-and-a-half minutes. Under normal circumstances he wouldn't have come in hot, but the call came in as police code 417, "person with a gun." He had fielded quite a few of those in his almost three-decade-long career but never from the County Courthouse. Thus, the sense of urgency became somewhat intensified.

Lieutenant Deputy Sheriff Gerard W. Jankowski was a twenty-seven-year veteran who had, by his own description, "seen it all, done it all." Those serving under him would derisively add "know-it-all" to his boast but never within earshot. The most aggravating part of it all was, the only thing that matched his arrogance was his ability. The man was undeniably successful in his assessments of almost every situation. Still, a smattering of humility would have been greatly appreciated by those he commanded.

An agitated and anxious Maria Cortez continued to fidget in her chair. "I don't understand why you just don't go *get* him."

"I understand, Miss Cortez," Jankowski replied calmly, seated kitty corner to her. "But we can't just rush in and make the situation worse than it is already, okay? I need a little more information from you so we can do this safely. I don't want anyone getting hurt, do you?"

"Of *course not*," she said, stiffening defensively, "but they could be getting hurt *right now!*"

"Then I need you to work with me here, all right?" Jankowski remained patient and cool, speaking softly in an effort to reduce her stress by association. "We're going to do everything we can to get everyone out as safely as possible. You understand that, right?"

She sucked in her lips and nodded quickly several times.

"Good. I know this is hard for you. Just try and stay calm. I know it was just a few seconds, but tell me exactly what you saw. It's very important that you tell me whatever it was that you saw. Just take a moment or two and try to remember, okay?"

"Okay," she agreed, leaning forward over the desk rubbing her temples with the tips of her fingers. "Uhhm, he was standing near the witness stand, and there was a girl there. I don't know her name, but I think I've seen her before. The judge was there too..."

"Good. Did you see the gun?"

"Yeah! How could I *miss* it? He was waving it all around, but—"

"But what?" Jankowski maintained his outward calm, but a thousand scenarios were playing out in his head at the same time. "What is it, Maria? What did you see?"

"He wasn't..." She paused, caught up in the rerun of memory. "He wasn't...*pointing* it at anybody. Just, you know...*waving* it around. Kind of like when you talk and you move your hands, you know?"

"Did you see any other people there, Maria?

"Yeah, I think so. There were two guys sitting on the floor, but I couldn't see if they—" She suddenly went wide-eyed. "*Oh shit! Oh my god!*"

Jankowski watched her carefully, knowing that she was picking apart the mental image and discovering significant facts. "Tell me what you saw."

"I think those two guys were *deputies*! They had on the same kind of shirt as *you*!"

Jankowski's stomach tightened as his eyes narrowed. "Did it look like they had been hurt?"

"No… I don't know. I couldn't see them that well. One of the tables was blocking them. I could only see their heads and shoulders."

"What table? Where were they? Can you remember?"

"The table where the lawyers stand. They were in front of the table but near the railing where they bring the prisoners in. I only saw them for, like, a second."

"You're doing great, Maria," he said with a reassuring smile and patted her hand gently. "Do you remember seeing anyone else in there?"

"Well, *Estelle* was there…which is why I went there in the first place. And she was on the other side with some other people—"

"How many people? Which side?"

"The left. Near the jury box. But I'm not sure how many there were—two, three, four—I don't know." She remained silent for several seconds and shook her head, staring down at the table, then repeated, "I don't know… I'm sorry."

"Don't be sorry, Maria. You've done great. You've been a big help." He stood, extending his hand out to help her up from her seat.

He opened the duty room door to reveal one of his deputies standing just outside. He motioned for his subordinate to escort Cortez back to the Family Services Office. He flagged another deputy, who responded immediately by walking swiftly toward Jankowski.

"Yes, Lieutenant?"

"Get me the docket for Courtroom 5. *Quickly.*"

30

Standing several feet back from his ex-wife, Corfinio squinted at her and furrowed his brow. He cursed himself for blowing up earlier. That would only serve to put her on the defensive, especially since she had a sympathetic contingency on her side. If he wanted to expose her for what she was, he was going to have to take a much different approach.

"Marsha, I'm going to ask you some questions. I'm not trying to trap you, fool you, or embarrass you. I'd just like you to answer some questions. I don't think anyone here seriously appreciates just what you've been through."

She sat huddled in the chair before him, wringing her hands in her lap with a forlorn, crushed expression on her face. She had acted out this scenario before, usually when she knew she could get more mileage out of portraying someone whose spirit had been broken. That was her forte, and it had always worked for her. It was astounding how many people around her felt the need to rescue her from her self-induced plight.

A sudden realization struck Corfinio as he watched her rubbing her hands one over the other. She wasn't nervously fidgeting; she was purposely toying with the diamond engagement ring that he had presented to her when he proposed. It may have appeared to be an innocent gesture to anyone who saw her, but he knew differently. "Marsha," he asked, "are you still wearing your engagement ring?" His voice sounded as if he was deeply touched by a deeper, long-absent emotion for this woman. In truth, he was hunting for a specific reaction from her.

She pretended to be equally touched by his seem-ingly genuine moment of tender, loving nostalgia. She nodded shyly, acting as if embarrassed at having been discovered.

"May I see it?"

She held out her hand toward him. Slowly, he cautiously reached over and grasped her wrist, pressing his thumb firmly against her pallid skin, raising it up as if inspecting it closer. He let her hand go gently and stepped back.

"Okay, so," he said, regaining his mindset, "before you and I met, you had previously been married to Ronald Anzalone, isn't that correct?" He spoke calmly and softly in a manner that one would use in speaking to a frightened child.

"Yes," she said hesitantly.

"How long were you married to him?"

"Just under a year."

"Was he a good husband, a good provider, a good man?"

"He was an animal!" she exclaimed, tears brimming on her lower lids.

"How was he an 'animal,' Marsha? Could you explain that a little, please?"

"I've *told* you this before!"

"Yes, you have," he agreed, "but I'd like for *them* to know what you went through. I know this is difficult for you…"

She sighed and lifted the back of her hand to her forehead. "He would go out with his friends at night and come home late. Then he would wake me up and make me cook for all of them, and if I didn't…"

"Go on."

"If I didn't do exactly what he wanted, he would slap me around." She paused, placing her palm flat on her chest as if it were difficult to breathe. "After his friends would leave—" She trailed off, shaking her head.

Corfinio waited several seconds before urging her on. "What would happen then, Marsha?"

"He would…force me to—" Her lower lip quivered as a single tear slid down her cheek. "To have sex. He was too strong for me to fight back. I-I couldn't…"

"It's okay," Corfinio said softly. "You don't have to explain any further. I think everyone understands."

She nodded appreciatively, wiping her face gently with the tissue supplied by LaTrina.

"How long were you married to him?"

"A year...then I filed for divorce."

"Right. Sometime after that marriage ended, you became involved with another man. A man you had known off and on for several years, correct?"

"Yes. Well, I *thought* I knew him. As it turned out..." She paused again, letting yet another tear roll freely down to her chin.

"What happened, Marsha?"

She stared at the floor as if reliving nightmarish moments. "He...he would hit me."

"And?"

"When he got drunk, he'd hold me down, demanding that I have sex with him. I would tell him no, but he was too big, and I couldn't stop him." She patted her brimming eyes gently with the tissue so as not to smear her mascara.

"So you got out of one abusive relationship only to find yourself in another nightmare. How long did stay with him, do you remember?"

"A little over a year. I threw him out."

"Of course, how could you not? And who would blame you for simply wanting nothing more than a safe, happy, and loving relationship. That's all *anyone* wants."

Corfinio sounded sincere without any trace of sarcasm or derision tainting his statement. He searched the faces of LaTrina, Goldman, Bari, and Avery. "Seriously, isn't that what we all want?"

They all nodded absently in agreement.

"So you tossed him out," Corfinio said, returning his attention to his ex-wife. "A short time later, you met a man who, by your own description, was someone who *did* make you feel; 'safe, happy, and loved.' *Me*. Remember?"

"That was a long time ago," she replied sadly, casting her gaze downward once again.

"And how did that relationship go?"

"It was good in the beginning, but it didn't last. You were so nice, and then…then you changed. You got to be very demanding. Then *you* started getting pushy."

"'Demanding' how?"

"You *know* what you did. You started demanding things and expecting me to be the perfect wife, and if I didn't snap to it, you'd haul off and *smack* me! And don't you deny it—you *know* you did!"

"I see," he replied in a calm that didn't betray his inner rage. "Although I don't recall those incidents, I would imagine that a man of *my* size 'hauling off and smacking someone' especially as petite as you are, must have done some noticeable damage."

"I had bruises for *weeks!*"

"I don't recall *that* either."

"That's because I *hid* them with makeup and long sleeves! I didn't want anyone to see them—I was too embarrassed."

"Was anyone else aware of the 'beatings' you took? Did you show the bruises to anyone else? A doctor? Friends, family?"

She hung her head, "No…no, I… I couldn't."

"You couldn't. You *didn't* because you were embarrassed or because they didn't exist?"

"I *knew* you'd do this," she said angrily, clenching her hands in fists of controlled rage. "I *knew* you'd try to make it look like it never happened! I told some of my friends what you did to me! You can ask *them! They* know what you're *really* like!"

Corfinio sighed. "These friends that you told about the beatings, you know, the ones you showed the extensive bruising to, were they *also* told about the rape sessions that supposedly occurred *after* the beatings? Did you tell them about that?"

"Why are you pretending like none of it ever happened? If I didn't give you what you wanted, I'd get another beating!" She buried her head in her hands and cried.

31

Lieutenant Deputy Sheriff Gerard Jankowski grimly perused several pages of docket sheets laid out on the duty room table. He mentally noted several items comparing them to the information he had garnished from Maria Cortez. He tapped his finger on a particular entry on the page and squinted several times, deeply engaged in deductive thought process.

Without looking up at his two subordinates, he pointed at each name on the docket, identifying them as he proceeded. "Here's what we got: the judge, his clerk, a woman from Family Services, some girl on the witness stand, an incapacitated bailiff, an incapacitated transport deputy with prisoner, the ex-wife and her lawyer, and John Corfinio and his lawyer. Possibly more."

"Lieutenant? You got three or four more people in there than Cortez accounted for. And you're saying that there might even be *more* than that?"

"She didn't account for the clerk. *He's* there." Jankowski's tone indicated that he was more than a little irritated by being questioned. "She also didn't account for the prisoner. I don't know where he is in there, but he's there. Maybe he's part of this whole thing or maybe not, but I'm sure he didn't run away. Especially with leg irons. There may or may not be other people in the courtroom that weren't in her line of vision. We don't know that yet."

"Are we going in, Lieutenant?"

"Only if you're hell bent on turning this situation into a complete disaster. Call SWAT." Jankowski faced his deputy head on. "Make the call," he ordered, exiting the duty room when he heard the exasperated sigh of the deputy followed by an unintelligible mumble.

Jankowski spun around, tension and anger boiling over. "You have something to say to me, Deputy?"

"No, sir."

"You *sure* about that?"

"Lieutenant, he's just *one* guy—"

"*One guy!* In case you haven't figured it out yet, that 'one guy' disarmed *two* officers! *One guy!*" he repeated emphatically, holding up one solitary finger inches from the face of the deputy. "And this 'one guy' has multiple weapons, at least *two* guns with *four* spare magazines, and a possible—*probable*—third weapon. And *two* Tasers. You go charging in there like Dirty Harry and you're going to get yourself—*or worse*—somebody *else* killed. This isn't like shooting paper targets at the range, this guy's going to shoot *back!* This is a *hostage* situation—are you prepared for that? Are you *trained* for *that?* I asked you a question, Deputy. *Are you trained for that?*" Jankowski's throat and forehead were beyond swollen, bulging veins throbbing, threatening to explode.

"No, sir."

"So why don't you do yourself a *big favor* and keep to what you know, taking key chains and belt buckles from idiots walking through a scanner!"

32

Segado lay on the floor, only half-listening to the verbal conflicts occurring behind him. Most of his attention was focused on getting to the handcuff key secured in Deputy Kennedy's service belt.

He had spent the last twenty minutes inching forward in his restricted fetal position, praying with every breath that his barely perceptible maneuverings would remain unnoticed. Three and half feet was all that separated him from the service belt that Corfinio had left behind on the floor after stripping it off of the fallen deputy.

His plan was simple. Get the keys, free himself, and run like hell for the stairs leading down to Prisoner Holding located on the lower level. The stairs were less than ten feet away, and even though he didn't know who or what he'd have to deal with once he reached the bottom, he figured his chances were a lot better than if he tried going through the main concourse of the courthouse, where he knew for sure there were anywhere from two to six cops from the sheriff's department. No, his best chance lay in going out the way he came in. Even a long shot was better than no shot at all. This would be the only opportunity he'd have now that everyone's attention was primarily focused on his gun-waving former cellmate.

Now only inches away from the object of salvation, Segado could plainly see the remaining equipment still attached to the belt: baton, pepper spray, flashlight, gloves, extra ammunition and a Taser. He didn't see the batteries, pens, and handcuff keys, but he knew they were there from several up, close, and personal experiences in the past. There were a few elements on the belt that he knew would aid him in his planned escape: the pepper spray, the baton, and the Taser for sure. But first, he needed to find the key that would free him from his metal shackles.

The service belt now lay within his grasp and completely out of sight of Corfinio's circus. Ever so carefully, slowly and deliberately, he unsnapped each pouch on the service belt, grimacing at the slightest sound, muffling it as best he could by pressing it up against his body. He need not have worried as no one was paying him any attention at all, being totally consumed by the ravings of the madman with the gun.

Segado reached into the third pouch and froze. Withdrawing his hand with speed challenging that of a snail, lightly grasped between index and middle finger, was the key. The handcuff key. The key to his freedom.

His hands were steady, but his palms were damp. His mouth was dry, but sweat dripped from his hairline. Still laying on his side, he felt the sweat crawl agonizingly from his temple toward his eye. He voluntarily shivered his head in an effort to deter its path, nervous that any greater movement may attract someone's attention. He gritted his teeth as the salty droplet found the corner of his eye in spite of his attempts at determent. Clenching his still aching jaw only reminded him again that Corfinio was the one who had delivered the haymaker that laid him out.

Tiny cramps assaulted his fingers as he tried to guide the key unseen into the handcuffs without success. He dropped the thin key twice, struggling each time to retrieve it without displaying any body movements that would indicate his intent. As long as Corfinio was talking, there was little chance that he'd be discovered, and actually, the only one who had a direct sightline on him was Judge Thompson in his elevated position, but he remained oblivious.

He still couldn't believe it, that *Corfinio*, of *all* people, would have been able to pull off this stunt!

Never would've figured him to disarm two cops, never mind one! And where the fuck did he come up with that third gun? He got some kinda shit going on.

Segado remembered that Corfinio was no street fighter. His kind of fighting seemed more calculated. After a few months in jail and well after he had seen Corfinio in a few dust-ups, he begrudgingly realized that Corfinio had been holding back when they fought each other. He also discovered that his pugilistic abilities weren't the only thing Corfinio had held back on. He found out much later that he had been in the military "briefly," but he never explained anything further. So maybe he had some kind of training—who knows? *Who cares?* he thought. *Doesn't matter… I'm going to kill him anyway.*

Segado continued fumbling with the key. Trying to maneuver in an immobile fetal position with hands cuffed and legs manacled proved to be far more of a challenge than he had anticipated. *Gotta be some kind of fucking Houdini to get out of this shit!*

33

Corfinio remained silent, nodding. He neither denied nor admitted her accusations. Instead, he addressed Donna LaTrina, head coordinator for DSS, who held a master's degree in family therapy. "Miss LaTrina, why do you suppose that the last three men that Mrs. Corfinio had intimate relationships with were abusive? Should one deduce from this record that *all* men are abusive or that she has simply chosen poorly?"

"Why would you care what I think?"

"I *don't* care what you 'think.' I'm asking for your professional opinion based on your experience and education. And I'm certain that you *are* someone whose experience and education make you the obvious choice to render an explanation that would be acceptable to the court."

LaTrina looked back at Corfinio with open hostility. "Well, I hate to *disappoint* y—"

Thompson's booming voice cut her off instantly. "Just answer the damned question, Miss LaTrina!"

She glowered first at Thompson, then at Corfinio. She hated having to give ground to this psychopath, rankling her beyond description. "*Fine!*" she said a bit too loud, attempting to gather some semblance of composure. "In my *professional opinion*," she mocked, "when someone is exposed to abusive relationships, usually during their childhood via parental example, they tend to repeat these past patterns of behavior in their own lives. Repetitive compulsion."

"I see. So what you're saying is 'She can't help but make bad decisions,' is that it?"

"I didn't say that."

"What if she *can't* make better decisions?" Corfinio asked, raising his voice. "What if she *can't* overcome this...this 'repetitive compulsion' disorder?"

She shouted out immediately, defensively, "*It's not a disorder!*"

"Disorder, compulsion, malady, condition, fucked-up-edness—*whatever* you want to call it—what if it *can't* be overcome by self-governance? *Is there* a solution?"

LaTrina fumed. Between gritted teeth, she acrimoniously hissed, "Yes."

"*Well?*" Corfinio asked, tipping his head toward LaTrina in an effort to draw forth the complete answer from her.

"Counseling or psychotherapeutic help is strongly recommended." She finished and hung her head as if she had just betrayed sensitive information to an enemy faction.

"And *yet*, Miss LaTrina, with *that* admission of probability, you and your organization deemed it preferable to entrust the safety of my son…*to her!*"

"It's still a better choice than to entrust his safety to a woman beater! *Especially* one who goes around half-cocked waving a gun around!"

"Touché, Miss LaTrina, touché." The corner of his mouth turned up with a barely noticeable smirk. "But in all fairness, I've highlighted three of her poor choices as opposed to my one. I understand that mine may weigh heavier in the balance, but at least my poor choice hasn't been repeated, over and over…and over."

Marsha grasped both arms of the chair in an effort to raise herself, but Goldman laid a heavy hand upon her shoulder, preventing her upward drive. "It's not my fault that you all turned out to be assholes! I shouldn't be blamed for what you did!"

"I'm not blaming you for anything," Corfinio replied evenly. "I'm trying to point out that the poor choices you made may not have been *your* fault at all."

Marsha looked confused. "Oh," she uttered meekly.

"*But*," Corfinio said looking skyward, "Miss LaTrina, I have another question for you. I'd like you to contemplate another possibility that no one seems to

279

want to admit *is* a possibility. Let's say that this 'repetitive compulsion' *thing* isn't relevant. Let's *also* say that Mrs. Corfinio *may be* the 'victim of mistaken thinking' concerning the demise of the relationships we've cited."

"I don't understand whatever nonsense it is that you're getting at," she replied haughtily.

Without looking toward the clerk's desk, Corfinio raised his voice and called out, "*Pete!* What do you have in your notes on Mrs. Corfinio's *first* husband?"

"Uhhh…" He flipped pages frantically.

"Come on, Pete, don't let me down!"

"Here it is! I got it!" he said victoriously. "Robert Anzalone—"

"Ronald."

"Yes, right. *Ronald* Anzalone, married one year, she suffered multiple beatings and aggravated rape…and, uhm…that's all I have."

Turning toward Masters, he remarked good-naturedly, "Not exactly *verbatim*, is it, Pete?"

"I'm… I'm sorry, Mr. Corfinio, but I can't write that fast."

"It's okay, Pete, it'll do." Sighing with a hint of satisfaction rather than disappointment at the terse recap, he faced LaTrina again. "Have *you* ever heard of a rapist filing for divorce? How about a wife beater or any kind of abuser for that matter? Personally, I *never* have, but then, I certainly don't have the exposure to these types of situations that *you* have in your line of work."

She stood silently, unwilling to participate fearing that he would turn this around on her and she'd look the fool.

"Yes? No?" he asked hesitantly. "You think about it, and I'll get back to you…" He turned once again to face Thompson. "What about *you*, Judge? Have *you* ever heard of such a thing? A rapist filing for divorce?"

"Where's the relevance in all this, Mr. Corfinio? For someone looking for 'truth,' you sure seem to be taking the long way around!"

"Just answer my question!" Corfinio scolded. "Have you ever, *ever*, in all your years on the bench, *ever* heard of an abuser, a rapist, or a known molester file for divorce?"

"No."

"*Me either!*" he announced triumphantly, spreading both arms out. "So then *this* news is gonna hit like the Fat Boy over Hiroshima! Court records—*filed and stored in this building*—indicate that *Mr. Ronald Anzalone*, after only *four months* of a something-*less*-than-blissful marriage, was the one who *actually* filed for divorce on the grounds of 'cruel and abusive treatment.'"

The uncomfortable silence stretched on for several seconds. Corfinio looked around the room, once again searching faces for reaction. He could see it plainly. They didn't believe him. They didn't *want* to believe him.

Disappointed, he continued, "Okay…tough crowd." He tapped the barrel of the Glock lightly on his thigh.

"Okay," he began again, "across the street from where I live, there's a church. Saint Clemenza's or Saint Clementine's or something like that. Every Wednesday night, there's a meeting in the basement that finishes about eight o'clock, and I see all these people coming out and some of them, I know. One of the guys that I happened to recognize was a guy named Wallace Piobar."

Marsha Corfinio's head shot up, her mouth agape, eyes wide.

Corfinio had hoped for that reaction and prayed that he wasn't the only one who had caught it. He continued talking, looking directly at his ex-wife. "Wallace was a regular at those meetings…had been for quite a while. As it turns out, he was celebrating six years of sobriety. Six years in AA."

"And just what bearing does *this* have on *anything*?" Thompson asked impatiently.

"Well, Judge, maybe you should ask Mrs. Corfinio if she knows who Wallace Piobar is."

Thompson shifted his irritated attention toward Marsha Corfinio, expecting some kind of reply but was instead rewarded with a shivering, shaking mass of emotional nerves.

Corfinio interjected, "Here, let me fill in the blanks for you, Judge. Wallace Piobar is the 'drunk' boyfriend that *allegedly* raped Mrs. Corfinio. After discovering from *other* sources that he was being accused of such vile deeds, *he* walked out. *He* left *her*, which in *my* mind is not quite the same as being 'thrown out.' But…in times of emotionally charged circumstances, we all tend to… recall things less accurately." He shrugged. "It's a human frailty."

Corfinio paced back and forth, shaking his head from side to side, pausing in front of the judge's bench once more. "It would appear," he said softly, "that Mrs. Marsha Hallet Corfinio either has an exceptionally poor memory brought on by extreme duress…or"—he paused, waving a single finger in the air—"she *may* have a tendency to fabricate stories that favor her position. *That's* the possibility I want you to admit exists."

"And what about *your* relationship with her?" Thompson asked. "Do you have an alternate version of *that* story as well?"

"Would it matter? I mean, who'd believe *me*?"

34

Jankowski designated the main concourse in the court-house as the command post. He instructed the remaining two deputies to make certain that all perimeters had been secured and that all non-essential personnel—specifically non-law enforcement—had been evacuated from all areas of the building. His orders were specific: "Get everyone out *quietly.* I don't want any commotion or noise signaling this guy that we know what's going on. *Yet.*"

He scanned the area quickly and pointed at one of a knotted bunch of local police officers awaiting orders. "*You!* I need you out front. SWAT should be here any second." Without making eye contact with anyone in particular but addressing anyone with ears, he waved a typewritten page above his head, announcing, "Does anyone around here have access to a computer or know how to get me background checks on every name on this list?"

"I'm on it, Lieutenant!" a random voice volunteered from the group of tan uniforms, walking over briskly to examine the list.

"Deputy!" he called out to the officer that he had chastised earlier. "Did you call in for SWAT like I told you?"

"Yes, sir, I radioed them ten minutes ago."

Jankowski went wide-eyed. "What...you did *what?*" Jankowski leaned forward and cocked his head to one side as if trying to listen better with his right ear. "You did *what,*" he repeated, "you *radioed* them? Did I *say* to radio them? I don't think I did. I said *call* them, didn't I? I said 'Make the call,' didn't I? *Didn't I?* Didn't I say that? 'Call,' as in 'phone call.' That's what I said, right? Isn't *that* what I said?"

Jankowski rattled off his questions without giving his subordinate the opportunity to speak at all. The officer stood dumbfounded by the barrage and was taken aback at having somehow raised the wrath of his superior once again in a span of less than ten minutes. Wisely, he remained silent as his stomach knotted and his bowels involuntarily clenched.

"That's great," Jankowski said sarcastically. "*Great!* Now we're gonna have half the fucking county here because *you* decided to *radio* them instead of picking up the goddamned phone! Half the fucking state is on that channel along with every television station, radio station, and weigh station clerk! Every two-bit chicken shit outfit is gonna come crawling out of every ass crack in the city so they can take a shot at being the next Geraldo Rivera. But *don't you worry*, Deputy, the extra three, four hundred people…" he said, scrunching up his face and tipping his hand either way, "that shouldn't have *any* effect at all on our ability to resolve this situation as quickly, efficiently, and safely as possible."

His scorn was palpable as he added, "Why don't you go find a bearded lady so we can sell tickets to this carnival!" Jankowski stormed off, leaving the dressed-down deputy contemplating which shitty traffic detail he'd be drawing tomorrow.

35

The late afternoon sun cast a long shadow across the granite stairway of the courthouse as an officer waved in the ebony BearCat SWAT armored rescue vehicle. Even before the vehicle had come to a complete stop at the base of the courthouse stairs, the double rear doors swiftly opened, revealing five armor-clad men, who immediately exited the vehicle in matched formation. The first two paired up on the left, followed by the second duo who automatically shifted right. The last remaining member of the squad stepped out and maintained center position as they climbed the stairway to the courthouse entry doors.

Their choreographed movements were clearly well-rehearsed, a veritable symphony of synchronized armored mobility. Verbal communication seemed unnecessary as each member assumed his position and path without conflict or confusion. Imperceptible nods or slight hand signing appeared to be sufficient for directives and acceptance. After nineteen weeks of intensive training and almost constant practice scenarios and simulations, it was imperative that they operate as one cohesive unit. Their lives and the lives of those they were sent to rescue would all be at stake.

Each man carried a HK416 assault rifle and a holstered SIG Sauer P220 handgun and wore a balaclava and helmets outfitted with eye protective goggles. Although all five men were virtually indistinguishable, being outfitted in almost identical non-rank insignia tactical gear, each moved with his own identifiable individualistic body language nuance. As opposed to Hollywood portrayals, none of the team possessed heroic physiques of monstrous proportions. None of the team were over six feet in height, and all were of medium to slender build, with the exception of the man in the center position.

Sgt. David Olson, acknowledged team leader, thick-chested, broad, and powerfully built, was by far the most accomplished member of the team, having resolved four high-profile hostage situations and nullifying three active-shooter scenarios during his eight years in SWAT. His high proficiency with handguns, long guns, and sub-machine guns qualified him as marksmanship trainer in Gunsite, a world-renowned firearms training facility in Arizona. Four years in the Marine Corp had earned him three expert marksmanship badges: distinguished marksman, distinguished pistol shot, and interdivision pistol. When Olson sighted the crosshairs of his weapon, there was only one question: "Where do you want the body sent."

Olson had recently hit the downside of forty, and while the other members of the force chided him about his 'advanced age', they were all well aware of his complete dedication. No one worked harder or trained harder, mentally or physically. Prior to volunteering for SWAT, he had served five years in the Boston Police Department, where he quickly attained the rank of sergeant. He seldom spoke of his four years in the Marine Corp and never discussed the incidents which led to his receiving the Bronze Star, Commendation Medal, Purple Heart, and the Distinguished Service Medal. The only reason anyone even knew about them was because his wife Jennifer insisted on displaying them proudly over the mantel.

The double courthouse doors suddenly opened like the waters of the Red Sea to admit Olson and his team into the confusion of the main concourse. Once inside, they assumed a spreading *V* pattern with Olson in the point position as they headed straight toward the hastily assembled command center set up in the middle of the expansive concourse.

"Command center" may have been a generous description given the limited amount of time and available equipment. Two conference tables had been enlisted from adjoining areas and were now covered with loose paperwork, three laptops, an ink jet printer, a landline telephone, and several radios. Jankowski stood some-where near the middle of the clutter and confusion barking abrupt orders to those manning the laptops. He caught a peripheral view of the approaching black-clad quintet but maintained his focus on the papers grasped in both fists.

"Sergeant Olson," he stated as a matter of fact rather than as a greeting. "Glad you could make it."

"Lieutenant Jankowski," Olson replied, removing his eye shields, stopping his advancement six feet from Jankowski. The men made eye contact with only the briefest of nods in an acknowledged greeting. In spite of the fact that they had worked several crises together, there would be no salutes, handshakes, or man hugs. The corner of Olson's lower lip turned up in what was meant to be a smile but could just as easily have been confused with a grimace. "How did you know it was me?"

"How'd I know it was *you*? Gimme a little credit, Olson. I'd know that walk if you were draped in a ninja robe wrapped in a black tunic on a moonless night. You move like an armored tank on ball bearings."

Although it didn't sound like praise, Olson knew that was about the highest compliment Jankowski would ever surrender. "Want to bring me up to speed?"

Jankowski moved to a sidelong table and puzzle fit several pieces of paper together. Olson followed, still cra-dling his weapon.

"You know the layout of the building," Jankowski explained, "but here's the floor plan anyway. I've marked the last known positions of everyone in the courtroom. You've got three entry points," he said, pointing to each in succession, "courtroom entry doors, judge's chambers, and Prisoner Holding. Suspect is well-armed."

"What's he got? Do we know?"

"Two Glocks, four magazines. I don't think he's too anxious to shoot anyone, otherwise he'd 'a done it by now. There's two officers down. I don't know the severity of their situation, only that they're incapacitated and unable to intervene."

Olson nodded, tapping a finger on the map. "I think the best—"

"*Excuse* me, *Lieutenant!*" a shrill voice interrupted Olson from behind. "*Lieutenant!*" repeated the emaciated-looking man wearing an ill-fitting tweed suit and wire frame spectacles, fumbling with a laptop that appeared to be his equal in body weight. His pallid white skin seemed almost translucent under the suspended fluorescent lights. Short, thick dark hair collected at his temples, emphasizing the gleaming bald expanse of his bare domelike head. There were sporadic individual hairs that had the appearance of being tiny ant legs that had been glued to his skull. He nudged by Olson, adjusted his slipping glasses as he stuck out a bony hand in greeting toward Jankowski.

"Who the hell are *you*?" Jankowski asked abruptly without returning the gesture, ignoring the pasty white hand thrust out in front of him. He looked questioningly toward Olson in hopes that he may shed some light on who this ridiculous-looking intruder was. Olson raised an eyebrow and shrugged.

The small, thin caricature of a man withdrew his abandoned hand and shoved his glasses back up the bridge of his nose once again. "Oh, yes...ahh, Hiawatha Abernathy, Jr.," he announced proudly, smiling weakly, darting furtive glances at both Jankowski and Olson, expecting them to respond in some manner, but they remained silent. "I'm, ahhhh, the *negotiator*."

"You." Jankowski said it like a factual statement. "*You're* the negotiator."

"Yes, sir!" he said enthusiastically. "Hiawatha Abernathy, Jr."

"Hiawatha?" Jankowski screwed his face up like he had just sucked on a lemon. "Like the *Indian* Hiawatha?"

"Hiawatha, like the *Native American*, Lieutenant. Yes sir, Hiawatha Abernathy Jr."

"*Yeah!*" Jankowski blurted. "I heard you the *first* six times Hiawatha Whoever-You-Are!'" Jankowski kept redirecting his attention toward Olson, who had backed up a step in order to hide the fact that he found this all very well amusing. He was convinced this was a prank that Olson was in on. "This is a joke, right? This is some kind of joke, right?" he repeated, again looking from Olson to Abernathy. "I don't know *you.*" Jankowski talked toward Abernathy then shrugged and aimed his next comment at Olson. "I don't *know* him! Where's Frankie Scutaro? *Him* I know!" He wagged a finger at Olson, anger visibly climbing. "Dave," he started to scold Olson, "I don't have time for this shit! I swear to *God*—"

Olson held up his free hand, palm outward, and shook his head back and forth but couldn't hide the amused grin that was building.

"*Lieutenant,*" Abernathy quickly cut in, "I can *assure* you this is *not* a joke. I really *am* the negotiator. My name really *is*—"

"Hiawatha Abernathy Jr.," Jankowski and Abernathy said in unison.

"Yes, correct. And," Abernathy added, shifting the laptop and pushing his glasses up one more time, "I *know* my name *sounds* funny and I *know* I look…*unconventional,* but I *assure* you, Lieutenant, I'm *very* good at what I do."

"You *better* be, *Hiawatha Abernathy Jr.* There's a dozen people down there whose lives might depend on it."

36

Marsha Corfinio sobbed into her hands while LaTrina attempted to offer her some solace for her unenviable circumstance and the horrifying experiences that she was being made to relive through this latest barrage of abusive treatment.

"You really *are* an asshole, you know that?" LaTrina said bitterly as she glared hatefully at Corfinio. "You're an even bigger asshole than I thought anyone could ever be."

"Wow," he said in a quiet, flat monotone, obviously unaffected by her assessment. "If I gave a rat's ass about your opinion, that might really bother me. But you didn't think so in the beginning, did you?"

"I had you pegged from *day one!*"

"Day one." Corfinio slowly and deliberately turned away from the trio and faced Thompson. "Judge, are you paying close attention to what's being said here? Miss LaTrina has just indicated that her estimation of me as a…'sphincter muscle' has been harbored since—in her own words—*day one*." Corfinio rubbed his chin as if entertaining a thought. "Now, Judge, I pointed out earlier that there quite obviously has been an overwhelming negative opinion toward me since the onset of this situation. *That* in itself compounds the likelihood of me being given an unfair and very biased judgment by *all*. Including *you*, Judge!"

Thompson and Corfinio stared icily at each other, each for different reasons but neither less bitter nor resentful. Not breaking the stare, Corfinio spoke in a low, angry tone parodying late night television ads. "But wait, there's more." Stepping slowly backward two paces away from the bench, he swept his left hand toward the two women as if introducing them in a stage production.

He glowered at the condescending DDS representative with open disdain, barely managing to keep his tone civil. "Miss LaTrina, I would imagine you've seen many examples of domestic abuse on every conceivable level, some of which are probably most disturbing. Isn't that true?"

With her arm still around the shoulders of Marsha Corfinio, she glared back without offering a reply.

"I know you're not a medical doctor, Miss LaTrina, but would you care to speculate what the likely result would be if someone of Mrs. Corfinio's 'dainty build'— what is she, five foot two, maybe a hundred and fifteen pounds? What kind of devastating *damage* would a woman of her petite physique suffer at the hands of a brutalizing attacker?" He bowed his head as if in thought, beginning to pace methodically once again in his contained arena. "A *large* man…a man of great physical strength. A man who is *twice* her body weight, a *foot* taller, and somewhat capable of doling out immeasurable injury through physical aggression. Would such a man—*man*, heh, we may as well call him what he really is, an animalistic, savage *beast*—leave evidence of his punishments? Would there be lacerations, bruising, perhaps fractures or broken bones?"

"I think you've described yourself *quite well*, Mister Corfinio," LaTrina answered coldly with blatant animus.

"Thank you…*and?*"

"There would be evidence."

"Would I be correct in stating that any bruises or lacerations begotten at the hands of such an 'animal' would last for several days?"

"More than likely. As Mrs. Corfinio has *already* said, she had bruises for *days*."

"Weeks." Everyone turned to gape at the source of the unsolicited remark issued by a suddenly emboldened Pete Masters seated at his work table.

Corfinio stared at the clerk in disbelief then asked, "What did you say?"

"*Weeks*, Mister Corfinio, she said 'weeks.' I got it right here." He held up his yellow legal pad, victoriously tapping it with his pen.

"Miss LaTrina," Corfinio said, redirecting his attention, "I believe you stand corrected!"

"*Weeks* doesn't work in your favor, you idiot!" LaTrina scolded him with fervor. "It only emphasizes the severity of the abuse…issued by *you!*"

"Miss LaTrina, tell me if any of what I'm about to say sounds familiar to you—it should because it's information that should be in your file. I was served with divorce papers and a no-contact order on the same day. Eleven days later, I was served with a restraining order citing 'physical abuse to spouse and minor child.' Do you remember that? You should—I believe it was at *your* urging that she file for the order."

"*That's* my job!"

"Calling it your 'job' doesn't make what you do right. Especially when you start to blur the lines. But let's get back to it—eleven days go by, and at some point, during those eleven days, Marsha waltzes into your office all teary-eyed, spinning a tale about how her monster of a husband repeatedly beat and raped her on a consistent basis. Did she happen to show you the grisly, raised welts, the purplish, hideous bruises, or the aberrations from past episodes? Well, *did she?*"

"No."

"Did you *ask* to see them?"

"No."

"The evidence of those beatings *should* have been fairly obvious if she had *really* been subjected to such an ordeal. Don't you think so?"

"They could have faded substantially by the time she spoke with us, and she already said that she covered them."

"Marsha?" Corfinio asked his ex-wife. "Do you have any black-and-blue marks on your body now? Maybe from bumping into something in the last few days?"

She shook her head without looking up and mumbled no.

"Miss LaTrina, Mrs. Corfinio. Would you both do me a small favor? Would you approach the Judge's bench, please?" Corfinio politely requested.

She looked apprehensive at the request but then, resolved to show no weakness, walked arm in arm with Marsha toward the front of the judge's bench. As they approached, Corfinio stepped aside, allowing them a wide berth.

"Your Honor… Judge, I'd like you to instruct Mrs. Corfinio to hold up her hands so that you can see her wrists."

Thompson sighed heavily, looked down at the two women standing before him, and nodded once, indicating that the request should be obeyed.

Corfinio turned his back on the two women and the judge, facing the broad, empty courtroom. "Judge, twenty minutes ago, I asked my ex-wife if I could see her ring. Now I'd like *you* to look at the *topside* of her left wrist. What you'll see there is a small bruise about the size of a quarter. *That* bruise is from *my* thumb when I grasped her wrist to inspect that ring." He turned back around and faced the bench and addressed LaTrina once more. "Twenty minutes and she's got a bruise from a *thumbprint*! And *you* want me to believe that bruises from an out-and-out *thrashing* would fade in less than *ten days* from *me* and my apparent Herculean strength? Even after *she admitted* that the bruises lasted for *weeks*!" Corfinio breathed heavily, chest heaving with built-up exasperation.

"*Weeks!*" he yelled. "She said weeks! And yet *after ten days...no bruise.*" He stopped, taking two breaths. "This doesn't look especially good for you, LaTrina... you, pushing heavily for Restraining Orders for reasons of physical abuse that you *can't prove*, saw *no* evidence of, and more than likely, *didn't exist*...nope, doesn't look good *at all!* The way I see it, you have two options here: one, you may want to reconsider your position on this or, option two, maybe you should look for a new job, because you really *suck* at this one!"

{ 37 }

Felix Segado was probably the only person in the courtroom who hoped that the disruptive chatter would continue for as long as possible. After all, that disturbance was the only shroud he had in covering his attempts at trying to free himself from his restraints. He managed to remove the handcuffs that secured the leg irons to the wrist cuffs, but he dared not straighten out for fear that someone would discover his partial achievement toward freedom.

His heart and breathing stopped instantly when he heard the soft *snick!* of the handcuffs as they released. He lay immobile for what felt like several eternities as he waited to see if the noise had alarmed anyone else in the courtroom. He need not have worried; everyone was still totally enthralled with the unfolding drama being played out forty feet away.

He handled the metal restraint like it was a volatile liquid explosive. Exercising great stealth and caution, he grasped the loosened handcuff and gently opened it to its full extent, disengaging it from the handcuff on his wrist then repeating the action to release the second oval from the leg iron chain. Once they were completely removed, he gently, silently, set the metal handcuffs down on the floor and removed the still-inserted key.

Lying still, he listened warily to the noise levels behind him, hoping only that the volume remain high so as to help muffle any sound he might accidentally produce in removing the next set of handcuffs.

38

Hiawatha Abernathy Jr. set his laptop on one of the assembled tables in the command center area, while Jankowski watched him warily. The little, shriveled bald man looked left and right at his surroundings and reluctantly addressed Jankowski. "Lieutenant," he squeaked cautiously, "is there, uhhh… I mean, do you think…"

Jankowski anticipated the end of the long, drawn-out request by shouting across the lobby, "*Deputy!* Grab me a chair, *pronto!*"

A chair appeared in less than twenty seconds, much to the relieved satisfaction of Abernathy. He sat and opened his laptop and hit the Power button then adjusted his posture. Raising one hand to his mouth, he cleared his throat, twisted his head from side to side, and then wiggled his fingers like a pianist about to begin a concerto. Reaching out with only his right index finger, he tapped one key, and the screen suddenly sprang to life. Eight different pages popped up in seconds, some scrolling, some blinking, others static.

An irritated Jankowski didn't want to admit it, but he was impressed with the flurry of information that appeared literally at the touch of a single key. Abernathy seemed totally absorbed, eyes darting from one item to the next, mumbling softly to himself. He caught Jankowski off guard when he declared authoritatively; "Lieutenant, I need information." Gone was the annoying vocal shrillness, suddenly replaced with a calming, subdued tone. Once he was totally absorbed in his work, his confidence went up, and his insecurities all but disappeared. "Who's our suspect?"

"John Corfinio, as near as I can guess."

"Who initiated the call and what time?" His questions were directed at Jankowski, but his eyes never left the computer screen as he noted each answer, fingers flying across the keyboard, inputting the information into several different applications simultaneously.

"Maria Cortez, maybe an hour ago."

"Explain."

Jankowski related the information of discovery through his earlier interrogation of Cortez.

"Is the suspect injured?"

"I don't think so."

"Who is he holding hostage?"

"Right now, everybody."

"How many is everybody?"

"Best guess is between eight and twelve. Two of them are my deputies."

"Are the deputies injured?"

"We don't know for sure yet. I have to assume that they are to some degree, otherwise they wouldn't be hostages."

"Has any contact been made with the suspect?"

"No."

"My understanding is that they're locked in an isolated courtroom?"

"Yeah, Courtroom 5."

"Floor plan?"

"Right here."

"Uh-huh… I see…you've marked the last known location of the suspect and hostages. Very good." He studied the floor plan carefully for several seconds. "I need available communication modes for that location: telephones, intercoms, PAs, anything and everything."

Jankowski ran his fingers through the hair on his temples and sighed heavily. "Well, you're shit outa luck there, pal. *One* phone. Landline, on the clerk's desk. That's it. That's all you got."

"Mmm. Okay…okay. I can work with that. What do you have for a profile on the suspect, Lieutenant?"

"Hold on…" Jankowski turned toward one of his deputy's seated at the adjacent table, diligently collecting information from county computer files. "Hey, Waller, what have you got for me on this guy?"

"Not much, Lieutenant," Waller replied, shaking his head with a frown, knowing Jankowski wouldn't be pleased with the answer.

"Not much," Jankowski repeated. Then exasperated, he asked loudly, "*Not much?* What does that *mean* 'not much'?" Wild hand gestures accompanied his raving. "You been banging away at that thing for almost an hour and all you can tell me is 'not much'? There's got be *some*thing. *Everybody's* got *some*thing. Parking tickets, speeding tickets, jaywalking, he stole a candy bar..."

"No, that's not what I meant, Lieutenant," Waller answered carefully. "In the last three years, he's got several restraining orders issued, did a year in county—"

"*Oh! Oh!* So he *does* have *some*thing*!* That's great, except we already *knew* that. What *else* do we know? What about *before* that?"

"Well," Waller said nervously, "uh...*that's* the thing."

"*What's* the thing? What *thing*?"

"I'm not finding *anything* on him before that."

"Do you know what you're doing?" Jankowski scolded, raising his voice. "*Do you?* You know *what*, Waller-"

Abernathy cut in quickly. "Hold on, hold on, hold on. Lieutenant? Give me his vitals, full name, birth date, driver's license, social security number, whatever you have."

Jankowski rattled off the information in the order it was requested. Abernathy stared at his computer screen, seemingly mesmerized, his fingers flying across the keyboard, screens exploding and compressing at warp speed. Jankowski stared, enthralled, unable to follow the pages scrolling by at terminal velocity, words flashing by until they looked like Egyptian hieroglyphic symbols etched on scrolled papyrus. And then, in shocking contrast, it stopped.

"Lieutenant?"

"Yeah?' Jankowski answered in complete awe. "What do you got for me, Abernathy?"

"Well, it appears, Lieutenant, that up until *three* years ago, our suspect didn't *have* an arrest record or any negative societal impact whatsoever. Completely clean."

"That's unusual. A guy just doesn't decide to go bad at *forty*. *Very* unusual."

"More unusual than you know."

"What's that supposed to mean?"

"*Seven* years ago, 'John Corfinio' didn't exist *at all*."

39

"So she's got a bruise on her wrist, *so what*?" Thompson leaned back and flicked the billowy sleeves, crossing his arms across his chest.

"Judge, can't you see that her claims of abuse have been wildly exaggerated, if not *completely* fabricated? How can you *not* see that? I thought that *you* of all people would plainly see that. LaTrina won't change her opinion or reassess *her* evaluation because it would only tarnish her reputation. She's afraid that if she goes back on what she said now, she'll look like a fool to her constituency. Just because she's sticking to her guns doesn't mean that she's *right*. Be honest, Judge, wouldn't *you* reassess *your* decision based on the facts I've supplied?" Corfinio's tone of voice almost sounded like a desperate plea.

"Heh-heh," Thompson laughed softly, pinching the bridge of his nose with his thumb and forefinger. "In spite of all your dramatics, Mister Corfinio, you haven't supplied me with any 'facts' at all. Just speculation."

"*Speculation?*" he asked, in awed surprise at Thompson's remark.

"You having a problem understanding that? 'Speculation'—conjecture, an *opinion*. You've got *nothing* to back up *any* of your wild accusations against anyone. Did you bring me documentation? Did you bring me witnesses? Did you offer professional assessments under sworn testimony? No? Shame."

"But *they* supplied *bogus* documentation, *false* witnesses, and shady professionals, and you're *perfectly* willing to accept *that* as…as *evidence?*"

"*Prove* it."

Sighing with disappointment, Corfinio's shoulders sagged heavily. "But 'reasonable doubt' should carry *some* weight."

"To a jury maybe. I need facts."

Corfinio hung his head down, seemingly admitting defeat. "Then I guess this is it then, isn't it?" He took a deep breath and let it out again. "This has all been for nothing," he said, his face flush with disappointment.

"And a complete waste of time. Congratulations on identifying the blatantly obvious." Thompson scowled sarcastically.

"Blatantly obvious," Corfinio repeated in a low, almost inaudible tone. His ire was rising quickly. His tone and volume increased as he reluctantly gave in to the anger that he had tried to keep in check for so long. He paced, agitated, animatedly waving his hands as he spoke, directing his wrathful tirade straight at Thompson. "Yeah, it's *blatantly obvious* now but *not* a complete waste of time. Because *now*, Judge, *now* I finally understand what this is all about. *Now* I *understand* how this whole *fucked-up* system of yours works. People come to court seeking justice, but that's not what they get, *is it*? It's *certainly* not about right or wrong, *is it*? It's not about finding out *the truth*, and it *never was*. All you're doing is driving a stake in the middle ground and tethering both sides to it. How stupid am I? How did I not see that before? It doesn't *matter* what *really* happened! It doesn't matter what the real *truth* is. *All that matters* is how you can make this all go away.

"*She...*" he yelled, pointing his gun hand in the direction of his ex-wife, causing the trio to flinch involuntarily, "*she...*withholds what is *rightfully, legally* mine, and I have to beg *you* for what should have *never* been taken from me. And what do *you* do? You make her throw me a bone from the meal that *I've* provided, and then you have the *gall* to tell me how *fortunate* I am to have *anything at all!*"

"You've got a pretty distorted view of reality, and I think I've heard about as much of your bullshit as I can stand. This has gone on long enough—"

"My *bullshit*?" he screamed, charging the bench in an explosive frenzy. "Are you fucking *kidding* me? Your *whole system* is nothing *but* bullshit! All she had to do was *walk in here* and claim that she was beaten, abused, or raped, and every one of your goddamned trained attack dogs trip over themselves with their 'socially corrective' programs to reform *my* intolerable behavior without ever—*ever*—considering that *she* was lying.

"And when the 'blatantly obvious' hits you in the face, *exposing* her lies, what did you do about it? Not a *fucking* thing! *Nothing! I'm* not the one who has to be 'fixed' here, Judge—*it's you!* I think maybe *you* need to get your head out of your ass!"

"Don't talk to *me* like that! You miserable piece of shit!" Thompson shot up from his chair, yelling back at Corfinio.

"*Sit the fuck down* and shut up!" Corfinio bellowed, waving the gun upward. "I'll say whatever the fuck I want!"

"You're just making this worse—"

"*Worse? Worse! How* could it *possibly* get *worse?* I'm going to fucking *prison* for this! *How* could it get any *worse*? What are you going to do, add five years on my sentence because I *offended* you?" Mild laughter escaped him as he resumed pacing back and forth until he found himself standing in front of the clerk's desk. He snickered once again. "Pete, not for anything, but how in the *hell* can you work for this guy? Has he *always* been this pompous and full of shit?"

Words caught in his throat like a chicken bone. Masters answered with an awkward shrug and a look of discomfort.

Looking up at Thompson once again, Corfinio continued with a small level of calm returning. "I'm sure that from where *you're* sitting, Judge, in your insulated cocoon, *you think* what you're doing is fair to both sides, *but it's not,* and we *both* know that now, don't we? Here's the way it *really* is. She walks in, starts whining. You sit there and go, 'Oh god, I don't want to listen to *her* shit all day.' So what do *you* do? You give her whatever the *fuck* she wants. Now *she* shuts the fuck up. I object. You tell *me* to shut the fuck up, *pay* the freight, or be in contempt and pay *even more. Everybody* shuts the fuck up. Judge goes home, pats himself on the back, and sips his Johnnie Walker Red…problem *solved.*

"I'm not saying that there aren't women out there who legitimately need protection, but *she* isn't one of them. She's learned how to use and abuse the system, and she's gotten a considerable amount of mileage out of it. She's done quite well with the lies you've encouraged her to tell."

He took a firm step toward the triumvirate. "She's nothing more than a *lying…*"

He took another step forward.

"*Deceiving…*"

And another.

"Vicious, self-centered…"

And another.

"Manipulating piece of *shit*…"

He stopped four feet from his trembling ex-wife, staring hatefully into her blackened soul, mentally reliving every injustice that she had played upon him in the last two years. His voice was flat and eerily demonic, as if forecasting an unnecessary tragedy.

"Yet our 'civilized' society *blindly* protects *her* against the punishments *she* truly *deserves*—a punishment that *she deserves* for polluting reputations, causing suspicion, wariness, and distrust toward people whose lives will be forever tainted because of *her* accusations. I *guarantee* all this crap would stop immediately if *she*—and the hundreds or thousands just like her—were subject to a punishment equal to that of the crimes she *alleges*…a punishment that solves *everybody's* problem once and for all."

Corfinio's chin dropped slightly, his eyebrows arching evilly over his festering dark-eyed stare. His left hand rose slowly, holding the gun steadily, aiming directly at her terror-stricken face.

"A fucking bullet in the head."

40

Probably because of his analytical personality and self-proclaimed "extensive professional experiences," shock was an unfamiliar reaction, but a clear display of shock was easily apparent on Jankowski's face. "*What?*"

"*Seven* years ago," Abernathy repeated automatically, "John—"

"I *heard* what you *said*!" Jankowski bellowed. "What does that *mean*, huh? 'Didn't exist'? *How? How* could he *not exist*? Answer me that. He's having a *hell* of an impact for a guy that *doesn't exist*!"

Abernathy wisely waited until Jankowski finished his rhetorical rant. "Lieutenant, all I can tell you is, there's no legal documentation existing for John Corfinio—including a birth certificate—until seven years ago. Nothing."

"Nothing," Jankowski repeated, stepping back from the table wordlessly, eyes darting rapidly across the room as if searching for the elusive answer as if it hung somewhere suspended in midair. Everyone waited anxiously for him to speak, but those who knew him well made sure not to make eye contact for fear that he would redirect his irritation toward them. The three men seated within close proximity all had the good sense—through prior involvement with Jankowski—to feign total absorption with their desk tops, computer screens, or fingertips. Jankowski wandered aimlessly in tight circles, rubbing his stubbled chin with his right hand, left hand shoved deep in his trousers pocket. Engaged in deep deductive thought, he would either nod several times with an affirmative grunt of "hmm" or shake his head with an accompanying "nah" during his circuitous journey to nowhere. His subordinates had seen this routine before and knew better than to interrupt. They knew that when he reached his conclusion, there would be no turning back on his decision. They also knew that his decisions were generally spot on, which only made it more infuriating. Several minutes passed before he made his way back to the tables and stood by Abernathy, addressing all within earshot.

"Fuck it!" he announced with finality, splaying his arms wide like an umpire calling a runner "safe."

The seated deputies eyed each other carefully across the tables, still not certain that it was safe to pose a question.

"Sir?" A surprised Waller asked apprehensively but thought privately, *Didn't see* that *coming!*

"I said *fuck it*, Waller. Fuck it *all*," he repeated, throwing one hand in the air. "I don't give a *shit* if he didn't *exist*. Doesn't matter. I don't give a *shit* who he *is*, *was*, or ever *will* be. Doesn't matter. *Whoever* the fuck he *is*, he's ours to deal with *right* here, *right* now. He's here *now*!" His last words were emphasized by stabbing his index finger onto the tabletop with the issuance of each syllable. He leaned down almost face to face with the negotiator. "Abernathy, you better be as good at talking this guy down as you are at playing with that computer there."

"Lieutenant," Abernathy said apprehensively, "my chances of success are considerably better if I have a little more background on the hostage taker. Right now, we've got next to nothing. Usually, I'd like to know why he's taken the hostages and what his demands are. I need some background information. That information gives me a starting point to negotiate."

It was uncomfortably obvious that Jankowski's ire was increasing rapidly as he snapped to a ridged standing posture, agitation winning out over patience. "Information," he said tensely, "you want information. Okay," he roared, "*here's your information!* You wanna know *why* he took hostages? *It's Wednesday!* He *hates* Wednesday! You want to know his *demands*? He wants it to be *Thursday*!"

Jankowski whipped around to his left and fiercely grabbed the landline phone seated in front of Deputy

Waller on the adjacent table. Waller leaned back reflexively, making every effort to steer clear. Flipping the cord like a bullwhip, freeing it of a snarled tangle, Jankowski charged back in front of Abernathy's table and slammed it down, rattling contents and nerves alike.

"*There's* your starting point to negotiate! *He's got hostages! Get them out!*" Jankowski spun around and yelled out, "Olson!" and stormed off toward the SWAT team leader.

As the cloud of heated emotions dissipated, Abernathy sat and stared at the phone, trying to formulate a reasonable approach and plan, but without some of the critical information available, it would be difficult to conduct a successful negotiation. It was hard enough *with* all the proper information supplied to assume that all would go well. Following suggested and proven negotiating protocol to the letter wouldn't guarantee successful results either. What worked successfully in one situation may result in a total bust on the next intervention. He hated to admit it, but even with the overall established success rate of 95 percent in terms of resolving a hostage crisis without fatalities, the 5 percent failure was responsible for his restless sleep and frightful nightmares.

How he approached the situation depended heavily on Corfinio's mental stability. He'd need to deal much differently with someone who was depressed or suicidal than with someone who was a cold, rational pragmatist. Abernathy's success hinged heavily on discovering why

Corfinio had taken the hostages in the first place and what it was he wanted. A psychological profile could be created from a telephone conversation if he paid close attention to his tone of voice, responses, and general attitude. It was always better to have eyes on them in one form or another—camera, closed circuit, or direct visual—but walking up to a potentially unstable gunman was never a good idea and could very well ensure unnecessary fatalities. Except in extremely rare cases, approaching an armed hostage taker seldom yielded a TV crime show's happily resolved ending.

Grabbing a pad, he rifled back through his hastily scribbled notes, quickly writing down four bullet points. Each bullet point contained one word. Completing his short list, he tapped the sheet nervously with the nib of the pen before crossing off one of the entries. He placed the pen down and leaned forward on his elbows, massaging his temples with the tips of his fingers. Picking up the pen once more, he carefully crossed out two more entries. The single bullet point remaining read only "why."

Setting the pen down one final time, he placed both hands flat on the table, closed his eyes, and sighed. He waited five seconds, opened his eyes, and reached for the telephone receiver.

{ 41 }

While Abernathy contemplated the best approach for a successful negotiation given his limited resources, Jankowski engaged Olson in a plan of action should the negotiator fail. Standing by one of the extremely large multipaned windows adjacent to the courthouse entry, they spoke in low tones.

"Olson, are you and your team ready?"

Olson looked questioningly at Jankowski. "Negotiation a bust?"

"He's working it out," he said without confidence then shook his head. "I dunno… I don't feel good about this one, Dave. What's your assault plan?"

"Our best shot is through Holding on the ground floor, come up through the stairs into the dock. If everyone else stays where they were, we should have a clear shot without compromising anyone else's safety."

After scanning the floor plan of the courtroom earlier, Olson had decided that of the three possible entry points, the best opportunity was through Prisoner Holding. This afforded his team the ability to approach the courtroom undetected from outside. Utilizing only one of the three triangle-point possibilities also ensured that his team wouldn't be putting themselves into a cross-fire situation that could possibly prove to be disastrous.

Prisoner Holding was directly under the court-room with a stairway leading directly into the dock, the segmented area of the courtroom typically reserved for felons awaiting arraignment. This position would afford them full view of the contained area and the remaining exits. The enclosed stairwell also gave them a point of refuge should there be a need in case things went totally sideways.

"Okay, okay," Jankowski readily agreed.

Glancing out the window revealed a scene of total disruption and confusion. At the instruction of the sher-iff's department, the local PD had cordoned off a perim-eter around the front of the courthouse while local traffic did its best to hamper their efforts. Shouted epithets, single social-finger waving, and horn blasts emphasized everyone's displeasure at being restricted from their homeward-bound objective. People were far more toler-ant of traffic detours and inconveniences *going* to work than they were on the way home. Adding to the confu-sion were the four television production trucks that had arrived complete with on-the-spot news reporters inter-viewing anyone with a face.

Jankowski groaned. "Ohh, for Christ's sake! Just what I need—a goddamned media feeding frenzy. In about ten minutes, they're gonna have the whole world believing this guy's a saint that's being persecuted by the injustices of a failed society or some such bullshit."

He waved over one of his men, putting his hand on his shoulder, and continued talking in a low tone. "I want you to make sure we have a clear path from here to Holding. Sergeant Olson and his team need an unobstructed path, do you understand? Make sure the perimeter is secure. Get the local PD to push everyone back across the street. Talk to no one else. *No…one!* Do you understand me? No news correspondents, TV people, or anyone with a cell phone, microphone, or a camera. The last thing I want to see on the eleven o'clock news tonight is your face smiling into a lens, got it?"

"Yes, sir."

"Good. You got three minutes. Clock's ticking. Go, go, *go!*"

Turning back to Olson, he stuck both thumbs inside his waistband and ran them around the front perimeter of his pants. "Your guys ready?"

"Waiting on you," Olson said with a wink before pulling his goggles back down into place.

"Your headset coordinated with TOC?"

Olson replied with a tap of his mouthpiece and a nod.

"Let me know when you're in position. If things don't work out with Abernathy over there," he said, tossing his head in the negotiators direction, "it'll be up to you to clean this shit up."

Olson pointed over Jankowski's shoulder back toward the negotiator. "Looks like he's got something. He's waving."

Jankowski turned to see Abernathy with the phone cradled against his ear. "Yeah," he replied, eager to get back to Abernathy. He stopped suddenly, turning back to Olson. "Hey, Dave? Do me a favor, will you?"

"What do you need?"

"If it comes down to it, don't waste this guy. I got a lot of questions."

Olson nodded. "No guarantees, Lieutenant, no guarantees."

42

Bang!

Marsha Corfinio instantly crumpled to the floor, a spreading pool of bodily fluids emanating from her collapsed form. Corfinio's sudden bellowing vocal of a gunshot sound had caused her to lose control of her bladder.

"Now *that*," Corfinio said, turning his head to face Thompson, "was *real* fear! Not like the theatrics she displayed earlier. *No!*" He faced his ex-wife once again as she remained seated on the floor in her own puddle of urine. "I bet you thought it was just an expression when people say '*I was so scared I peed myself.*' Well, *there* you have it! It's a *real* thing!"

LaTrina piped in indignantly, "You really *are* a *bastard*, d'you know that?"

"Yup."

"Are you happy with yourself," Goldman added bravely from behind LaTrina, "now that you've—"

"Shut the *fuck* up, Goldman," Corfinio scolded. "Don't pretend like you've got a set of balls *now*, especially after you've been hiding behind *her* all day."

Marsha sobbed quietly, more from embarrassment than anything else. Corfinio felt oddly gratified watching her finally express an emotion that truly was the result of reaction rather than a rehearsed situation of her choosing.

"You *can't* expect her to *sit* here like this," LaTrina chided, "while you...play out your little *game!*"

"Ohhh, *sure* she can," Corfinio answered. "I sat in jail for a whole year while she played *her* little game. I think she'll be just fine...a little soggy perhaps, but outside of the humiliation, she'll be fine."

"*You're an asshole!*"

"And you're a twat." He sighed and continued calmly. "As much as I'd *love* to continue this biologically stimulating conversation with you, I'm afraid we're going to have to cut it short. I have some questions for my ex-wife."

He walked over slowly toward the table adjacent to where Masters sat, still dedicating his time to taking thorough notes.

"You doing okay, Pete?" he asked quietly.

"Yes sir, but..."

"What's wrong, Pete?"

Masters looked sheepish. "Well, it's my hand—it's getting a little cramped."

"Yeah, I'm sure it *is*," he replied in agreement. "Take a little break then, go ahead."

Masters set the pen down and looked inquisitively at Corfinio for approval.

"Yeah, go ahead…you're good. Shake them a little."

Masters shook his hands vigorously, trying to get the stiffness out and some blood flowing.

"*Mister Corfinio!*" Thompson bawled. "*Do* you *mind!*"

Refusing to face Thompson, he merely held up the flat of his palm toward the judge and continued to speak to the court clerk.

"You good now, Pete?"

Masters nodded appreciatively, once again picking up the pen.

Thompson, insulted and infuriated at having been shushed, erupted in outrage. "Don't you blow *me* off!" he thundered. "This is *my courtroom*—"

"Was!" Corfinio yelled back, cutting Thompson off. "*Was* your courtroom…now it's *mine*! You've been voted out of office by me and *Mr. Glock* here." He brandished the 9mm pistol and waved it tauntingly in the air. "*None* of this would be happening if you had just done your due diligence instead of 'playing it safe.' And that goes *for all of you!*" He made a wide, sweeping motion with his gun hand and stared them all down with a look of disgust and revulsion. "'*Playing it safe*'…playing it safe by infringing on *my rights! Now* if you *don't* mind, and even if *you do*, I really don't *give* a shit. I'd *like* to continue and *be done* with—"

Brreeeet! Brreeeet! A sharp, chirping sound emanated from the corner of Masters's desk. One of the sixteen buttons blinked green, accompanying the pitchy sound of the black polymer phone. Masters looked from Corfinio to the phone several times, unsure of what to do as the signal went on unabated.

Corfinio stared down at the phone in something just short of awe. He pointed at the phone and directed his question to Masters. "That thing actually *works?*"

"Uhm, well...yeah," he replied as the phone continued to ring.

"For how long?"

Masters seemed confused by the question. "Until you answer it...that's kinda how it works."

Brreeeet! Brreeeet!

"No, I meant, will it go to voice mail or something?"

"No, this line isn't equipped with that option."

"Do you know who it is?"

Brreeeet! Brreeeet!

"Well, no. I have to pick it up," he explained nervously. "Shall I answer it?"

"Well, *Jesus*, Pete! It *is* kind of annoying!"

"So I *should* answer it?"

Corfinio rolled his eyes. "*Yes! Yes! Answer* the damned thing before I shoot it! But, Pete..."

Masters nodded, understanding the unspoken directive, then hesitantly reached for the phone when the light stopped flashing and the chirping ceased. His hand remained suspended above the handset as if afraid to lift it off the cradle. "It *stopped*!" he declared. Shrugging his shoulders, he looked up at Corfinio from his seated position and seemed genuinely perplexed.

"So I see." Corfinio thought for a moment. "I'm pretty sure that wasn't someone calling in a lunch order. Will someone come—"

Brreeeet! Brreeeet! The chirping sound resumed its single-tone musical symphony.

Masters looked at Corfinio, waiting for direction as the chirping continued. Corfinio grimaced and begrudgingly nodded.

Masters lifted the receiver. "Yes?" Looking down at the scarred surface of his desk, he listened for several seconds before finally replying. "Yes…yes, of course." He held the phone receiver out toward Corfinio. "It's for you."

{ 43 }

Abernathy waved his arm high in the air as a signal to Jankowski that he had made contact with the hostage taker.

Using hand-slicing gestures across his throat, Jankowski motioned everyone in the area into silence. "Put it on speaker," he demanded in a harsh whisper. He pulled out the chair adjacent to Abernathy and set his left foot on it, resting his folded arms across his knee and stared intently at the phone.

*****

In Courtroom 5, ignoring the proffered phone receiver, Corfinio's facial expression asked the obvious question without having to utter a word.

"I don't know. I didn't think to ask," Masters replied guiltily.

His stomach knotted with a pang of paranoia, his hand involuntarily clutching and loosening his grip on the pistol. There were no windows in the courtroom, but he recognized that there were two exits with doors, one leading to the corridor and the other leading to the judge's chambers. Neither door had glass panels to reveal if someone was on the opposite side. The third exit was the stairway leading down to Prisoner Holding, but he could plainly see there was no one there.

Corfinio took the receiver apprehensively and held it to his ear, involuntarily holding his breath. Straining to listen, he heard muted background noise and the breathing of the caller. Pressing the receiver closer to his ear, he squinted his eyes in an attempt to increase his hearing capacity, but his efforts yielded no significant results.

"Hello?" Abernathy offered.

"What do you want?" Corfinio asked abruptly.

"I believe it's more a question of what *you* want." Abernathy kept his tone low and calm, almost pleasant, and quite disarming.

Mind racing, bouncing in a hundred different directions, Corfinio stood rock steady for several breaths without uttering a sound. When he finally spoke, it was aimed at Masters. "Can you put this thing on speaker?"

Masters nodded once and held out his hand to take possession of the receiver once again. He pressed the speaker button on the console and set the receiver in the cradle, again nodding to Corfinio, indicating that the speaker function was engaged.

"Hmm, well, let me see—what...do... *I*...want. How about money? No, I'm all set. Getaway car? No, too cliché...maybe the release of political prisoners being held in Russian gulags? Nope. I guess you're shit out of luck! What *I* want *you* can't give me. So before we get into any Freudian discourse over how sucking the cream filling out of a Twinkie is a latent homoerotic desire, let me assure you that whatever psychological profiling you're trying to establish is going to fall several feet short of whatever they taught you in Negotiation 101. You *cannot* fulfill my demands, so let it go."

"Why don't you tell me your demands and I'll see what we can do?"

"Let me guess," Corfinio said while he carefully scanned every exit of the courtroom, "you must be the guy who's supposed to talk me off the ledge, right? Then we go on Doctor Phil, and we hug and cry and become best buds after I do my twenty-year sentence."

"Not at all," Abernathy replied steadily. "I think you realize that you're in a very difficult situation, and I'd like to help you sort it out. Perhaps you could help *me* by telling me what it is you need."

Corfinio studied the phone attentively, listening to the tinny voice through the speaker, and began walking around the table in a slow circuit. "How very *gracious* of you, allowing *me* to assist *you* in *my* time of need." There was a definite trace of sarcasm evident in his speech, which was not lost on Abernathy.

"I should have been more precise," Abernathy apologized. "How can we work this out?"

"You just don't know when to quit, do you? There's nothing to work out. This is over. Save your breath."

"Will you at least let me know if any of the people with you are in need of any medical attention?"

"Well, to be honest, Judge Thompson looks like he could use a Xanax, and in my opinion, Officer McCorken would benefit *greatly* from a low-carb diet, but other than that, no, I think we're good."

Abernathy paused for a few seconds then continued cautiously, "I'm glad to hear that the hostages are unharmed. With as many as you have there, I'm sure that it must be taking quite a toll on you to keep them all under surveillance. I can only imagine that several of them by this point are becoming quite impatient and cranky. It may be in both our interests for you to divest yourself of the…*more irritable* ones."

Corfinio continued his circular pacing, listening carefully to the unruffled speech of the negotiator. The voice was practically soothing in its delivery. Almost *mesmerizing*.

He stopped pacing. Walking over to the phone, he reached down and picked up the receiver and spoke into the mouthpiece. "Can I get back to you on that? I'd like to think it over." Without waiting for a reply, he carefully placed the receiver on the cradle, ending the call.

"Pete," he said, "do you have an extra piece of paper?"

"Yes, of course." Masters tore out the back page of the notebook and handed it outward toward Corfinio.

"Do me another favor, Pete. Write this down for me," he said, leaning over and whispering his dictation so that only Masters could hear. Upon completion of the short dictation, he resumed his normal tone. "In a little while, that phone is going to ring again, and when it does, I want you to take that piece of paper and hand it to Miss LaTrina and have her recite the contents of that note to the caller. Will you do that?"

Masters looked down at what he had written, and a genuine grin filled his face. "Yes, sir! I can do that!"

44

Snick! The second set of handcuffs' locking mechanism released after much hand cramping and uncomfortable maneuvering. No one paid him any attention at all. It was like he was a non-entity at this point, which suited his purposes just fine.

Segado smiled, laying the handcuffs ever so gently on the floor next to the first set, thinking, *You got a big set of cajones, Johnny. You ain't got no brains, but you got cajones! You don't be reprimanding no fucking judge! Gun or no gun, judges don't forget shit like that!*

He flexed his hands a few times and rubbed his wrists where the cuffs had left the skin raw. He took a deep breath before attempting to turn his attention to the last remaining set of restraints, the leg irons. These would prove to be more difficult because of the attached length of chain, thus more likely to make noise. He inched his legs up slowly toward his torso to better reach the lock when suddenly all the noise behind him stopped. He froze instantly, thinking he had been discovered, but there was no expected cry of alarm, no pattering of approaching footsteps, only an annoying, incessant sound that he couldn't identify.

Segado closed his eyes and listened hard to the lack of noise behind him and was relieved to finally hear Corfinio's voice. "Can you put this thing on speaker?"

Letting out a long, controlled sigh of relief, Segado realized what the sound was and returned his attention to the leg irons. *It's a phone! He's on the fucking phone. Only a dumbass fucking wop would decide that now's the time to call for a fucking pizza!*

His legs were stiff and aching from lying on the hard floor and being in the same position for a long time. He reached down and inserted the key into the ankle lock, using his alternate hand to muffle any sound. He turned the key and held his breath, rotating the key until he heard the *snick!* of release. Realizing that he couldn't completely remove the leg irons without being detected, he loosened the clasp but let them remain in position.

Reaching out slowly and carefully, he edged the deputy's service belt closer to his bent form. Corfinio's voice droned on behind him, still engaged in telephone banter. *You keep talking, Johnny. I just need a little more time.* He released the Taser from the looped holster and slowly tucked it into his waistband, taking several agonizing minutes to complete the task. Blinking away salt-laden sweat from burning his eyes, he reached out once more and retrieved the baton, clutching it firmly in his left hand. He opted to leave the extra Taser cartridges and flashlight as useless for his immediate needs. The pepper spray might come in handy, though, especially if he needed to subdue more than one adversary in a non-lethal fashion…not that he had a problem with that should it come down to it. This was do or die, baby.

45

"That's *it*?" Jankowski asked, rising from his bent position. "What the fuck was *that*? We got *nothing*, Abernathy! *Nothing*!" The frustration and disgust at the failed negotiation was plainly obvious on Jankowski's contorted face as he scolded Abernathy.

Abernathy sighed and sat back in his chair. "Lieutenant," he drawled, "we actually do have *some*thing."

Jankowski walked around to stand directly in front of Abernathy, placed both hands flat on the table top, bent from the waist, and shoved his enraged face within two feet of the negotiator. His lip quivered. "We don't know *who* this guy is! We don't know *why* he's doing this! We don't know what *the fuck* he wants! We don't have *any released hostages*! That looks like a big, fat, fucking *nothing sandwich* to *me*, Abernathy!"

The slightly built, pasty-faced negotiator was wholly unruffled by the intimidating antics of Jankowski.

Abernathy raised his head, looking Jankowski in the eye. "Here's what we *do* have, Lieutenant: We've got a gunman who is basically in control of his situation. Although you may not agree with my assessment given the situation and its circumstances, he's emotionally stable. He's also analytical, probably a bibliophile—"

"A *what*?" Jankowski interjected, instantly confused by the unfamiliar term.

"Bibliophile. He's a reader. He reads books."

"So? So he reads books, so what? How is that relevant?"

"Readers tend to recall scenarios they've read about and are able to apply them with some success to real-life situations. Those who are not avid readers tend to fail more often because they have less to draw from given the same circumstances."

"Or maybe he's just a whack job."

"Highly doubtful."

"What else?"

"He's neither depressed nor suicidal. He is, however, to be considered somewhat dangerous—and not by virtue of his available weaponry but rather by his rational, pragmatic nature and cool, under-fire attitude. He's unshakable."

Jankowski backed off slowly from the desk and squinted at the negotiator. He wasn't quite sure if he believed everything Abernathy was telling him, and his patience was wearing thin. "Abernathy, I think you should get *back* on the phone and get this resolved before someone gets hurt or maimed or killed. Tell him whatever you have to—just get it done."

"Lieutenant, this situation will not be resolved by negotiation. *Of that* I am *quite* sure."

"Call him back," Jankowski demanded, pointing at the phone.

"Lieutenant—"

"*Call him back!*"

"He won't *answer*, Lieutenant, I—"

"*Yes, he will!*" Jankowski grabbed the receiver off the console and shoved it toward Abernathy. "*Call him back, goddamn it!*"

The negotiator sighed heavily. Everybody's nerves were frayed, and he understood exactly why Jankowski was being so adamant about the call. Even though he had dispatched the SWAT team for a possible assault, Jankowski didn't want to give them the go-ahead to storm the courtroom and risk a fatality. Once the SWAT team engaged in an assault, there was no going back. They would complete the mission by disarmament or by fire if warranted. Despite all his bravado and bluster, Jankowski didn't want to be the man giving the order that could result in the death of anyone, even if they had earned it.

Abernathy reached for the phone and pressed the call button for Courtroom 5 and then immediately pressed speaker.

The phone rang twice.

Three times.

Four times. Abernathy tapped his finger on the receiver.

Five times. Abernathy heard a click as the receiver on the other end was picked up, but no one answered.

Uncertain anyone was there at all, Abernathy asked, "Hello?"

A woman's voice replied, "I'm sorry, the person you are trying to reach is unavailable at this time. Please try your call again later."

46

"*So!*" Corfinio exclaimed brightly after hanging up the phone. "It appears our time here is coming to a close. I'm sure none of you will be disappointed with that conclusion, having been 'persecuted' as such by a 'crazed gunman.' But I can tell you one thing for certain: You'll be talking about this day for *years* to come."

"How *very* narcissistic of you," LaTrina said, not trying to hide her snarky attitude. "What makes you think *anyone* will want to remember even *ten seconds* of your life?"

"Ahhh, the dim, bottle blonde *reeking of ineptitude* regales us with her noble and courageous sentiments once again!" Corfinio raised his index finger in the air rather playfully, as if declaring a victory over his adversary. "On the *contrary*, I wasn't talking about *me* at all. I was talking about *you!* About how you'll cover up your inadequacies and blemishes that have *caused* this entire situation. You'll cover your negligence, your errors, your *rash* judgments…but *especially* your lies. Which incidentally, brings us *right back* to where I keep getting sidetracked from." Motioning toward his ex-wife, he said, "*Her.*"

He walked back toward the table where Masters sat. "Pete?" he said in slightly more than a whisper, "I, uhhh… I know this is going to sound insincere given all that has happened. But you didn't deserve this today. You were just in the line of fire. I'm sorry for…dragging you into all this crap. I shouldn't have—"

"Mister Corfinio," Masters suddenly interrupted, holding up his hand palm outward, elbow on the desk and tapped his notepad with the pen. "We need to *finish* this…okay?"

Corfinio held Masters's confident stare. "Okay."

Masters nodded. "Okay. Proceed."

Corfinio turned his back on Masters and leaned his ass against the heavy oak desk and slumped slightly with legs stretched out in front of him. He crossed his arms across his chest, Glock still held in the right hand, and tapped it gently against his left biceps repeatedly before he finally spoke.

"Marsha, why don't you explain to all these nice people why you've gone to extraordinarily ridiculous lengths to keep me away from my child? Tell them why you fabricated story after story about how I *abused* you or tried to *murder* you and kidnap our son. Why don't you explain to everyone how your intent right from the very beginning was to have a child so that you could use him as a meal ticket? I'm sure you have a *perfectly* legitimate reason for completely fucking me over, so maybe you could share that with us. Care to explain?

"No? Okay then, why don't we go back—*way back*—back to when your mother left you on a doorstep. That's when it all started, isn't it? All the abandonment issues? She tucks you into a little wicker basket with a note that says 'Love me' and *dumps* you on a doorstep because she doesn't want you, right? So she throws you away! She doesn't have *time* for a baby. She had *things* to do, *places* to go—she couldn't be *saddled* with a baby. That would have cramped her lifestyle as a party girl, so she *dumped* you. *Plop!* Hit's the buzzer and *bam!* She's off like a shot! Doorbell ditch! *See ya!*

"And then...*then* what happens? Well, then that family takes you in and adopts you. But instead of being the caring and loving parents that every child deserves, you're treated like Cinderella with an evil stepmother that forces you to assume the servile tasks of the household. You're practically an indentured servant! They punished you undeservedly, repeatedly, for nothing more than cross words or simple disobedience. Until they finally tire of your fatiguing existence, and *they too* cast you out, leaving you *no* option but to fend for yourself in a cruel world that *also* doesn't want you. And there you are, only sixteen years old, *alone* once *again*, abandoned by those who should have offered you the security, the safety, and the love that you so craved." Corfinio unfolded his arms, placing the heels of both hands on the edge of the desk. "That's what happened, right? That's what you told me…didn't you?"

Marsha sat as if in a trance, staring at the floor. She nodded slowly without looking up.

"Yeah, I remember when you told me that. At the time, I thought, 'Oh God! What kind of *monsters* would *do* such a thing!' But we both know…that's not what *really* happened, is it? Just like the horrific tragedies you told about your ex-husband and former partners—none of it was true, was it?

"Yes, it was," she offered weakly.

"No, Marsha," Corfinio said, shaking his head disapprovingly, "no, it wasn't. Your mother *didn't* leave you on a doorstep in a cute wicker basket. There *was* no basket…and there was no note that said, 'Love me.' Oh, it makes for a good story and very heart wrenching, but it wasn't true. She gave you up for adoption after struggling for two years because she couldn't care for you properly."

"That's not true," she whispered. "You don't know…"

"She wanted to provide better for you, but she knew she couldn't. She wasn't cut out for it. Financially, emotionally, she couldn't do it. There was only one option for her if she wanted you to have a stable life in a good home, and that was to give you up—"

"No, that's not true—" she said, barely louder.

"For adoption. It *is* true. She *loved* you. She loved you enough to make the ultimate sacrifice that a mother can make—"

"*No!*" Marsha yelled. "*No! If she loved me, she would have kept me!*"

"She did what was best for you whether you want to believe that or not."

"*She gave me away! How could she do that?*" Tears rolled down her face freely as her screamed replies reflected an inner turmoil never resolved.

"She did the right thing, and you know it. Deep down, you *know* it."

"*No, it's not!* None *of that is true!*"

Corfinio kept a steady, calm tone. "Oh yes, it is. She couldn't bring you up by herself—no job, no money, no skills, hardly any education, and no promising prospects. What else could she *possibly* have done? And your father—*whoever he was*—walked out on her as soon as she informed him of her pregnancy."

"*No! That's not what happened!*"

"I'm afraid so. *He* was the one who didn't want to be tied down. *He bolted. He* didn't want any *part* of you. You were a weight, a responsibility, an obligation that he did *not* want to own up to."

Marsha continued to cry real tears, burying her face in the palms of her hands, denying every truth as it was presented.

"But here's where it gets kind of interesting." Corfinio stood up, tapping his left forefinger on his upper lip. "Your adopted parents decided that it would be best to tell you that you were adopted. And that in itself is not a bad thing. You have a right to know that, but *that's* when the trouble started. They wanted you to know the truth of how you came to them, but they also wanted you to know that you were *selected*, you were *wanted*, and that you were *loved*. You didn't just 'happen'—they *picked* you. They wanted you to know that. They wanted you to know that they *chose* to love you!"

"They were *cruel*. They *didn't care* about me! They didn't *love* me!"

"Yes, they *did*, and they still *do*. But *you* turned on *them*, didn't you? Instead of realizing that you had a home with parents that actually loved you, you chose to focus on the parents that *gave you up*, the ones who *abandoned* you. *That* became your entire obsession, trying to escape rejection and abandonment by driving *everyone* away. As soon as anyone gets inside, your defenses go up and you shove them out before they can hurt you or leave you. Your adopted parents didn't *throw* you out. They didn't *ask* you or *tell* you to leave. *You left!*

"You did it to your *parents*, you did it to your *husband*, you did it to *every man* you've had a relationship with, you've done it to *every friend* you've ever had, you did it to *me*, and guess what, Marsha, you're going to do it to *your son* too! You'll drive *him* away just like you've

344

driven everyone else away in your life! *Is that what you want? Is* THAT *what you want?* Is IT?" Corfinio finished, shouting his closing remarks.

"Nooo!" she screeched. "*You won't take my son from me!*" She jumped up, screaming, wild-eyed, clenching her fists. "*He's* MY *child! You can't…*NO!" Specks of foamed spittle hung on the edge of her lip in her crazed state. Her throat-searing screams were evidence that she was beyond all rationality.

"*Marsha!* MARSHA! *Stop!*" Goldman grasped her by the shoulders and shook her violently in an effort to keep her from continuing her self-destructive rant, all to no avail. She was wholly within the dreadful grasp of overwhelming emotions, pushed the very precipice of insanity.

"*You fucker! You won't take him! He's* MINE*! I'll do whatever I have to—anything I have to do!*" she screamed. "*You won't get him! I'll make sure of it, you'll see! I'll keep you from getting him from me! You'll never see him again! Never!* NEVER!" She let out a final ear-piercing screech and collapsed, sobbing and exhausted, shaking violently from the rush of adrenaline. Goldman lifted her gently and quietly guided her to a chair.

Corfinio breathed in deeply and let it out again. Turning away, he walked one careful step at a time until he reached the center of the bench. Slowly turning ninety degrees, he faced Thompson, who simply stared down at him most unkindly.

"Judge, I believe court…is adjourned."

47

Sergeant Dave Olson, SWAT team leader, signaled his team with nothing more than an inconspicuous hand gesture and a nod. To anyone unfamiliar with tactical training, it appeared as if the five men assembled as if by mental telepathy. No verbal directive had been uttered as to sequence, position, or individual task. Each man knew his role within the team and had practiced this scenario several hundred times in training.

The training sessions occurred continuously under ever-changing circumstances and conditions, weather, time of day, residential, educational, or commercial buildings, ground floor or multi story. Every contingency was introduced and considered as highly probable, no matter how unlikely. The drills were physically and mentally exhausting, but the proven methods yielded positive results for team members and those they protected.

The cordoned area was pushed back thirty feet from the sidewalk bordering the courthouse, reducing pedestrian and automotive access to an uncomfortable and dangerous minimum for unobstructed passage. News media thronged the area and shouted out unintelligible questions, each attempting to outshout the other in an effort to maintain their status as "the most informative news station serving the greater Boston area."

In situations like this, basic and honest news reporting took a back seat to journalistic sensationalism. Having a complete lack of factual data did nothing to dampen their enthusiasm for creating a "highly compromising situation" with a "gun-toting, maniacal madman threatening to kill random hostages if his demands are not met." It didn't matter if it was true of not; it kept the viewing public glued to their television screens. As soon as the SWAT team appeared on the courthouse steps, one reporter was quick to announce into the camera, "SWAT is now lodging a full frontal assault," which was nothing more than an inconclusive assumption or, as Jankowski had said earlier, "bullshit."

The team exited the courthouse and descended the wide granite stairway leading down to street level. They automatically assumed well-practiced and measured positions, allowing each member safe distance, unlike the clustered "pod" assemblage frequently seen on high drama TV police shows. Olson, taking point, led the team from the front of the building and turned left at the street corner, which also paralleled the courthouse. Paying little attention to the pressing throng of bystanders, they trotted down the sidewalk until they came to a wide, well-worn asphalt driveway that ramped downward toward the lower level of the building.

At the bottom of the ramp, an iron-strapped door opened outward, allowing access into the basement of the courthouse. Upon entering, a short hallway with exposed iron piping, dented ductwork, and peeling paint-lined walls and ceiling alike. Small iron cages surrounded struggling incandescent bulbs, casting peculiar shadows as the heavily armored men made their way stealthily through to the Prisoner Holding Area.

Olson held up his hand, indicating "hold position," as he advanced slowly forward toward the location of the stairway leading up into the courtroom. Padding deftly across the concrete floor, he approached the stairwell in complete silence—a seemingly impossible task given his body mass, the armored tactical vest, and full equipment adding another forty-six pounds of weight. Looking up into the stairwell, he climbed four stairs and stopped, waiting and listening, keeping his head well below the floor level. He could clearly hear what he assumed was the hostage taker's voice arguing with a woman. He waited several seconds, picturing the floor plan of the courtroom and trying to assess the distance between himself and the hostage taker. Satisfied with this mental image, he backpedaled down the four steps and rejoined his team. He radioed Jankowski and spoke only two words: "In position."

48

Jankowski stared at the phone. "What the fuck was *that* all about, huh?"

Abernathy shut the speaker off and disengaged the call. He could have said, "I told you so," but that wouldn't have served any purpose other than to aggravate the living crap out of Jankowski, who was already angry enough without adding more fuel to the fire.

"We both know *exactly* what it is, Lieutenant," Abernathy answered. "He's done talking."

Jankowski remained silent, staring at Abernathy. He *knew* the negotiator was right. He knew *before* the second call was made that Abernathy was right. But he didn't *want* him to be right. He wanted Abernathy to talk this guy down, release the hostages, and clap the bracelets on him nice and neat. No fuss, no muss, get on the bus, and go home. But it didn't work out that way.

"I'm sorry," Abernathy offered sincerely, pushing his glasses up, his squeaky, annoying tone beginning to return. "There's only one option available here, Lieutenant. Advance your team."

Jankowski fumed, turned, and walked away. Lifting the handheld radio to his chin, he pressed the Send button and issued the order.

"Go."

49

Segado dared to turn his head when he heard Marsha Corfinio screeching like a complete lunatic. This was it. This was the opportunity that would gain him his freedom. Now was the time to make his move.

Kicking off the loosened leg irons, he scrambled to his feet and stumbled. He had been immobile for far too long, but he didn't have the luxury of waiting around for a message therapist to get the blood flowing. He clomped heavily to the head of the stairs, Taser and baton in hand.

As he reached the landing, he looked down into the stairwell and saw the startling black-clad, ominous figure of SWAT Team Leader Dave Olson, who had just begun his ascent. Both men reacted to the other's sudden unexpected presence in a split second.

In a reflex moment born of pure panic, Segado raised the Taser and pulled the trigger. The twin prongs sailed fast and true, lodging just below the shoulder strap of Olson's impenetrable Kevlar vest.

At the same moment, Olson's raised HK416 assault rifle fired one round, striking Segado in the left side of his chest, creating a dime-sized hole piercing the left ventricle of his heart, killing him almost instantly. His body vaulted backward almost five feet, resulting from the close range of the impact, splaying him on the floor like a discarded rag doll.

Olson charged up the remaining stairs, shoulders stooped, knees bent, and rifle held high as he spun to his right at the top of the landing. He never gave as much as a sidelong glance to the fallen Puerto Rican con. He knew Segado was dead. He also knew that Segado *wasn't* the hostage taker. That much was clearly obvious from the orange jumpsuit, which meant that the primary target was still active and armed.

The crack of the gunshot froze everyone in the courtroom. Only Corfinio and the two incapacitated officers understood the significance of the sound immediately.

To the others it was a loud foreign noise, similar to a tin can being hit with a bat. When Segado's body pitched backward, landing on the floor in a heap, the confusion only intensified. Complete lack of visual comprehension of the situation descended into mounting fear and absolute bewilderment. The sudden appearance of a black-clad, armed invader, seemingly erupting from the depths of a sinister hell, proved a complete mental overload, eliciting gasps of horror. The screams followed as the remaining members of the SWAT team were dis-gorged from the stairway as if shot from a canon. Each member selected critical points of offensive and defensive advantage in milliseconds, each with their weapons trained exclusively on the lone gunman.

"WHOA, *whoa, whoa!*" Corfinio yelled desperately. "*Stop!* This is *not* what I want!" Both arms were extended forty-five degrees from his body, the Glock still clutched in his right hand.

Olson took one step forward and addressed him calmly, "Put the gun down. I *will* shoot you!" He bobbed his head and the muzzle of his weapon slightly downward, indicating by gesture the direction he wanted Corfinio to follow.

Corfinio hesitated, fearing only that if he moved too quickly, his actions may be misinterpreted, but he didn't doubt for a second that Olson would carry out his threat. Looking over at the prone and lifeless body of Segado, whose unseeing eyes stared blankly at the ceiling, was direct proof of that.

"You want to end up like him? Three seconds." Olson's baritone voice was commanding and unemotional…and issued without compromise.

Corfinio harbored no fantasy of "dying in a blaze of glory," and he could tell from Olson's no-nonsense directive, stance, and attitude that this was *not* the man to test.

"Okay," Corfinio agreed.

"Three…"

Corfinio lowered his gun hand slowly toward the surface of the adjacent table, never taking his eyes off the reflective surface of Olson's ebony eye shields.

"Two…"

The Glock made a small *clunk* sound as it made contact with the wooden tabletop. He released his grip, slowly spreading his fingers outwardly, trying to give every indication that he no longer had any contact with the weapon.

"Good." Olson nodded once again, pointing at the pair of weapons tucked into Corfinio's waistband. "Thumb and forefinger, low on the grip."

Corfinio brought his right hand back toward his waist slowly, still not wanting to give anyone the impression that he was about to make an aggressive or suicidal move. His left hand remained out from his body, suspended in midair like a retail store mannequin.

Pinching the grip panel firmly between thumb and forefinger as directed, he lifted gently upward, releasing the gun from his belted waist.

Olson motioned toward the tabletop once more. The reflective surface of his eye shields prevented anyone from knowing which direction he was looking in or focusing on, but Olson's sight was locked onto Corfinio's eyes. He had long ago discovered that if there was any way to accurately read someone or their intent, it was through the eyes. Every move was forecasted by a squint, a rove, or a tic. Every lie was forecasted with a darting glance or refusal to make eye contact. Every truth had an open innocence.

Olson didn't like what he saw in Corfinio's eyes at all. The man should have been shitting his pants with five HKs pointed at him, and yet he was ridiculously calm. No trace of desperation or panic. Nothing. Nerves of steel, ice water in his veins. Olson knew the gunman couldn't see through the dark lens of his eye shields, but it felt like he was looking him right in the eye. His stare was steady the entire time, no wide-eyed, wild gawking or sorrowful pleading. He appeared to be as cool and collected as if he were standing in his own backyard watering the lawn on a Sunday afternoon. Olson didn't like it at all.

Corfinio pivoted his right arm from his waist to the tabletop and slowly lowered the second Glock. He laid it down gently, every movement carefully deliberate.

Olson nodded one last time. "Same thing."

Corfinio nodded back in compliance and repeated his slow, methodical movements in retrieving the last firearm from his waist. No one but Corfinio knew that this last "weapon" was actually the plastic gun, nothing more than a harmless toy. *There are five highly trained men with Heckler & Koch 416 assault rifles that could literally turn me into a human block of Swiss cheese if I were to mishandle this toy gun.* As he pinched the grip panel, he smiled at the irony.

"*Stop!*" Olson yelled out. He saw the smile. This was the type of signal that usually preceded an action of disastrous results. Was he breaking disposition? Was he going to try something insanely stupid?

Corfinio froze instantly, his smile melting quickly, unsure of what changed.

"*Hands!*" Olson yelled out to Corfinio.

He moved his right hand away from the grip of the pistol and extended it out to his right side to match his left.

"*Turk! Jackson!*" Olson called out, never turning his attention away from Corfinio.

Two members of the team rushed forward from their perimeter positions and approached the gunman from either side. "Hands behind your back," ordered Jackson.

Corfinio brought both arms from their extended positions in toward his back. Once his hands touched, Jackson quickly and expertly zip-tied his wrists.

Turk reached across and removed the last remaining pistol from Corfinio's waistband. As soon as he touched it, he realized exactly what it was. Looking down at the toy in disbelief, he hefted the lightweight pistol. "Sarge," he said, incredulously addressing Olson, "it's a *toy!* It's a *goddamned toy!*"

Turning back to face Corfinio, he said, "You did all *that*…with *this*?"

Corfinio shrugged.

Turk shook his head in continued disbelief. "Holy *shit*, dude!"

Olson spoke into his mouthpiece. "Target in custody. Area secured."

50

Jankowski yelled out across the courthouse concourse recently turned command center, "*Deputies! Courtroom 5!*" He grabbed one deputy by the arm as he passed. "Hey, what's your name, Deputy?"

"Tordiglione, Vincenzo, sir."

A look of confusion washed across Jankowski's face. "Uhhh, yeah—"

"They call me 'Tordy,' sir."

Jankowski looked relieved at the reprieve. "Okay, *Tordy*, are the EMTs still out front? If they are, get them in here. Bring them to Courtroom 5."

"Yes, sir, right away," Tordy replied and disappeared.

"Everyone else, *let's go!*"

Jankowski led the parade of officers down the east corridor and through the storage room leading to Courtroom 5. He burst through into the courtroom entry, shoving both doors hard in a grand entrance followed immediately by half-a-dozen officers. As he made his way toward Olson, the deputies attended to the comfort and safety of the former hostages.

"Sergeant Olson."

"Lieutenant Jankowski."

"Casualties?"

"One." He looked over to where Segado's body still lay on the floor, upper torso now covered with Corfinio's suit jacket.

"EMTs are on the way in. How are my deputies?"

"A little worse for wear and tear, but that's about it. Neither one is hurt...*physically*, anyway."

"Meaning?"

"They were disarmed by a guy with a *plastic gun*. They couldn't have known it at the time, but they're both going to beat themselves up over it. You *know* that."

"Yeah." Jankowski sighed.

"And when the press gets a hold of *that*..."

"They *won't*."

Olson nodded, fully understanding that Jankowski would do everything in his power to keep that from getting out. Every branch of law enforcement suffered from bad PR. Public opinion was always the loudest voice, demanding more stringent training procedures and an overall de-escalation in aggressive tactics. The problem was, the public was the least informed and by far the least qualified to criticize procedure. But that never stopped them from passing judgment.

"Where is he?" Jankowski asked ambiguously.

Olson didn't need to ask who "he" was and pointed to a corner of the jury box where Corfinio was flanked by two of the SWAT team members. "You want to talk to him?"

He scrutinized the man who had turned a mundane courtroom case into a catastrophic calamity. Jankowski breathed heavily, anger and hostility apparent. "No," he finally said. "No, I…yeah, *I do*."

Fists clenched, Jankowski walked over to where Corfinio sat in the jury box and leaned on the rail in front of him. The two men stared at each other for a full five seconds.

"Tell me something," Jankowski said, "was it worth it?"

Corfinio sat silent, but held his glare.

Aiming his thumb over his own shoulder, Jankowski pointed toward Segado's corpse now being removed by the EMTs on a covered stretcher. "That's on *you*."

Corfinio started to lean forward from his seated position when one of the SWAT officers grabbed his shoulder and forced him against the backrest of the chair. "We *all* have sins."

Jankowski let go of the rail and stood up straight, continuing to stare Corfinio dead in the eye. "Who *are* you?"

"I'm nobody," Corfinio replied. "Nobody."

"Oh, you're *somebody*…you're somebody," Jankowski repeated.

He backed off a pace and turned to leave when one of the deputies caught up to him. "Lieutenant? What do you want us to do with him?"

"Lock him up. He'll be arraigned soon enough, and then they can put him away for forty years." Jankowski scanned the courtroom one final time. "Oh, hey, did you get everyone's names? Get everyone's name. Don't let anyone out of here until you get names *and* statements. We need statements from *everyone*—even Judge Thompson," he added, realizing he was nowhere in the courtroom. "Where the hell is he anyway? Where'd he disappear to?"

"He's in his chambers, sir."

51

Thompson stood in front of the Russian red mahogany credenza holding a cut crystal decanter, pouring out the amber liquid in a generous portion into his glass for the second time. "Lieutenant?" he said, motioning to the glass tumbler.

"Still on duty, Judge, no thanks," Jankowski declined.

Thompson shrugged, walked to his desk, and sat in the posh leather chair, took a gulp of the smooth liquid, leaned back, closed his eyes, and sighed heavily.

Across the room seated on a leather couch sat Donna LaTrina and Estelle Avery. Marsha Cortinio was using the bathroom facilities.

Jankowski waited impatiently as Thompson took another generous gulp from his glass. "I told the ladies they were welcome to use the bathroom before having to deal with..." He paused, rotating his hand in an attempt to urge the remainder of his thought into words. "Uhhh, everything else."

"Judge, what exactly happened here?"

"Oh, he was pissed off about some decision that didn't go his way. Common for about 50 percent of the people in 100 percent of the cases I sit on! 'Can't please all the people,' as they say. He just took it to another level. Stupid bastard."

"Excuse me, Your Honor," Estelle Avery mildly offered, "he *was* right."

"*Right?*" Thompson scoffed. "About *what*, Mrs. Avery?"

"All of it."

52

Masters sat on the plump blue vinyl cushion of the diner's booth holding a white porcelain coffee cup filled with black, steaming liquid. Two middle-aged men sat across the booth from him each with their own coffees in hand.

The older of the two, Anthony J. Terranova, was the current serving Massachusetts attorney general. The other man, Eddie Grunicki, was a reporter for the long-standing *Boston Globe*.

"Thanks for meeting me at such short notice," Masters began. "I do appreciate you taking the time out. I know you've both got tremendously busy schedules…"

"Don't mention it," placated Terranova. "But I am a little curious about the 'why.' You were pretty vague over the phone."

"Speaking of vague," Grunicki said with a wink, "what happened in that courtroom last week? You've been pretty tight-lipped about the whole ordeal."

Masters smiled broadly, reached down on the seat, and produced a sheaf of yellow note paper. He dropped it in the center of the table, where both men looked down at it questioningly. "Funny you should ask…"

ABOUT THE AUTHOR

Dale DeLillo grew up in the suburbs of Boston one hundred years ago before there were tall buildings and Fenway Park was the only place that had grass. A debut author, he attributes his writing skills to being an extremely irritating student in grammar school, where he wrote 846 compositions as punishment for "bad behavior." During that time, he also acquired the ability of a skilled liar while fabricating extensive narratives as to why the homework assignments were never completed and writing creative book reports for books that never existed. When asked what he wanted to be when he grew up, he replied, "tall." In that regard, he has been most successful.

He now resides in the foothills of California with a stuffed monkey and a metal goat. Although he showers daily, no one visits because he doesn't have cable.